"You look like you could use a drink."

Alyssa waved the glass away. "I'm not allowed alcohol."

"This is just ginger ale. You don't have to worry."

Didn't she? Alyssa sniffed the contents of the glass before taking a cautious sip, not trusting Adam now that she recognized the extent of her vulnerability.

Adam sat down in the chair opposite her; the austerity of his expression softened. "You know, maybe we should stop circling each other and try sharing what little we know."

"When did you decide that?" Alyssa asked, her voice brittle. "A few minutes ago you were accusing me of faking amnesia."

"That's not precisely what I suspect."

"Why would I fake amnesia?"

"Because you're scared," he said quietly. "Because you're into something way over your head. I saw you the day before you caught that fatal flight, and underneath all the bluster, you were terrified."

Dear Reader,

You asked for it, and we're delighted to bring it to you—two more Harlequin Intrigue novels each month!

Now you can get a double dose of derring-do as all your favorite Intrigue authors bring you even more heart-stopping suspense and heart-stirring romance.

Our exciting new cover promises the best in romantic suspense—and that's just what you'll find in the four Harlequin Intrigue novels each and every month.

Here's to many more hours of happy reading!

Sincerely,

Debra Matteucci
Senior Editor & Editorial Coordinator
Harlequin Books
300 East 42nd St., 6th floor
New York, NY 10017

Nowhere
To Hide

Jasmine Cresswell

Harlequin Books

TORONTO • NEW YORK • LONDON
AMSTERDAM • PARIS • SYDNEY • HAMBURG
STOCKHOLM • ATHENS • TOKYO • MILAN
MADRID • WARSAW • BUDAPEST • AUCKLAND

To Malcolm,
even though he moved me to Cleveland

Harlequin Intrigue edition published September 1992

ISBN 0-373-22194-0

NOWHERE TO HIDE

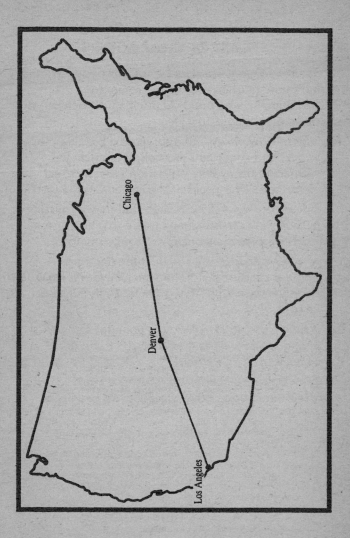

CAST OF CHARACTERS

Suzanne Swenson—Her fiancé betrayed her, and her plane crashed—all on the same day. Sometimes it was easier to put the past behind you and start a whole new life.

Alyssa Humphrey—She survived a blazing plane wreck, and America's most eligible bachelor wanted to marry her. Why didn't the prospect excite her? Why couldn't she remember her past?

Adam Stryker—Three million dollars was missing from Alyssa's trust fund—and he was the trustee. Had he stolen the money, or was he set up?

Matthew Bradford—The best-looking, most popular senator Illinois had seen in years. He was deeply in love with Alyssa. At least, that's what he said.

Jackie Humphrey—Alyssa's younger sister was hiding secrets. Were they teenage trivia or something more deadly?

Tony Delano—He and Alyssa were married once, a few years ago. What would he do to win her back?

Prologue

"What you need," said Rex Clancey, "is a wife. Damn it, Matthew, I'm tired of giving you the same advice over and over again."

Matthew Bradford, junior senator from Illinois, yawned. "Good grief, doesn't the wife I already have cause us enough problems?"

"Marisa's an ex-wife," Rex said wearily. "Eight years into your past."

Variations on this conversation had been played every week for the past month, and Matthew Bradford was heartily sick of it. Damn it, he didn't want a wife; he was perfectly content with the collection of mistresses he already had. Sipping his wine, he listened with half an ear as Rex nagged on.

"Ex-wives don't count, Matthew. The great American public likes to think its political leaders are safely married. Makes them feel secure."

"Makes them feel we're sharing their own misery is more like it."

"Maybe. But you're not going to get elected unless you're married."

Matthew poured himself another glass of white wine. He would have preferred a stiff bourbon, but nobody could accuse him of being unwilling to make sacrifices for the cause. The presidency of the United States was worth a few months of semiabstinence. Maybe it was even worth taking on the burden of another wife. He could tolerate the right woman, one who knew her place and kept to it without complaint. Because Rex was right, damn him. Even if Mr. and Mrs. Joe Average had more sense than the political hacks assumed, the party insiders would never risk political suicide by putting a single man at the head of the presidential ticket.

Matthew sipped his drink, Rex's advice churning sourly in his stomach. He scowled into his glass. "Hell, what I need is three or four million dollars that can't be traced back to me. Then we could cut Van Plat out of the race, and I wouldn't need to clutter up my life with another stupid wife. Marisa was enough for a lifetime."

Dick Humphrey, the third man in the cosy, oak-paneled study, spoke for the first time. "If you married my sister, maybe you could have the money and a wife who's no trouble. My father left Alyssa a ten-million-dollar trust fund."

Matthew jerked around in his armchair. "Your sister?" he murmured. "Would she be willing to get married again?"

"She could be persuaded," Dick said. "She's ambitious and she's felt bored these past few months. She spends all her time organizing charity balls and looking for her name in the society columns. If she's going to use her energy getting her picture in the papers, she might as well do it for a useful cause."

Matthew thought fast. Dick Humphrey was a hard-hitting wheeler-dealer, who wouldn't come across with a single penny of his sister's millions unless Matthew agreed to marry her. On the other hand, Alyssa was exactly the sort of woman he could mold to his tastes. Shallow, spoiled and eager to be entertained, she was ripe for manipulation.

"She's a good-looking woman and she sure knows the score," he commented. "I agree, Dick, that she'd be an asset to the campaign."

"That's debatable," Rex Clancey argued. "She's divorced, and the electorate doesn't like divorced women."

"She was the innocent party," Dick interposed hastily. "Everyone will understand she was just a kid when she got married.'' He hurried on before Rex could voice any more objections. ''Denver's society matrons love her. My sister's raised enough money for worthy causes that our publicity people could write up her résumé so that she sounds more noble than Mother Theresa.''

The senator stared thoughtfully at his wing-tip shoes. He had an outstanding memory for names, faces and biographical details. It was one of the talents that made him a politician to be reckoned with. He mentally reeled off his inventory of information about Alyssa Humphrey. A blonde. Above-average height. Gray eyes. Wore her clothes well. Married to a nobody she'd met her first year in college. Divorced before her classmates reached graduation. Wealthy background, but her father had been a self-made man. Self-made millionaires went over okay with the voters. All in all, marrying Alyssa Humphrey might not be a bad idea.

We could have a fancy wedding right before the Iowa caucuses, Matthew thought. *People* magazine could be counted on for a cover spread. Hell, the publicity alone would be worth it.

''Well, you know, that's a real interesting idea, Dick,'' he said, giving his campaign chief a warm, approving smile. ''I certainly think it's worth exploring. Let's find out how your sister feels about becoming first lady. When could you arrange a quiet meeting for us?''

''Hey, hold on a minute here.'' Rex jumped up and began to pace the floor, clearly not happy. ''Alyssa's not the perfect candidate by any means. Apart from the problem of her divorce, she's too young—''

''Thirty-one,'' Dick said. ''And the media will love her. Think of the contrast with Mrs. Van Plat. My God, Rex, have you ever taken a close look at Van Plat's wife? My cleaning woman's got more style! Alyssa will be the most elegant woman in politics since Jackie Kennedy.''

''That's all very well,'' Rex said. ''But for every male voter who loves her, there'll be a fat wife who hates her. Tell us exactly what you meant about her money, Dick. If the senator married your sister, her contributions to the campaign would be scrutinized more closely than ever."

"That's true," Matthew agreed. "What we desperately need is three or four million dollars off the books. I don't see how we could get that from Alyssa."

Dick smiled. "I've already worked out a way to take care of that. And having my sister as first lady would be worth a few million dollars to me. Of course, once you were elected, I'd expect you both to remember who put this whole deal together."

Greedy conniver, Matthew thought, but he fixed his features into their best professional smile and hoped that his eyes had taken on their famous sincere glow. "When I'm president, we'll have you right at the top of our appointments list, Dick, you can count on it. How does ambassador to France sound? Or we could promise something really cushy on the White House staff, couldn't we, Rex?"

Rex struggled visibly between the desire for Alyssa's millions and dislike of the power Dick Humphrey was gathering. "Not quite chief of staff, but getting up there," he agreed. "However, we need some specifics of how you would work the cash end of the deal, Dick."

"My sister's trust fund. It would be a cinch. I'm the sole family executor, and I could siphon off a couple of million dollars with no trouble at all. I already know exactly how I can do it."

Rex looked doubtful. "Would Alyssa agree?"

"She never pays any attention to the details of her trust fund so long as I pay off her charge cards every month."

"But the fund must have professional trustees. Wouldn't they notice if several million dollars suddenly vanished?"

"Yes, there's a professional trustee—Jerry Hershel. Banking friend of my dad's and smart as a whip. We'd never get anything illegal past him. But I can take care of Jerry. I'll replace him with somebody guaranteed not to ask awkward questions."

"Got anyone special in mind?" Matthew asked.

"Sure have. Guy who was in college with me. Looks like he was born wearing gray pinstripes. Earnest, hardworking, honest as the day is long. Just bright enough to make it through law school. You know the type? The guy's too slow-witted to spot a trust-fund manipulation if it stood up and bit him on the nose."

Matthew stretched luxuriously, feeling a glow of well-being pervade his system. "Sounds ideal. How much of a contribution do you think you can swing?"

"Two million. Three if you can persuade me it's really necessary."

Matthew nodded slowly. "Three million should do the job. In today's market, that can buy a lot of guns."

Dick glanced up. "You've decided to go with the South African scheme, then?"

It was Rex who answered. "I decided that. Van Plat's more vulnerable on civil rights than anything else. And Matthew's record on minority legislation is impeccable."

"Black, white, yellow. Jew, Christian, Moslem or Buddhist, they all make important contributions to our great nation and I love them all." Matthew stood up and took Dick Humphrey's hand in an enthusiastic clasp. "Dick, this has been a great meeting. I'm thrilled to think you may become my brother-in-law. Let's set a date when Alyssa and I can get together to talk things over."

Dick flipped open his pocket diary. "How about next Saturday? Lunch at our home in Denver."

Matthew turned to his aide. "Does that work for us?"

Rex nodded. "We can swing it."

"Make a note, will you please, Rex?" Matthew lifted his wineglass and smiled. "I propose a toast," he said. "To Alyssa Humphrey, my lovely future bride."

Rex acknowledged the toast, then added one of his own. "To three million untraceable dollars," he said. "And guns for Daniel Schaak's army."

Chapter One

Suzanne Swenson couldn't get the horrible pictures out of her mind. Harry and Marianne. Her fiancé and her best friend. *Harry lying in the middle of the bed, hands cradling the swell of Marianne's breasts, his tanned thigh pressed against her sleek body, his mouth covering hers in a passionate, seeking kiss.*

The all-too-vivid image played through Suzanne's mind for the hundredth time. Anger built inside her, frightening in its intensity, and she stared at the airline clerk on the other side of the counter, not really seeing him as she struggled to regain her self-control.

Pulling a tissue from her jacket pocket, she blew her nose and sniffed back the tears that kept threatening. She never made scenes in public, and she wasn't about to indulge in one now. She wasn't going to fly apart at the seams because her best friend was having a love affair with her fiancé. Think how lucky you are that you hadn't already married him, she told herself briskly.

The airline clerk had been tapping at his computer for five or six minutes, and the line of customers waiting behind Suzanne was growing longer. Judging by his hunt-and-peck fumbling, the clerk couldn't have received more than a couple of days' training before being thrown into a Trans Allied uniform. Suzanne gritted her teeth and willed herself to patience. She wouldn't yell at this poor little guy because she wanted to murder Harry.

The clerk's face was suddenly wreathed in smiles. He scribbled on Suzanne's boarding pass with a flourish. "This is your lucky day, Ms. Swenson. Economy is overbooked, so I'm upgrading you to first class." He smiled as he pushed her ticket back across the counter. "Seat 1A, right at the front. Your flight leaves from concourse B, gate 10, and we're about to start boarding."

Suzanne picked up the ticket and her garment bag, choking back a gasp of hysterical laughter. More luck like today, and she'd start wishing for a hefty dose of misfortune. Tears threatened again, but she swallowed hard, rejecting self-pity. *Damn Harry, anyway.* She wasn't going to waste any more time thinking about him.

Outwardly composed, Suzanne walked to gate 10. Contrary to the clerk's warning, the flight wasn't yet boarding, so she searched out a corner of the waiting area and curled into a hard plastic chair.

Her thoughts resumed their relentless circling. How ironic it all was! The new family unit she'd hoped to establish with Harry would have been as flawed as the alcoholic family she'd left behind. Kensington Bennett Associates paid her thousands of dollars a year because her professional judgment was good. But somehow where people were concerned, her wonderful judgment seemed to vanish into thin air.

In which case she might as well stop worrying about her personal relationships and concentrate on work. Suzanne reached for her briefcase and took out the notes for her upcoming presentation. If she reread her notes, maybe she would stop thinking about Harry. Please, God, she would stop thinking about his betrayal.

Studying her presentation didn't work its usual magic. However much she tried, she couldn't summon any enthusiasm for perfecting her sales pitch on the wonders of white llamas as an advertising motif for New Age cosmetics. Suzanne's mouth twisted into a grim smile. Her talents would be better utilized developing a public service campaign on the dangers of women trying to marry themselves into a feeling of self-worth. With ruthless honesty, she admitted that she'd become engaged to Harrison Quentin III in part because his family was everything hers had never been. However sleek and sophisticated her exterior, she could never quite believe that the scared kid from the wrong side of the tracks wouldn't show through.

"Miss Humphrey?" A light, female voice penetrated Suzanne's gloom. "Miss Humphrey, your brother has been looking for you. He missed you when you left the check-in counter to go to the ladies' room."

Suzanne quelled a moment of disorientation. "I'm sorry," she said politely, looking up at the woman in a Trans Allied uniform. "I don't know what you're talking about."

The woman smiled with obvious deference. "I'm Tracey, one of the attendants on your flight today, Miss Humphrey. We met earlier. Your brother is searching the terminal looking for you. He'd like you to go to the Aviation Club lounge and meet him there."

Suzanne's addled wits finally grasped the simple message. "I'm sorry," she said. "There's been some mistake. I'm not Miss Humphrey." She hesitated for a second, then continued firmly, "I'm Suzanne Swenson. Ms. Suzanne Swenson."

The flight attendant stared at Suzanne in mingled confusion and embarrassment. "I'm sorry, Ms. . . . er . . . Swenson. Your hair . . . your figure . . . From a distance, you looked just like Miss Humphrey. Now I can see the difference, I guess. I mean, you're not even wearing similar clothes. Although you could have changed in the ladies' room."

The woman sounded positively suspicious. Suzanne took hold of her temper, but she couldn't manage a smile. On another day she might have felt curious about the missing Miss Humphrey. Not today. At this moment she wanted nothing except to be left alone to wallow in her misery.

"Good luck in your search," Suzanne said with pointed disinterest and returned to reading her presentation.

She scarcely noticed the attendant's departure. Kensington Bennett's art department, she realized, had delivered her an entire set of diagrams that bore no clue as to what they represented. Wonderful! She just needed to look like a total idiot in front of her bosses to complete a perfect day. Suzanne's pen slashed across the offending page with vicious intensity before she realized what her hand was doing. She stared at the ruined page in disbelief. Good grief, she was destroying her own presentation. She was going crazy!

Her hands trembled so violently it took three attempts to stuff the charts back into her briefcase. She got up and walked quickly to the window, gazing with blind eyes at the luggage being hoisted into the belly of the aircraft. Control, she reminded herself, pressing her shaking hands against the cold glass. As long as she kept control over her emotions, she would be safe.

"Boarding all passengers for Denver flight number 127. Please have your boarding passes ready to show the gate agent."

Getting out of Chicago would be a relief, Suzanne decided, as she joined the long line of boarding passengers. She needed distance to get her feelings into perspective. A broken engagement wasn't the end of the world, even if it did mean the loss of your best friend along with your fiancé.

At the door to the aircraft, Suzanne hung up her garment bag in the narrow closet and walked past the galley to the front row of the first-class cabin. A fair-haired man, thirtyish and drop-dead handsome, sat in *her* seat, absorbed in reading the contents of a thick manila folder.

She scowled at the man's Greek-god profile, then checked her boarding pass, spoiling for a fight. Bright green ink announced her entitlement to seat 1A. Either the ticketing clerk or this passenger had messed up. Or perhaps both, this being the sort of day for maximum application of Murphy's Law. Any minute now, she would be bumped back to economy.

Suzanne cleared her throat. The man continued to read. If he wasn't deaf, his powers of concentration were awesome.

"Sir," she said. "Sir, you're sitting in my seat." She hoped he would argue so that she would have an excuse for yelling. Right now she was in the mood to yell.

The man looked up. Shock, followed by uncertainty, followed by rage chased across his handsome features. "The joke isn't funny," he said harshly. "What the hell are you and Alyssa playing at?" He gripped her hand and pulled her into the seat next to his. "Sit down. You're holding up the rest of the passengers."

Suzanne slid into seat 1B, too shocked to protest the man's aggression. She tilted her chin defiantly, meeting the man's gaze head-on. That was a mistake. He examined her with loathing, then gripped her arms and leaned close.

"I don't know what you and Alyssa are trying to achieve," he muttered into her ear, his voice tight with fury. "But it isn't going to work, babe. Your hair and body may be a good match, but your nose has a bump on it, and your chin's far too square. You don't even have the clothes right. Alyssa wouldn't be seen dead in a school-marmish suit."

"Get your hands off me, or I'll call the flight attendant!"

"Look, lady, if this is a trial run, you've blown it. You're not going to deceive anyone who's seen Alyssa more than a couple of times. And Bradford's seen all of her. In intimate detail."

"Whoopee! Let's score one for good old Bradford. Now get your hands off my arm or I'll scream."

"Right, and let the whole plane know you're masquerading as Alyssa?"

The man had to be high on something, Suzanne thought, trying to get a glimpse at the pupils of his eyes. Or could he possibly be making an honest mistake? Remembering the flight attendant who'd approached her in the airport lounge, she decided to give her seatmate the benefit of the doubt.

"I think you're making a mistake," she said, trying to sound calm and reasonable. "I'm not masquerading as anybody. I'm me, Suzanne Swenson, and I'm on my way to Denv—"

"I don't give a darn who you are, or what you call yourself." The man's cultured accent was at odds with his abusive manners. "Look, honeybun, take it from me, whatever Alyssa's paying you, it isn't enough. She closed out her options weeks ago. Now she can damn well live with the consequences. She knows she has to be in Denver tomorrow night for dinner with Bradford, and you haven't got a hope in hell of passing as a substitute. You'd better get on the phone when we land and tell her to get herself out here on the next plane. And you can get right back to wherever you came from."

A flight attendant, carrying a tray of crystal glasses, walked down the aisle. It was the same woman who'd confronted Suzanne in the waiting area, and they eyed each other with mutual wariness.

"Good evening, Miss Humphrey," the woman finally said. "I see you found your brother. I apologize for the slight delay, but there's a minor problem with the latch on the cargo hold door. Would you care for some champagne while we wait for clearance to take off?"

"I've told you before, he isn't my brother and no, thank you—"

"Yes, she'll have a glass," Suzanne's seatmate said.

Something hot and primitive exploded deep inside her soul. She was sick and tired of people telling her what to do. Sick and tired of trying to live up to other people's expectations. Sick and tired of a life that seemed to have taken a totally wrong turn. Suzanne turned to her seatmate.

"I don't know you," she shouted. "What's more, I don't want to know you. If you dare to answer for me ever again, I'll take the darn champagne and dump it straight into your lap. Do we understand each other, Mr. Whoever-you-are?"

"Keep your voice down!" Her seatmate growled, looking furious. The flight attendant backed away, shielding her tray of champagne as if she expected Suzanne to grab a glass and make good on her threat at any minute.

"It's been a long, hot day, hasn't it?" she said with all the professional aplomb she could muster. "Er...Mr. Humphrey, would you care for some champagne yourself?"

"No," he growled. "I'd like a bourbon on the rocks. No water."

"We'll be pleased to get that for you after takeoff, sir."

He grunted his thanks, then added. "Let's hope this damn plane gets moving real soon."

"As I explained to your sist—to the lady sitting next to you, the captain is experiencing a little difficulty with the cargo door." With an obviously strained smile, the flight attendant turned to the passengers on the other side of the aisle.

Suzanne tightened her seat belt and fought with an overwhelming urge to burst into tears. Why, in heaven's name, had she lost her temper? From the day her father ruined her graduation from junior high by tumbling down the school steps and breaking his arm, singing "Danny Boy" all the while, she had sworn never to make a scene in public. And now, not only had she yelled at her seatmate with all the elegance of a fishwife, she could already feel the anger starting up again. If Mr. Humphrey said one more rude word to her, she was likely to brain him with her briefcase.

Suzanne decided she'd better smooth matters over with her seatmate. "My boss is waiting for me in Denver," she said with what she hoped was firm, but courteous, finality. "Since you and I both have to take this plane, perhaps we could agree to ignore each other for the rest of the journey."

The man scowled. "Lady, I have no interest in your supposed plans. God only knows where Alyssa found you. Looks like she's picked a real doozy this time."

"If your sister is a woman called Alyssa Humphrey, I have never met her. What's more, I have no desire to meet her at any time in the future—"

"You surely don't expect me to believe that a dead ringer for my sister has taken the seat next to me by complete coinci—"

"I don't expect you to believe anything, Mr. Whoever-you-are. I just want you to keep quiet and let me get on with my work."

"My name's Dick Humphrey. As if you didn't know."

"I didn't know. And I don't care. I plan to ignore you from here to Denver. Have a good flight, Mr. Humphrey."

Suzanne snapped open her briefcase and pulled out a collection of papers virtually at random. She could feel Dick Humphrey peering at the pile of papers stacked in her briefcase. He squinted sideways to get a look at the headings on her various charts. His shock at what he saw was almost palpable. When he finally jerked his head back up to stare at her, Suzanne sensed confusion and a softening of his attitude.

He coughed to get her attention. "Look, Ms....er...I'm sorry. I wasn't listening when you told me your name."

"I'm Suzanne Swenson. I work for the Kensington Bennett Associates advertising agency in Chicago."

"Yes, I noticed the heading on your papers." He coughed again. "Well, look, Ms. Swenson, it seems I may have made a mistake."

"You certainly did."

"You're on your way to Denver to make a presentation to a client?"

"I am."

In contrast to his former behavior, her seatmate now oozed charm. He displayed white, even teeth in a broad smile. "Look, I'd appreciate it if you'd forget what I said earlier, and I can't apologize enough for the—er—unfriendly attitude."

"It would have been nice if you'd given me a chance to speak before jumping to wild conclusions."

"You're absolutely right." He gave another apologetic smile. "The fact is, my sister's not the most reliable of people and she's supposed to be joining me in Denver for a very important meeting. When she gave me the slip at O'Hare, I immediately assumed she was up to something. I'm sure you'll understand that it just seemed too much of a coincidence when you suddenly turned up to claim her seat. You and Alyssa really do look a lot alike, you know. Same body build, same eye color, same hair..." His voice trailed off into renewed suspicion as he listed the similarities.

Suzanne's powers of reasoning had taken a beating over the past few hours, but she could still think clearly enough to realize that Dick Humphrey's apology left several loose ends floating in the breeze. "Aren't you worried about your sister?" she asked. "If she disappeared, something might have happened to her at the airport."

"Not to Alyssa," the man said bitterly. "She's decided to screw us over—" He bit off the explanation and gave a chuckle. "Well, there's no need to go into all the boring details, but I'm sure Alyssa will be all right. I'll find a message from her waiting in Denver."

Since Dick Humphrey didn't strike Suzanne as a man given to naive optimism, she assumed he had far better reasons for believing his sister was safe than the ones he had given her. Mentally she shrugged. She had enough problems to handle right now without bothering about the missing Alyssa.

Thank goodness Dick Humphrey seemed no more interested in continuing the conversation than she was. The plane finally taxied into position for takeoff, and he stared out of the window as if fascinated by the dreary vista of tarmac and straggling grass. Suzanne opened her file of notes, and once again tried to immerse herself in the facts and figures relevant to the Astral presentation.

The sandwiches and fruit served as a snack were edible, if not exciting, and once she had eaten, Suzanne found she was finally able to focus her attention on her papers. Her intense powers of concentration had always been a matter of pride, ever since childhood days in Peoria when she had learned how to complete her homework even when her father was smashing up the furniture—or his wife. She was relieved that those powers seemed to be returning at last.

The flight attendant had to tap her on the shoulder before Suzanne heard what she was saying. "Miss Humphrey, we're passing through some unexpected air turbulence. The captain has turned on the seat belt sign. Please buckle up."

"My seat belt's already fastened and I'm not Miss Humphrey," Suzanne started to say, when a plummeting swoop of the aircraft deprived her of breath. Another violent lurch left her stomach feeling as if it hung in space several yards higher than the rest of her. When her stomach and body finally reunited, the stewardess had gone. Suzanne gave up. Dick Humphrey might have changed his opinion, but as far as the flight attendant was concerned, she was obviously destined to remain forever Miss Humphrey. The way she felt right now about her own life, Suzanne wasn't sure that she cared.

The second officer's voice came over the intercom, uninflected and slightly bored. "Captain Baker asks everyone to sit down and return their seat backs to an upright position. Cabin crew, please check that all passengers have their seat belts tightly fastened. We apologize for any discomfort you may feel, but we're encountering unexpected pockets of air turbulence. Fortunately we're only fifty miles out from Denver and we expect to be landing on schedule at seven-thirty local time. Thank you for your cooperation, and thank you for flying Trans Allied."

Suzanne pressed the button and straightened her seat back as requested. Dick Humphrey stared out of the tiny window, his hands clutching the armrest as if his life depended on it.

"We're coming in much too low," he muttered. "My God, we have to be five thousand feet too low!"

Suzanne was prepared to be sympathetic, even if the guy had behaved like a demented toad earlier in the flight. She had been a white-knuckle flyer herself until sheer boredom of constant travel had changed fear to mild discomfort.

"I'm sure the pilots know what they're doing," she said soothingly. "Perhaps air traffic control has given them a lower flight path because of the turbulence."

With visible effort the man tore his gaze away from the darkness outside the window. "There's smoke coming from one of the engines."

"Smoke? You mean the plane's on fire?" Mouth dry, heart pounding, Suzanne twisted around and leaned across to stare out of the window. Visions of leaping red flame and imminent death crowded her mind.

The sight that greeted her was a touch less dramatic. A few clouds scudded across the star-spangled night sky. A scattering of lights, from streets and houses on the eastern fringe of Denver, illuminated the ground. To the west she caught a shadowy glimpse of distant mountains. The only sign of fire was the exhaust smoke that belched in occasional puffs from the far left tip of the wing. Suzanne almost smiled. Her seatmate was working himself into a frenzy over nothing.

Dick Humphrey's fear of flying made him seem much less threatening. Suzanne felt almost benign as she leaned back in her seat.

"I've flown into Stapleton before," she said reassuringly. "The mountains cause updrafts or downdrafts or something like that. It's often a really bumpy ride for these last few minutes. You don't have to worry."

Dick Humphrey blinked in disbelief, his grip on the armrest not relaxing by a millimeter. "Damn it, I fly in and out of Denver almost as often as the pilots! I tell you, we're too low!" He grappled with the buckle of his seat belt. "Where's the damn steward anyway? I'm going to see what's going on!"

"I don't think you'd better get up—"

She was too late. Dick Humphrey jumped out of his seat just as the plane got caught in another massive pocket of turbulence. He bounced upward, his head crashing with bone-crunching force into the overhead storage bins. His body lurched forward, hit the front panel, then slid slowly onto the floor, landing face up across Suzanne's feet. His eyes rolled upward.

"Oh, my God! Somebody help, quickly!" Suzanne moved instinctively toward the inert body, but she was restrained by her seat belt. Simultaneously the plane shuddered into a rattling sideways dive, and a woosh of air sent the loose papers on Dick Humphrey's seat hurtling backward. Suzanne realized that the roaring noise she heard in her ears was real, not a nervous reaction of her own blood system to Dick Humphrey's accident. She felt a movement against her legs and saw one of his hands flop in a grotesque parody of intimacy between her knees.

An attendant rushed by, and Suzanne grabbed her. "I think he's—" She swallowed hard. "I think maybe he's dead."

"Throw a blanket over him," the attendant replied curtly. She edged along the walls of the aircraft to the galley and slammed shut a storage bin that had flown open, spilling plastic cups all over the floor. She didn't even glance again in Suzanne's direction before proceeding to the cockpit.

Suzanne arranged a blanket over Dick Humphrey's body as carefully as she could, given the violent bucking of the plane. She knew he was dead. His body felt like lead on top of her feet. Somehow, though, it seemed obscenely disrespectful to extricate her feet and rest them on top of his dead body.

The scream of horror tore from her throat before she could force it back. From somewhere in the rear of the plane, she heard its echo, followed by another and another, each more frantic than the last.

Suzanne forced her head around to the window. The dark night sky was dark no more. A sunburst of orange fire blazed with deadly beauty at the edge of her vision. Dick Humphrey had been right all along. At least one engine was on fire, possibly more. And the plane was heading precipitously downward.

The plane was going to crash. And they would all die.

Until this moment Suzanne hadn't realized how much she wanted to live. She hadn't realized how very much she wanted to marry and have a child. Now, when it was almost certainly too late, she was filled with aching regret because she had never known how it felt to push a baby out from her womb and hold him in her arms, wrinkled, squalling and alive. Waiting to be loved. Waiting to learn all the lessons of life and love that Suzanne had never learned. With a bitter sense of irony, Suzanne wondered if she had wasted twenty-nine years of her life so that Harry could write on her tombstone: She Made it to Account Executive at Kensington Bennett.

"Your attention, please." The voice that came over the intercom this time was no longer bored. "This is Captain Baker. We've lost power in two of our engines. The control tower at Denver's Stapleton airport has been notified and we are being guided in. Emergency equipment is standing by. Cabin crew, prepare for emergency landing."

White-faced, the flight attendant emerged from the cockpit and once again braced herself against the wall of the galley. Voice shaking, she instructed passengers to pad themselves with pillows and blankets.

Suzanne did exactly as she was told. She even cushioned her body with a couple of extra pillows lying on Dick Humphrey's vacant seat. But she no longer felt any fear, only regret. Dear God, she'd wasted so much *life!*

The hysterical screams from the rear of the plane grew louder. Following the flight attendant's instructions, Suzanne obediently tucked her head onto her knees, cushioning her face with the pillow. "I'm sorry," she whispered to Dick Humphrey's inert body, when her movements jostled him against the wall. "My God, I'm sorry." She was no longer sure to whom she apologized.

The plane had stopped lurching from air pocket to air pocket. Even with her head on her lap, Suzanne could feel its hurtling, uncontrolled descent.

The noise was the worst thing, she thought. The roar of the single remaining engine, straining to hold the nose of the plane at the correct angle to the ground. The blast of the wind against fatigued metal. The muttered prayers of the woman across the aisle, praying for God to forgive her sins.

She should be praying, too, Suzanne realized. *Dear God, don't let me die now when I've finally realized what a waste I've made of my life. Please God, let me live long enough to find out who I really am.*

Her prayer didn't seem to be answered. The ground rose up to greet the plane, taking the burning metal into its concrete embrace with bone-jarring, life-extinguishing force. The belly skidded over the ground, and friction turned black smoke into leaping points of scarlet flame. Screams of anguish were mercifully obliterated by the clang of sirens and the thunder of foam pouring onto the exploding engines.

"Get that blasted hose over here! And the damn ladder! If there's anybody alive up front, we could get them out. *Move, curse you! Move!*"

Pain detonated through Suzanne's body, twisting her muscles into a hundred different pinpoints of agony. She lifted her head a scant inch from the pillow and flicked her gaze sideways. The orange flame no longer blazed at the tip of the wing. Now it danced in triumph over the entire horizon.

The pain thrust a little deeper, a little harder, just to remind her there were levels of torment beyond her darkest imaginings. Her head fell forward onto the pillow.

Suzanne closed her eyes and willed herself into unconsciousness. Deprived of its victim, the pain retreated, biding its time. Suzanne relaxed.

Once you got used to it, dying wasn't so bad after all.

Chapter Two

Doctor Reinhard gave a sigh of relief as he stepped into the elevator. "I hope that's the last press briefing I have to give for a while. Most of those journalists make vultures look tame."

Adam Stryker nodded. "But at least the out-of-town reporters seem to have gone home. The reporters today were nearly all from Denver."

"It's five days since the crash. Old news. The great American public wants to know that Alyssa Humphrey is still alive, but by now she merits nothing more than an inside paragraph. Thank goodness the pilot and crew were taken to Denver General instead of here. At least the other survivors take some of the heat off us."

The hospital was fortunate, Adam thought, that Alyssa happened to be a rich, thirty-one-year-old woman. Her plight didn't provoke the same fever of national interest an orphaned child might have done. He allowed himself a grim smile. If the journalists knew that Senator Matthew Bradford was sitting at Alyssa Humphrey's bedside right this moment, the fax machines would start working overtime. For all but the most sober journals, a romance between the Senate's most eligible bachelor and a survivor from doomed flight 127 would be major headline material.

The elevator arrived at the third floor. "Do you think Alyssa might regain consciousness today?" he asked.

Doctor Reinhard gave a noncommittal grunt. "She had a restless night," he said finally. "She's not about to sink into a coma if that's what's worrying you."

"To be honest, I'm worried about the legal practicalities of the situation. I'm the trustee of Alyssa's money, but we're not personal friends."

Which was an understatement, Adam thought wryly. As soon as Alyssa regained consciousness, she was more than likely to order him back to Chicago. Rich, sophisticated and beautiful, Alyssa was accustomed to dazzling every man who came into her orbit. Adam had infuriated her by refusing to be dazzled. Almost from their first meeting he had seen right through the bold, glossy exterior to the lonely and confused young woman hidden within. A month ago he had committed the cardinal error of allowing Alyssa to see just how completely he understood her. She had never forgiven him for his insights.

Doctor Reinhard mumbled a greeting to a passing nurse, and pushed open the door to Alyssa's room. Adam followed him inside.

Four expectant faces turned toward the doctor. Four voices murmured "Good morning." Nobody paid any attention to Adam, who was able to retreat to a corner of the room and observe the proceedings with as much detachment as he could manage to dredge up. Ever since Su-lin died, hospitals reminded him of a lot of things he'd rather forget. He carefully wiped his mind clear of painful memories and concentrated on his professional reasons for being in the intensive care unit.

Senator Bradford stood in his usual position at the side of Alyssa's bed. Even after a twelve-hour vigil, he appeared fresh, alert and amazingly good-looking. No wonder he was so widely touted as a leading contender in the next presidential sweepstakes, Adam thought cynically.

Rex Clancey, the senator's chief aide, was making another of his eternal phone calls. Adam had yet to see the man when he didn't have a phone growing out of his ear. Jackie, Alyssa's teenaged sister, lounged in a chair, scowling as she flipped through *Rolling Stone* magazine. For the third day in a row she wore a scarlet and black outfit, complete with veiled hat and high-button boots.

Senator Bradford barely waited until the doctor closed the door before seizing his hand in a firm clasp. "Glad you made it up here, Doctor. I have to leave Denver by noon and we're waiting on tenterhooks to hear your latest progress report."

Reinhard checked a couple of monitors, then looked at his patient, who lay as still and silent as ever. "I'm sorry, there's no way of knowing when she's going to regain consciousness, Senator. Believe me, I wish I could tell you something more positive."

The doctor's manner was gruff, but Adam saw how gentle his fingers were as he checked a tiny seepage of blood on one of Alyssa's facial bandages. Alyssa cared a lot about how she looked, and Adam hoped for her sake that Reinhard had managed to reconstruct her face. The doctor was reputed to be one of the best maxillo-facial surgeon in the country, so Alyssa might be lucky.

Bursting with self-importance, Rex Clancey hung up the phone. "Senator, we must get back to DC right away. The president has invited us to breakfast with him tomorrow. Privately."

Matthew Bradford gave an easy laugh. "Calm down, Rex. Much as I enjoy chatting with the president, we don't need to leave right now."

"The president wants to ask your opinion about the new appointment to the Supreme Court." Rex puffed out his chest and checked to make sure Doctor Reinhard was listening. "The president always asks our opinion when he has judicial appointments to make."

Adam wondered if being a pain in the neck was a job requirement for political aides. Doctor Reinhard seemed equally unimpressed with the senator's breakfast date. "Congratulations," he said dryly. He held out his hand for Alyssa's chart. "How's she doing?" he asked the nurse.

"Her vitals have been stable for six hours. She took liquid nourishment by mouth at five this morning, then went back to sleep without speaking. But I have the feeling next time she wakes up, she's going to stay awake for a while."

"Let's hope our patient has the same feeling," Reinhard said.

Senator Bradford stepped up to the bedside. "Do you see some signs of improvement, Doctor? She's barely moved a muscle all these hours. Alyssa was always so *alive.*"

"Miss Humphrey is still very much alive, Senator. I assure you, she isn't in any danger of dying."

"That's a miracle in itself." The senator's piercing blue eyes darkened with emotion. "But be honest with me, Doctor. Those bandages on her face don't look too good. Is Alyssa going to be badly scarred?"

"She isn't going to be scarred at all," Reinhard promised briskly. "Right now there's a great deal of swelling and bruising, but when the bones mend and the surgical incisions heal, her face will be as good as new. I've spent thirty years putting people together again after automobile accidents. Unfortunately, drunk drivers provide me with lots of experience. From my point of view, Miss Humphrey's case was moderately difficult, but not unusual, or one that required novel techniques."

"That's great news to take away with us." The senator's entire face suffused with relief and pleasure. "I'm glad Alyssa will look just the same as she always did."

"I didn't quite promise you that, Senator. Miss Humphrey won't appear *radically* changed, but her features won't be as you remember them. I had to do a fair amount of rebuilding in an emergency situation, so you're going to notice some changes."

"But she'll still be good-looking?" Matthew asked.

The doctor's mouth twisted into a cool, professional smile. "I'm happy to put your mind at rest, Senator. Your fiancée will emerge from those bandages with a face pretty enough to launch a thousand ships. Or an election campaign, if that's the particular launch you all have in mind."

Bradford laughed easily. "You're jumping the gun, Doctor. I'm not a presidential candidate. Our party has any number of qualified people who've already said they're willing to take on the burden of running for president."

"Yes, but none of them look as good on television as you do, Senator. Particularly with a wife like Alyssa Humphrey at your side."

For a moment Bradford appeared taken aback by the doctor's bluntness. Then he laughed again, showing no sign of offense. "The American people have more horse sense than the media and pollsters realize," he said. "Believe me, you can't sell the voters a handsome TV package with no substance behind it. The people of Illinois vote for me because they approve of my policies, not because they like my hairstyle."

"Perhaps the national electorate would like your policies as much as the voters in your state."

"That's a possibility for us to think about, of course. But not now. Not when Alyssa is suffering so badly."

Adam found that, as always, the senator was beginning to irritate him. He walked quietly across the room, standing at the end of Alyssa's bed, willing her to regain consciousness.

Come on, kid, you can do it. Wake up and smile for your fiancé. Or fight with me if that seems like more fun.

Nothing. It had been crazy of him to imagine the tiniest flicker of eyelashes between the bandages.

"Why doesn't Alyssa manage to stay conscious for more than a couple of minutes at a time?" he asked the doctor. As always when he felt worried, his voice emerged sounding flat, almost bored. "Is she unconscious now? Or simply sleeping?"

"She's sleeping, Mr. Stryker. Perfectly normal sleep."

"Is she drugged?"

"We've cut down on the painkillers every day since surgery. The narcotic level is currently minimal. I hope she'll soon be alert enough to show a more active response to our presence."

"You *hope*, Doctor? Are you warning us to anticipate some long-term degree of impairment to Alyssa's mental processes?"

Great, Adam told himself. *You sound like a typical prissy-mouthed lawyer gathering ammunition for a lawsuit.* No wonder Doctor Reinhard was looking at him so sourly.

"My patient suffered cracked ribs, two broken cheek-bones, one where her face impacted her knee and the other where she was hit by a falling suitcase. She has a broken nose, crushed fingers of the right hand and superficial cuts and bruises over eighty percent of her body. If her brother's body hadn't somehow fallen in front of her—and the experts tell me they've no idea how that happened—she'd be dead. As it is, she's in pain, Mr. Stryker. A lot of pain. Her body probably got smart and decided it would be a hell of a good idea to remain dormant for a while."

Adam still hadn't heard what he wanted to hear, but he'd had a lot of experience pressing doctors for answers when Su-lin was dying, and he asked his question again. "When Alyssa regains consciousness, Doctor, can we anticipate any long-term impairment of her mental processes?"

"I'm a surgeon, not an oracle," Reinhard snapped. "But the neurologist has run plenty of tests and sees no physical reason why Miss Humphrey shouldn't recover fully. Does that satisfy you, Mr. Stryker?"

"Yes, thank you, Doctor. You've answered my question."

Jackie spoke without moving from her chair. "My sister's waking up."

Adam glanced down at Alyssa. To his surprise he saw that Alyssa's eyelashes were actually fluttering. He watched as Alyssa stretched the uninjured fingers of her left hand, then tried the same movement with her right. Her eyes jerked open.

"Hurt," she whispered. Her mouth scarcely moved between the enveloping bandages. She lifted her left hand and put her fingers against the dry, cracked skin of her lips. "Thirsty."

"Nora will give you some apple juice to drink." Reinhard's voice was soft, kind, totally unlike his earlier acerbic tones. He stroked Alyssa very lightly on her arm. "Nora here is one of the nurses helping to take care of you. Do you like apple juice?"

A long pause ensued. "Yes." The murmured word was barely audible.

Reinhard nodded to the nurse, who stood ready with a small container of juice and a special drinking straw. The senator started to speak, but Reinhard waved him away with an impatient gesture. "Let's not crowd her," he said, turning back to his patient. "Let's take this slowly."

Jackie positioned herself at the foot of the bed, directly in her sister's line of vision. She'd taken off her hat, but her makeup was strictly of the ghoul variety, including stark white lipstick and quantities of black eyeliner. Enough to scare anybody back into unconsciousness, Adam thought wryly. The doctor gave him a brief nod of approval when he drew the girl to one side with a softly voiced question about Alyssa's favorite foods.

Nora spoke quietly. "She's finished the juice, Doctor."

Reinhard hooked a chair with his heel and pulled it up to the bed. When he sat down, he was at comfortable eye level with his patient. "We're all very glad you've woken up, Alyssa. Your sister and your fiancé are both here, waiting to see you."

"My...fiancé?" Alyssa turned blank grey eyes toward the doctor. With most of her face swathed in bandages, her eyes appeared enormous. Adam watched intently as gray blankness turned to panic. "Can't...remember...anything..."

The doctor touched her hand in reassurance. "It's normal to have blurred recollections after a major trauma. Your plane crashed as it came in to land, but you're safe, Alyssa. You're in the hospital in Denver and getting better every day."

"Fire! By the window! I didn't believe him!"

Reinhard calmed the agitated clawing of her fingers. "The firemen reached you in time, Alyssa. Only the back of the plane caught fire. You're safe. You'll soon be well again."

She touched her face, patting the bandages. "Burned?"

"No, you're not burned. Those bandages are to keep surgical dressings in place."

"Surgery?"

"Your nose and cheeks were broken and I had to fix them. And you've had tubes down your throat, which is why your voice sounds so raspy. You also have lots of cuts and bruises which are making you ache all over. Right now you probably feel too lousy to believe this, but in less than a month you'll be as good as new, and that's a promise."

The panic in her eyes didn't seem to be fading. "Alyssa Humphrey," she whispered, the words sounding oddly like a question. "Dick Humphrey."

"Yes. You were flying to Denver with your brother."

"Dick...banged his head. Fell...onto the floor." Her damaged throat distorted the sound she made into a horrible croak. "His blood was all over my hands."

Adam felt his gut tighten in sympathy, but before he could speak, the senator burst out, "For God's sake, Doctor, I can't stand this! Let me speak to her. *Please.* I should be the person to tell her about Dick." Without waiting for permission, Bradford took hold of Alyssa's uninjured hand and dropped a tender kiss on her knuckles.

"Darling, it's me. Welcome back. I've been so worried about you."

Alyssa stared at the senator without any sign of recognition. When Bradford finally released her hand, Adam was sure he saw a flicker of relief in her eyes. What the hell was going on here? Some confusion after an accident was to be expected, but Alyssa's reactions were too tense, too wary, to be natural.

"Dick sat next to me on the plane," Alyssa said finally. "He tried to warn me about the fire...."

Bradford put his hand on her shoulder, then quickly drew it back when she gave a little moan of pain. "Honey, I have bad news for you. You have to be strong, because this news is going to cause you grief, whatever way I try to tell it. The truth is, honey, that Dick didn't make it."

"The paramedics—"

"Honey, he was dead by the time they got to the plane. It's a miracle you were taken out alive. If Dick's body hadn't cushioned you—"

Reinhard gave a sharp, angry shake of his head, and the senator stopped immediately. This clearly wasn't the moment to tell Alyssa that she'd survived the crash because her brother's body had somehow become interposed between her and the shattered front panel of the plane.

Bradford took her hand again. "Your brother didn't suffer, Alyssa, honey."

Alyssa, honey. How strange it was, Alyssa thought, that the images of Dick Humphrey's death were so clear, so brutally vivid. Whereas her impressions of the people right here in the room wouldn't come into any sort of focus. Why didn't she recognize the handsome man who had just now kissed her hand? Why did the idea that he was her fiancé evoke this faint but definite feeling of repulsion?

Her mind skittered away. Dick hadn't suffered, according to the man who called himself her fiancé. Maybe he hadn't. He'd fallen at her feet the moment he banged his head. "Dick was angry," she said, trying to shape her thoughts into words. Another memory nudged at the edge of her brain. "Dick was angry with me."

She saw the people around her bed exchange worried glances. She wondered what she'd said to upset them, then decided she didn't care. Once upon a time she'd cared a lot about what people thought of her. But now she was Alyssa Humphrey she didn't have to care anymore.

An odd-looking child, wearing a pathetic shield of badly applied makeup, suddenly appeared at the side of the bed. Alyssa felt an immediate surge of sympathy for the child, although she didn't recognize her any more than the other people in the room. But this girl was hurting; Alyssa was sure of it. Hurting in the way only a badly neglected child can hurt.

"You have to get better first," the girl said. "Then you can worry about Dick. He was always mad about something or other, that was his way. But right now you have to get well. That's the most important thing."

The poor kid sounded so earnest, so anxious, beneath her veneer of defiance. Alyssa tried to smile, but the skin on her face congealed into a solid mask of pain. She reached out and touched the tassled fringe of the girl's silk scarf, wishing she could *make* the girl feel happy.

"I like your scarf," Alyssa said. "Scarlet looks good on you."

"Do you think so? I found it in the attics." The girl made an odd snuffling sound, then wiped her nose with the back of her hand. "I'm glad you didn't die, Lyss."

Lyss. Alyssa squirmed on the bed. The very sound of her name made her uneasy. She searched through her mind with growing alarm, trying to call up some memories, seeking some clue as to the person she really was. Nothing. She could summon up nothing except flames, lighting the blue-gray interior of the plane as it dived into the concrete runway. And something to do with champagne. Dick had told her to have champagne, and she'd been furious with him. Was that why they'd been arguing?

"I don't like champagne," she said petulantly. "Why didn't Dick remember? I never drink alcohol. Daddy—" Her mind ran smack into a solid brick wall. She didn't want to remember anything about Daddy. Not now. Not ever.

The doctor was holding her hand again, talking. He had a nice voice and nice eyes. She listened to what he was saying.

"Do you want to talk to us about your father, Alyssa?"

"No." That, at least she knew with absolute certainty. She might not remember much, but she knew with unshakable convictions that she didn't want to discuss her father. "Daddy's dead," she said flatly.

"She doesn't know who we are, does she, Doctor?" The man they had called her fiancé asked the question. He had a nice voice, like the doctor. But she didn't think much of his eyes.

Another voice spoke, one she hadn't heard before. "Is this your definition of *no mental impairment,* Doctor Reinhard?"

Alyssa squinted in the direction of the new voice. It came from a tall man wearing horn-rimmed glasses and a navy blue pin-striped suit. The voice was cool, faintly ironic, and it inspired Alyssa with a distinct feeling of annoyance.

I'm sick, she thought angrily, glaring at the man. *I've survived a flaming death. You're supposed to sound worried.*

"Disorientation and selective memory loss are normal after a period of unconsciousness, Mr. Stryker." That was the doctor.

"She seems to remember the accident better than anything else. I was under the impression that it was usually the immediate short-term memories that disappeared."

"You're right." The doctor again. "But I'm not an expert in this field, Mr. Stryker. In thirty years of dealing with accident victims, I've learned that the mind plays some very odd tricks. My personal opinion is that by this time tomorrow, we'll be seeing an entirely different person."

What nonsense the doctor talked, Alyssa thought sleepily. How could she become a different person? She was Alyssa Humphrey, and that's who she was going to stay.

"You have to understand, Doctor, that there are a great many legal matters awaiting Miss Humphrey's attention. A ten-million dollar estate, left in only the loosest form of trust, requires a capable mind in charge."

"Then isn't it fortunate, Mr. Stryker, that she has you?"

The voice Alyssa didn't like—the blue, pin-striped voice—had spoken again. Cool. Ironic. Just the way it had sounded before. *Ironic.* That was a neat word, Alyssa thought, full of subtle resonance. Resonance was another big word. She couldn't have forgotten anything important if she remembered big words like *resonance* and *ironic*.

"Miss Humphrey's good fortune is questionable, Doctor Reinhard. I am a lawyer, not a detective. And I am currently quite unable to determine the whereabouts of approximately three million dollars in the Humphreys' family assets."

A crash shattered the shocked silence of the room. "Sorry," Rex Clancey mumbled. "The phone slipped. Three million dollars is a hell of a lot of money. Good heavens, how did you manage to lose three million dollars?"

Good question, Alyssa thought. A darn good question. Funny, too. She would have laughed if she hadn't been so tired. "I didn't lose three million dollars, Mr. Clancey." The lawyer sounded as bored and unperturbed as ever. "I merely discovered the loss and am now reporting it to you."

Alyssa closed her eyes, ignoring the sudden babble of voices. Poor little Alyssa Humphrey! Missing three million dollars, which meant that she was down to her last seven million. Somehow, she couldn't feel sorry for her. For herself, that was.

When she got out of here, when she was well again, she would have quite a lot of fun spending seven million dollars.

Chapter Three

The nurse carefully fluffed Alyssa's limp hair around her bandages. "You're looking great this morning, really great. It must be because you're going home."

Alyssa picked up the hand mirror Nora held out to her. An Egyptian mummy crowned with dirty-blond hair stared back. *This* was looking great? Alyssa would have smiled, except that she had learned her lesson. Smiling hurt.

"Okay, Nora. Tell me how somebody buried in bandages looks great. Or rotten. Or anything except ready for a part in a horror movie."

"With their eyes," the nurse replied, unabashed. "You're not in pain anymore and your eyes are sparkling. Also, your lips aren't swollen, which makes your mouth look halfway normal again. You're lucky you didn't lose any of your front teeth. And your dress looks great. Red suits you."

Alyssa gave another squint into the mirror. Maybe her eyes did look cheerful this morning, and it was true her lips had healed. And her body felt almost human again. With a mutter of exasperation, she tossed the mirror onto the bed, ashamed of her need to be reassured.

"You're a terrific nurse, Nora. Here I am, about to go home to a house I don't remember, to a sister I could swear I'd never set eyes on before last month, and you've got me convinced everything's peachy keen."

"Sure, why not? From what people tell me, it's a very comfortable house with a cook and a chauffeur and a cleaning woman who comes in daily. Sounds like heaven to me. You don't have to remember all the tiny details to know luxury feels wonderful.''

"Don't you?" Alyssa got up from the chair and walked restlessly to the window. She stared down at the uninspired view of parked cars. "I want to feel sorry that my brother's dead, but I can't. I can't mourn somebody I don't remember."

The nurse's bracing tones softened. "Your memories will come back soon enough, Alyssa. The neurosurgeon says you've no permanent brain damage, and he's a cautious man. Usually we have a tough time getting him to agree in writing that Tuesday is Tuesday. If he says your memory loss is psychosomatic, then you can take his opinion to the bank."

"Is it better to know I'm nuts rather than neurologically damaged?" Alyssa asked wryly.

"Temporarily nuts."

"How temporary is temporary?"

"However long it takes your brain to come to terms with the trauma, I guess. You survived a terrifying plane crash that killed your brother and a hundred and forty-three other people. Your body was bruised just about everywhere a body can be bruised. Your face was banged all to blazes, and Doctor Reinhard had you in surgery for eight hours pinning you back together again. You need time to heal and then your memories will come back."

"And if they don't?" Alyssa whispered, keeping her gaze fixed firmly on the parking lot.

"They will." Nora spoke with confidence, then gave a gurgle of laughter. "And if it doesn't, you can tell Senator Matthew Bradford he has to make you fall in love with him all over again. Honey, that ain't such a bad prospect. I'm willing to trade places!"

Alyssa didn't share in Nora's friendly laughter. Instead she smothered a pinprick of uneasiness. The mere thought of Matthew Bradford made her stomach clench tight with nervous tension. Why? She searched her mind for some clue, some connection, but nothing came. *Damn,* but she hated this sensation of floating free in the ether.

A brisk knock at the door cut through her mounting agitation. Nora opened the door.

"Oh, hello, Mr. Stryker, you're right on time. Alyssa's ready to go home as soon as we can get the orderly up here with a wheelchair."

"Good morning, Nora." The lawyer walked into the room and nodded to Alyssa. "Miss Humphrey."

She returned his nod with one equally cool. This morning Stryker had forsaken the gloom of navy blue pinstripes in favor of funereal charcoal, highlighted by a gray-on-gray tie. His button-down shirt was starched stiffly enough to crackle, and his face wore its habitual expression of aloof, vaguely patronizing patience. When he walked past her to set his briefcase on the small table, Alyssa caught a momentary breath of expensive, musk-based after-shave. An odd prickle of physical awareness raced down her spine. It changed almost at once into irritation. Alyssa had realized during the past week that Stryker's mere presence annoyed her. Just seeing him created a childish desire to say something startling enough to shock the neat gray dots off his sensible, all-wool socks.

Nora's beeper buzzed. "Oh-oh! I have to go. I'll call the orderly from the nurses' station. See you folks in a while."

"No hurry. The chauffeur won't be here for another fifteen minutes." Stryker took off his glasses and pressed his thumb and forefinger to the bridge of his nose. He looked tired, and it occurred to Alyssa for the first time that Dick's death and her own loss of memory must be causing Stryker a considerable amount of extra work. Not to mention the problems caused by the missing three million dollars.

"Did you steal the money that's vanished from my account?" she asked, then snapped her lips closed in frustration. "I'm sorry," she said. "One of the more interesting side effects of having no memory is that I've lost most of my social inhibitions. As soon as I form a question in my mind, I tend to ask it."

Stryker put his glasses back on. "Your question was perfectly valid, Miss Humphrey. And my answer is—No, I didn't steal three million dollars of your money."

She would have liked him better if he'd shown at least a hint of anger, but he showed no emotion at all. "Is there any reason I should believe you?" she asked, wanting to needle him.

"None that I can think of. At least until I find the missing funds and return them to you."

"Can you do that?"

"I *will* do that, Miss Humphrey. You can count on it."

"I could fire you and hire somebody I know is reliable."

"Yes, you could. I would still look for the missing funds, however. And I would find them."

A hot flare of irritation flickered deep inside her. "You're arrogant, Mr. Stryker."

"So are you, Miss Humphrey. As far as I can see, your accident hasn't changed that characteristic in the slightest." He sounded faintly amused.

It was disconcerting to realize that although she knew almost nothing about the man standing in front of her, he knew all sorts of things about her. Alyssa sank down into the room's only armchair, finding a certain black humor in the situation where two seconds earlier she had felt nothing but aggravation.

"What's your first name, Mr. Stryker?"

"Adam."

"How old are you, Adam?"

He looked at her consideringly. "Is this a job interview?"

"Maybe."

"I'm thirty-five."

"How long have you worked for me?"

"I don't work for you, Miss Humphrey. I work for the Humphrey Family Trust."

"A distinction without a difference."

"Lawyers are fond of those."

She sighed. "Answer the question, please, Adam. How long have you worked for me?"

"Two months." He paused, then added. "Your brother hired me when the previous trust officer resigned. Dick and I attended law school together."

"And you graduated top of the class, right?"

"No, Miss Humphrey. I graduated slightly above the middle. In the forty-fifth percentile, to be precise."

His answer surprised her. Somehow she had gained the impression that a very bright intellect lurked behind Adam Stryker's unapproachable, phlegmatic facade. But since she couldn't imagine him blowing off his studies, she could only conclude he wasn't as smart as he appeared. The conclusion was obscurely disappointing.

"Why did my brother hire you? He must have known your law school record was mediocre."

Adam's voice contained a hint of mockery. "No doubt he considered my honesty above reproach, Miss Humphrey. My plodding honesty was worth something, even if my legal qualifications seem less than stellar."

So his law school class ranking was a sore point with Adam Stryker. Interesting. "Oh for heaven's sake stop calling me Miss Humphrey," she snapped. "You sound like the faithful family retainer in a bad Victorian novel."

"Until today you made a point of insisting that I was not allowed to use your first name." The lawyer's mouth twisted in a faint suggestion of a smile. "You disliked me just as much before the plane crash as you do now."

Alyssa felt a tiny curl of amusement unfold inside her. "How nice to know that I'm consistent."

"At least where your feelings toward me are concerned," he agreed without heat.

"How did you discover the money was missing from my trust fund?"

"That's the wrong question," he said quietly. "The real question is how could responsible executors take so long to discover funds were missing?"

"All right. Then answer your own question. Why did you take so long to find out I was being robbed?"

His hesitation was so brief, she almost missed it. "The cover-up was so simple it was virtually foolproof," he said. "Somebody converted three million dollars of your assets into zero-coupon bonds. They're a perfectly legitimate form of investment which pays no interest until maturity, at which point the face value of the bond is doubled or sometimes tripled. Investors often buy them for tax reasons."

"If zero-coupon bonds are legitimate, why have I lost three million dollars?"

"Because your particular bonds are fakes. The certificates look genuine, but they're forgeries."

She frowned. "Surely whoever took the money must have known the forgeries would be discovered the first time my account was audited?"

"Not at all. The bonds don't pay interest, as I explained. Anybody auditing your account would simply check that you held the paperwork for the appropriate amount of money and that would be that. You aren't expecting to receive interest payments on the bonds, so you would have no reason to question the certificates—or even look at them—until they fall due fifteen years from now."

"But you obviously questioned them. Why? Was it something to do with my brother's death?"

"No. When I took charge of the trust, I reviewed your portfolio of assets. Three million dollars seemed an excessive amount of money to hold in non-interest-paying bonds. The week before your plane crash, I suggested to you and your brother that one or two million dollars' worth of bonds should be converted back into income-producing funds."

Considering her assets in million-dollar blocks gave Alyssa an intense desire to giggle. She looked away so that Stryker wouldn't see her laugh. "Why was my brother so closely involved with all this?"

"He is—was—the other executor of your trust. I was legally obligated to consult him on all financial decisions until your thirty-fifth birthday."

"Did that annoy me?"

"Yes."

"Another area where my feelings are consistent."

"Your father seems to have cherished some rather old-fashioned beliefs. The provisions of his will suggest that he didn't trust women to make financial decisions."

"Whereas you, of course, are an ardent feminist."

"Of course," he replied, his voice bland. "A paid-up member of NOW."

"Right," she said with heavy sarcasm. "And you think women can handle money as competently as men."

"I've seen no convincing evidence that male hormones are a prerequisite for understanding finance."

She grinned beneath her bandages. If you spent long enough with him, Adam's pompous way of speaking became oddly attractive. She cut off the grin and spoke quickly to cover a sudden flare of confusion. "Why don't you just trace back the transactions until you find out who sold three million dollars' worth of my assets? There must be a paper trail."

"Unfortunately not. The transactions were made through an electronic financial clearing house in New York, so the orders were placed either by wire or by computer." Once again Alyssa detected a fractional hesitation before Adam continued. "The name on the purchase orders is your brother's."

"My own *brother* was stealing my funds?"

"I didn't say that. Anybody could use his name on a computer transaction. I explained all this to you the day before your accident. Are you sure you don't remember anything about our conversation?"

"Why do you sound so doubtful, Mr. Stryker? I don't remember *anything* prior to my accident except boarding the plane in Chicago. If I don't remember my fiancé or my sister, why would I remember a conversation about converting zero-coupon bonds into stocks? That's not exactly a subject to set my heart palpitating."

"Perhaps not. Except that you were annoyed when your brother wouldn't agree to the sale of the bonds. You accused him of exercising petty tyranny over you through the terms of your father's will. You made some pretty dramatic threats."

"Like what?"

"Like taking your case to the ACLU in a blaze of publicity and claiming you were being penalized for having married a man your father disliked—"

She felt as though a knife had been plunged into her stomach. "My God, what do you mean? How can I be married? I thought I was engaged to Senator Bradford!"

Adam looked at her searchingly, then the aloofness of his expression softened. "You were married and divorced right out of college, Alyssa. Your father disliked your ex-husband, which must be why he wrote his will the way he did. If your second choice of husband meets with your brother's approval, you gain immediate control of your inheritance. If you marry without his approval, then the trust continues."

"But Dick is dead."

"Yes," Adam agreed smoothly. "Permission for your marriage now has to come from me. That's only in legal theory, of course."

"And—in legal theory—Mr. Stryker, do you approve of my forthcoming marriage to Senator Bradford?"

"You're an adult, Alyssa. I approve of adults making their own decisions."

He hadn't quite answered her question, but she didn't pursue the topic. She swallowed, moistening her dry throat. "This ex-husband person. What's his name? What does he do?"

"His name is Tony Delano. I don't know what he does now, but at the time of your divorce he was planning to become a movie star."

"Is he—was he a good actor?"

Adam's voice was very dry. "There is no evidence to suggest he had the slightest talent for acting. He did, however, have a remarkable talent for spending your money. Of that we have ample proof.''

Alyssa absorbed the information in silence. She couldn't remember the details, but somehow she knew the man she loved had betrayed her in the worst possible way. Pain exploded inside her head, and she gave a tiny, involuntary groan. Dear God, she didn't want to think about the man she had once loved.

''Alyssa, what is it?'' Stryker was at her side in few swift, silent strides. He eased her gently onto the bed. ''Do you want me to call the nurse?''

''No. I'll be okay. I had a sudden memory flash, that's all.''

''Not a pleasant one, obviously.''

''No, it wasn't pleasant.''

He handed her a glass of iced water and she sipped it thirstily. ''What did I do before the crash?'' she asked. ''What was my job?''

''You chaired a great many charity events,'' Adam said. ''You're very much in demand for organizing balls and fund-raising banquets. You've never actually sought paid employment.''

''It's amazing how much disapproval you can pack into a supposedly neutral statement, Mr. Stryker.''

For a moment she thought she saw laughter dancing deep in his eyes. He put his glasses back on, then turned and looked straight at her. Beneath her bandages she felt her skin grow hot.

''It's amazing how much disdain you can pack into saying a person's name, Alyssa. I thought we'd agreed that you were going to call me Adam.''

''Yes, we did.'' She cleared her throat to get rid of a sudden huskiness. ''Why don't we make an effort not to rub each other the wrong way over the next couple of weeks? We'll need to spend a fair amount of time together, and it would be easier if we could be polite.''

Adam turned away to open his briefcase. ''It's a deal,'' he said.

"Good. You'll call me if you discover anything about the missing money?"

"I'll come and see you next week with a full report of everything I've discovered." He handed her a business card. "One of those numbers will always reach me. Let me know when you feel up to talking business."

"Thank you." She took the card and pushed it into the pocket of her dress. Silence expanded awkwardly between them, all the harder to break because there was no reason for the sudden tension. They both jumped at the sound of a light tap on the door. Alyssa looked up and saw her fiancé. The senator strode into the room, breathing vitality and the subtle aura of command.

"Matthew!" She greeted him with a pleasure inspired chiefly by relief. Adam Stryker kept all her nerve endings jangling, and she wanted their tête-à-tête to end. When the lawyer looked at her, she had the weird impression he peered right inside her skull, seeing too many things she would rather have kept hidden. *Damn the man, anyway.* He had nothing to be so all-fired conceited about. And she had nothing to hide. What could a rich society woman possibly have to hide other than the unlisted phone numbers of Denver's upper crust?

Matthew's blue eyes sparkled with delight when he realized Alyssa was up and dressed. "You look fabulous, sweetheart. You remembered that's my favorite dress."

She shook her head. "I still can't remember much, Matthew. Jackie chose this outfit for me."

"I'm astonished at her good taste," he said, holding her hand to his cheek. "Mmm, I sure have missed you this week."

Adam cleared his throat. "I'll go and check on that orderly and the wheelchair," he said. "I'm sure the two of you would like a few minutes alone."

Matthew smiled his thanks. "We sure would. I can't wait to get Alyssa home where we can have some real quality time together."

Adam left the room and Matthew guided her to a chair. "We mustn't tire you out," he said. "Honey, I have a big favor to ask you."

"What's that?"

"I want to announce our wedding date before you leave the hospital. It's what you were originally coming to Denver to do."

Alyssa recoiled. "Oh no, Matthew, let's not! The reporters will be all over us!"

He stroked her hand soothingly. "Honey, there's no way for either of us to avoid the huge crowd of reporters lying in wait downstairs. Why don't we give them something to sink their teeth into? That way they won't harass us with dozens of prying questions."

"I hate the thought of exposing our personal lives to public gossip."

He smiled reassuringly. "Sweetie, I'm an old pro with reporters. Trust me, I'm suggesting the best way to get them off our backs. I've been trying to convince them for weeks that I'm not a candidate in the next presidential election. If I tell them we're getting married next month, and that we're planning to start a family right away, they'll believe me."

A baby. Matthew wanted to have a baby! He was giving up a chance to run for president of the United States just for her! A lightning shaft of memory blazed through Alyssa's mind.

"Do you know, that was what I regretted most when the plane was going down," she whispered. "All I could think about in those last few minutes before the crash was how much I wanted to have a baby."

For a moment Alyssa had the odd impression that Matthew was disconcerted by her reply. Then he reached out and touched her gently on the arm. "Hey, I'm so glad you're seeing things my way. We're going to give those reporters a *real* story to phone home."

"What story is that?" Adam asked, returning to the room.

Alyssa looked at the lawyer. "That Matthew and I are getting married next month," she said with a touch of defiance.

"That I'm definitely, categorically and absolutely not running for the presidency of the United States," Matthew said.

Adam's expression revealed no more than mild interest. "My, my," he said. "Dick would have been surprised. By both of you."

Chapter Four

Alyssa stared out of the tinted windows of the limo, trying to conjure up a few memories. She must have driven along these streets a thousand times, and yet nothing looked familiar. If she hadn't known better, she would have sworn that she had never seen this part of Denver in her entire life.

She didn't want to confess her ignorance to Matthew, but in the end the need to feel some sense of orientation won out over pride. "Where are we?" she asked tersely.

Matthew betrayed no sign of impatience when he spoke. "This is Sixth Avenue, and we're traveling east toward Monaco. Your house is on the other side of town, near the Denver Country Club."

Alyssa had been told that she'd lived in the same house on Maple Street since early childhood. She hoped—passionately—that going home would provoke emotions strong enough to break through the mental barriers she had erected against the past. Despite the neurologist's assurance that she had suffered no permanent brain damage, she secretly feared that some vital nerve had been severed in the crash, and that one morning she would wake up a raving, gibbering lunatic.

"This is the intersection of Sixth Avenue with Holly Street." Matthew's voice intruded into her gloomy thoughts. "It's pretty, isn't it?"

"Yes, it is," she agreed. This section of Sixth Avenue was divided by a central strip of grass, shrubs and trees wide enough to form a linear park. Joggers panted around flower beds, mothers strolled with babies, and senior citizens walked their dogs among the bushes. Alyssa watched the passing blur of red geraniums, bronze chrysanthemums and yellow dahlias and thought how bizarre it was that not a single thing about this distinctive street looked familiar.

"You are a stupid, dumb subconscious," she muttered. "How can I work through my problems when you won't let me remember what my problems are?"

"What did you say, sweetheart? Are you sure you're feeling all right?" Matthew leaned over her, adjusting the mohair blanket and fussing with the pillow he had tucked behind her head as they left the hospital.

Alyssa gritted her teeth so that she wouldn't yell at him to leave her alone. "I'm feeling wonderful," she said with determined cheerfulness. She stretched out her legs and eased the crick of tension that had somehow appeared in her neck. "I was enjoying getting reacquainted with my hometown."

"Once we're married, Chicago will be your home. And Washington, DC, of course."

Alyssa shrugged off a tiny chill. Her jitters about marrying Matthew were too irrational to worry about. They were simply another phobic reaction to the plane crash, and she would ignore them.

"Where do you live in Chicago?" she asked. "Are we going to live in the same place after we're married?" She gave a frustrated laugh. "This is ridiculous, isn't it? Having to ask my own fiancé where he lives."

"Don't worry, I understand how you must feel. And the answer is that I have a town house in Georgetown, almost in the heart of Washington, and an apartment in Chicago with a fabulous view of the lake. You particularly liked my Chicago apartment."

"Whereabouts in Chicago is the apartment?"

"Water Tower Place, although I don't suppose that'll mean anything to you."

"But it does!" she exclaimed, surprised and delighted by the instant flash of name recognition. "Water Tower Place is a huge development in downtown Chicago. There's a shopping complex and a major residential tower right next door."

"Why, yes, that's wonderful, sweetheart! You're absolutely right."

The picture of Water Tower Place that sprang into Alyssa's mind was complete in every detail. She could visualize each floor of the shopping plaza, and knew exactly where she could buy her favorite handmade chocolates, and which boutique carried leather belts and purses imported from Italy.

But could she remember Matthew's apartment building, the famous Water Tower Place? *Yes!* In her mind's eye, she saw the lobby, complete with its reception desk and complex security system. She knew how she would turn to get to the elevators. She knew that the elevators were mahogany-paneled inside.

"Oh, Matthew, it's beginning to come back! This is one of the most precise memories I've had since the accident." She was thrilled by the break in the curtain veiling her past. "But I wonder why I remember your apartment building so much better than my own house here in Denver?"

Matthew's mouth curved into a smile. "I can think of a couple of excellent reasons, sweetheart." In deference to the chauffeur he lowered his voice and leaned across to whisper in her ear. "My Chicago apartment is where we made love for the very first time. Do you think that might have something to do with why you remember the place so clearly?"

But she didn't remember his apartment, Alyssa realized in sudden despair. She remembered the lobby and the elevator, then her memories of Water Tower Place came to a total halt. She had no idea how Matthew's apartment was decorated, or what his bedroom looked like, much less how she had felt when they made love. Her stomach knotted with fear. My God, surely this was a sign that she was crazy, not just amnesiac! It was totally insane to remember the lobby of a building, but not the place where your fiancé had made love to you for the first time.

Alyssa pushed at the stubborn wall of blankness. She tried to visualize herself lying in Matthew's arms. The harder she tried, the more nauseated she felt, but she kept on pushing. And then the ghastly image swam into focus.

A handsome blond man, crouched in the middle of the bed, hair tousled, skin sweaty, eyes defiant. And a woman lying next to him, elegant even in her nakedness, with tiny diamond studs decorating her shell-like ears.

Alyssa pressed her hand to her eyes, willing the image away. She had fought so hard to bring this memory into being, and now that it was here, she wanted no part of it. But the image lingered tenaciously, mocking her with its clarity before shifting into a hideous series of moving pictures.

The man kissed his lover with a passion and tenderness that made Alyssa feel sick with hurt and the sense of betrayal. She couldn't see the woman, couldn't see the details of the bedroom, but somehow she knew that the couple were making love in *her* room, in *her* bed. She knew with equal certainty that whoever it was writhing in silent ecstasy under the blond man's smothering embrace, she didn't want to identify that person.

Alyssa bit down on her knuckles, forcing back an anguished cry of betrayal. The scene was unbearably painful to her. Who was the blond man on the bed? Not Matthew, that was for sure. Could it be Tony, her ex-husband? Perhaps that was why her first marriage ended within two short years. Tony must have been an adulterer. And his adultery had been a shattering blow to her.

To Alyssa's relief the limo drew to a halt before Matthew could ask why she had suddenly become so stiff and silent, and in the flurry of removal from car to driveway, the unwelcome images finally vanished.

"Here we are, sweetheart, home at last." Matthew beamed with pleasure as she glanced around the beautiful yard. "Everything looks splendid, doesn't it? The yard crew have done a good job. Those dahlias make a wonderful show."

She heard the note of hope he couldn't quite eliminate from his voice, and wished that she could give him the answer he was longing for. The garden did indeed look splendid. But it didn't look in the least familiar, which was what Matthew obviously wanted her to say.

"The dahlias are beautiful," she said, wanting to give him something. "They're a family tradition, aren't they?"

"See! You're beginning to remember!" His face lit up with such excitement that she didn't have the heart to tell him she'd made a lucky guess. Alyssa walked slowly up the flight of stone stairs to the double oak doors of the house where she had supposedly spent all her childhood and a good many years since. She recognized literally nothing.

Before either she or Matthew could ring the bell, the door was thrown open and a neatly dressed, middle-aged woman greeted Alyssa with a smile.

"I was watching from your room upstairs," she said. "I'm Barb Mackintosh, the nurse's aide the senator hired for you, Miss Humphrey, and I'm sure we're going to have you feeling better in no time."

"Thank you. Please call me Alyssa. I'm glad to be home."

"I'm sure you are. Well, come on in, Alyssa, my dear. You'll be wanting to rest, I don't doubt. Coming out of the hospital is always a lot more tiring than we think it's going to be."

If the car journey hadn't tired her, Barb Mackintosh's chatter was surely guaranteed to finish her off, Alyssa reflected wryly. Barb was already launched into a monologue on the comforts awaiting Alyssa in her bedroom when a door to the left of the hallway was thrown open, and Rex Clancey burst into view.

"Senator!" he exclaimed with as much joy as if he and Matthew had been parted for weeks rather than minutes. "Senator, the spin they're putting on your speech is outstanding. Everything we'd hoped for, and more. The CNN commentator has already said that this speech is simply another reason to hope that you'll stay in the r—"

"Great," Matthew said calmly. "Glad you're staying on top of things, Rex. I'll talk to you when I've seen Alyssa to her room."

Rex blinked, visibly tamping down his euphoria. "Alyssa, I'm sorry. I should have welcomed you home before starting on business. I hope the journey didn't tire you too much?"

"I'm fine, thanks."

"That's good, very good." Rex glanced at his watch. "Oh, my, it's two-thirty already."

"We're not in any rush," Matthew said.

"Well, actually I'm afraid we are. I have a piece of unfortunate news for you and Alyssa. The thing is, Matthew, you're needed back in Washington."

Matthew frowned. "I thought we'd cleared my calendar for the next two days."

"Yes, we did. But there's a tight vote coming up on the budget, and the chief of staff called from the White House. I only just hung up from speaking to him as you walked through the door. The president is counting on your vote, Matthew. He needs you back in Washington right away."

Sighing wearily, Matthew took Alyssa's hands into his. "Sweetheart, I'm sorry, but you do understand, don't you? I have to go. The president's counting on me."

"Of course you must go, Matthew." Alyssa quelled a rush of guilty relief. For some reason it felt terrific to know that Matthew was leaving town. Perhaps the relief sprang from the fact that Rex Clancey would leave, too. Matthew's aide was about as pleasant to have around as a cockroach.

Matthew returned her hands carefully to her sides. "What a wonderful senator's wife you're going to make, sweetheart."

Alyssa pushed her mouth into a smile and thought wistfully of her bed. This was the longest she had remained standing since the crash, and her legs were beginning to shake from the effort of holding her upright. She was actually relieved when Rex Clancey cut short Matthew's tender goodbyes with a curt "We really have to leave now, Senator."

Her afternoon nap was refreshing enough to inspire Alyssa with a determination to eat dinner downstairs. With Barb Mackintosh's help she washed, combed her hair and dressed in a white satin robe trimmed with fake swansdown. Alyssa would have preferred something less exotic, but the other robes hanging in the vast clothes closet were all transparent. She wondered what happened when the doorbell rang unexpectedly, then realized that in a house filled with servants, she never needed to open the door. Strange how the details of her past life seemed to belong to another person. Somehow she knew she would never loll around the house wearing transparent robes.

"The housekeeper's making dinner early," Barb said, plumping up the pillows on the bed, while Alyssa puffed herself with talcum powder. "Jackie's going to come down and join you as soon as she's finished her homework."

Jackie. Her sister. *Good grief, she'd completely forgotten about Jackie!* Now that she was in her own home again, she would have to get to know her young sister a lot better. Alyssa had a hunch that Jackie was sorely in need of some loving attention.

Barb was still talking. "Mr. Stryker suggested chicken breasts in lemon sauce and a sorbet for dessert. Light enough, but a bit tastier than the boring hospital food you've been having."

"Mr. Stryker!" Alyssa exclaimed. "Here? What's he doing here in my house?"

Barb looked surprised at her patient's vehemence. "He needed to speak to you about something, I believe."

"He *always* needs to speak to me about something," Alyssa muttered, marching toward the door. "Is he downstairs?"

"In the TV room, last I saw him."

Alyssa stormed down the graceful, curved stairs. She was in the entrance hall before it dawned on her that she hadn't the faintest notion where the TV room was located. The realization did nothing to sweeten her mood. She threw open a few doors at random and finally came across Adam Stryker in a small, dimly lit room, furnished with a large television and several comfortable chairs.

Adam stood in front of the corner bar, mixing himself a drink. In the shadowy half light, he appeared taller and more powerful than her memory of him. His hair shone almost unnaturally black, and his face appeared taut with hard, uncompromising intelligence. He looked up as the door banged against the wall, and his eyes seemed to gleam with momentary amusement behind his glasses. An indulgent father, humoring his child. Alyssa seethed inwardly.

"Hello, Alyssa. Did you have a good rest?" He gestured to the impressive array of beverages. *Her* beverages. He was being mighty generous with *her* drinks. "Could I fix you something? There's juice here, if you're not allowed alcohol."

"Don't you have any work to do?" she demanded. "Why are you here?"

"Waiting to talk to you." He raised his glass and took a sip, not reacting to her rudeness. "I wondered if coming home had helped to trigger any of your memories. I hoped very much that it would."

"No, it hasn't." Disappointment because the return home had achieved so little made her speak more sharply than she'd intended. "Are there any other questions you need answered before you leave?"

"Several." He grimaced ruefully. "But I wonder if I'm likely to get accurate answers to any of them."

"Try me."

He glanced up. "Very well. Here's the first. Have you really lost your memory, Alyssa? Or is this all a pretense?"

She was too stunned even to feel anger. "Are you crazy?" she asked. "Of course I've lost my memory. Why in the world would anyone pretend to have amnesia?"

"I can think of many situations where it might be convenient."

"Believe me, this isn't one of them."

"If you say so." He had his neutral face on again, so she had no idea if he was convinced. "Question number two. How badly do you want to be first lady? Would you lie for the job? Cheat? Rob? Kill?"

He *looked* sane enough, Alyssa thought, edging toward the door. But then, not every lunatic foamed at the mouth. "I don't want to be first lady at all," she said, trying to keep her voice soothing. She nodded her head toward the television, where the local news broadcast had just come on. "You were at the press conference this morning. You heard what Matthew and I said. He's not running for president."

"Isn't he? My reaction to Matthew's announcement this morning was that I've rarely heard a more brilliant campaign speech."

The guy was not only mad, but half-witted as well. "Matthew called the press conference to announce that he *wasn't* running for president," she explained patiently. "Which also means that I have no chance of becoming first lady."

Adam picked up a remote control and turned up the sound on the TV. "Come and sit down," he said. "Why don't you try listening to what your fiancé really announced this morning? If you honestly don't know what's going on this might be an eye-opener for you."

Alyssa sank down into a recliner in a rustle of satin and swansdown. News had apparently been short on the ground during the past twenty-four hours, and the usual two-minute sound bite had been increased to three. Alyssa listened carefully as Matthew twice proclaimed that his personal circumstances—here he shot loving glances in the direction of Alyssa and her bandages—would not permit him to mount a realistic campaign for the presidency at this time.

Adam waited until the segment was over, then cut off the sound. "Well?" he asked. "Wasn't that the niftiest invitation to ignore the early primaries that you ever heard from a candidate?"

Losing her memory hadn't turned her into a total fool. Only a partial one, Alyssa thought wryly. There was a subtext to Matthew's speech that she'd not noticed this morning, but she was sure it was unintentional. It had to be unintentional if the things he'd been saying to her in private were true.

"Matthew is definitely not running for president," she assured Adam. She spoke with absolute firmness in the hope of squashing her own niggling doubt. "We're planning to start a family as soon as we're married. Naturally he didn't want to come right out and announce our personal plans to the whole of America. I expect that's why you heard messages in his statement that really aren't there."

Adam looked at her consideringly. "Maybe I misunderstood," he said at last. "Third question, and this is what I waited around to ask you about. Has anybody mentioned the name Jerry Hershel to you recently?"

"Nobody. I'm sure I've never heard the name. Who is he?"

"He was my predecessor," Adam said. "A banker friend of your father's."

"I'm sorry. I don't remember him. Did I know him well?"

"He was like an uncle to you," Adam said, adding another ice cube to his drink. "He was the main reason you asked to meet me a couple of days before the plane crash. You had several things on your mind. Chief among them was the fact that your brother had removed Jerry Hershel as trustee without consulting you. You asked me to find out what had happened to Jerry. Apparently he'd disappeared. Your brother claimed he'd gone on an extended vacation."

"Had he?"

"No. Jerry Hershel died two weeks after he surrendered the trusteeship."

"I'm sorry," she said, and it was true, although she could feel only an impersonal regret for a man who had no physical reality in her mind.

"He died in a sailing accident on Lake Michigan," Adam continued, his gaze intent as he looked across at Alyssa.

"He wasn't an experienced sailor?"

"On the contrary, he had years of experience. A friend of mine who's a cop has been looking into what happened, checking a few police reports and so on. He got back to me just this afternoon. He tells me the accident was almost certainly no accident. The police are convinced Jerry Hershel was murdered."

Chapter Five

Murdered. Alyssa rubbed the goose bumps on her arms, trying to dispel a sudden chill. She had no memories of Jerry Hershel, no idea whether she'd liked the man when he was alive. But the news of his death pierced the emotional fog that had surrounded her ever since she regained consciousness after the plane crash. The three million dollars missing from her trust account no longer seemed like Monopoly money. All at once, three million dollars seemed like *real* money—a sum quite large enough to tempt people into every sort of crime. Jerry Hershel had been in charge of the Humphrey family trust when the money disappeared. Alyssa couldn't make herself believe that his death was coincidence.

Concentrating hard, she closed her eyes and ran the images through her mind, trying to force a memory: trust fund, three million dollars, Jerry Hershel. Nothing came, not a glimmer of light in the midnight emptiness. But this blankness no longer seemed a welcome escape from a past too bleak to contemplate. Instead, Alyssa recognized a new sense of personal danger. How could she trust anyone or anything when the details of her own life were a mystery to her?

She sprang to her feet, unable to sit still beneath Adam's cool scrutiny. Why had it taken her so long to realize that her amnesia left her vulnerable, at the mercy of anyone who chose to manipulate her? How in the world was she going to know if someone lied to her? She had already noticed an odd prickle of awareness whenever Adam was in the vicinity. Perhaps some buried knowledge in her subconscious was sending her a subliminal warning to beware.

She heard Adam approaching and swung around to confront him. "Why do the police think Jerry was murdered?" she demanded. "Do they know about the missing money?"

"No, I haven't discussed your trust fund with the police. Their suspicions about Jerry's death are based on the autopsy report. Jerry seems to have been dead for at least an hour before he fell into the lake. Some abrasions suggest he was dragged on board the yacht after dying elsewhere."

"His murderers must have been pretty dumb not to realize what the autopsy would reveal."

"They may have hoped the lake currents would take the body out of reach of the police divers until it was too decomposed to reveal anything. Or maybe they were confident enough not to care. Just because the police suspect Jerry was murdered, it doesn't mean they have a clue as to who did it or why."

"In other words, the murderers have every right to be confident. They're getting away with killing Jerry."

"So far, it seems."

She gripped the back of the sofa, hoping Adam wouldn't notice her sudden need for extra support. But of course he did. "Why don't you sit down?" he suggested and went to the bar, returning with a full glass, chinking with ice cubes. "You look like you could use a drink. I'm sorry if my news upsets you."

She waved the glass away. "I'm not allowed alcohol. I'm still taking painkillers."

"This is just ginger ale on the rocks, nothing added. You don't have to worry."

Didn't she? Alyssa sniffed the contents of the glass before taking a cautious sip, not trusting Adam now that she recognized the extent of her vulnerability. The icy soda tasted good, free of any taint of alcohol and comfortingly familiar, as if ginger ale were her favorite drink.

Adam sat down in the chair opposite her, the austerity of his expression softened by the tiniest hint of laughter. "If you were a porcupine, every one of your quills would be quivering with hostility," he said.

"How fortunate for you that I'm merely a woman, and my hostile vibrations can do you no damage."

"Can't they?" he asked, his voice wry. He hesitated for a moment, then put down his drink. "You know, we're both in something of a dilemma. Maybe we should stop circling each other like two dogs staking out their home territory and try sharing what little we know. Three million dollars are missing from your trust fund, but neither of us have any idea why, or who took it—"

"My goodness, when did you decide that?" Alyssa asked, her voice brittle with politeness. "A few minutes ago you were accusing me of faking amnesia. Presumably that's because you think I stole my own three million dollars—"

"That's not precisely what I suspect."

"Why else would I fake amnesia?"

"Because you're scared," he said quietly. "Because you're into something unsavory way over your head, and you want to let certain people think you don't remember anything about their activities. I saw you the day before you caught that fatal flight out of Chicago, remember, and underneath all the bluster and hostility, I know you were terrified."

Alyssa didn't want to accept that she had reason to be frightened, so she answered him with deliberate sarcasm.

"Which people do you think I was scared of?" she demanded. "The Mafia? My next-door neighbors? The housekeeper?"

"None of them," he said. "I think you were afraid of your brother."

For a split second her heart seemed to stop beating, although what she felt wasn't exactly shock, more an icy sense of foreboding. "Are you accusing my own brother of robbing me? That's pretty despicable, since he's dead and can't defend himself."

"I'm not in a position to accuse anyone. I know exactly how the trust fund was manipulated, but not why, or who did it. You were furious with your brother right before the plane crash, but you weren't willing to tell me why he'd made you angry. I'm throwing out suggestions, Alyssa, not making accusations."

"Would you expect me to betray my own brother, even if there's something to betray? I scarcely know you, and we both agree that I never liked you."

"We know each other better than you might expect," he said tautly. "And no, I didn't expect you to betray your brother." He turned away, lifting his shoulders in a shrug that struck Alyssa as strangely defeated. When he turned around again, his stern expression had softened into a rueful smile. "I just hoped you might come to me for help," he said. "It's unreasonable of me, I know, but I keep wishing you could bring yourself to trust my integrity, even if you can't manage to like me."

His smile altered the whole of his face, changing his expression from remoteness to warmth, tempered by a hint of strong intelligence. Alyssa felt a tug of attraction until her emotions, always capricious since the crash, switched with lightning speed back to anger.

"Your integrity seems to consist of accusing your predecessor or my dead brother of some nameless crime. I may not have any memories, Adam Stryker, but I haven't lost all my powers of reason. Do you want to know what I think happened? I'll bet that before the crash I'd collected proof that *you* stole the damn money yourself, and this 'let's be friends' act is your way of keeping tabs on me."

"If I'd stolen three million dollars and gotten away with it, don't you think I'd be smart enough to have flown off to South America by now?"

"I don't know. Maybe not. Based on your law school record, you're not very smart."

"And if I'm a thief and a murderer, those sort of remarks on your part could be considered downright stupid."

Adam was white-faced. They were both tight-lipped and breathing hard. On the brink of yelling out a furious retort, Alyssa's rage vanished as swiftly as it had come. In truth, Adam was right. For whatever combination of crazy reasons, she didn't believe he was a thief. Oddly enough, considering how prickly and restless he made her feel, she trusted his professional integrity. In fact their mutual antipathy seemed an easier and more honest basis for a relationship than the love she was supposed to feel for Senator Matthew Bradford. Her fiancé. She closed her eyes and leaned back against the sofa cushions, woozy with sudden fatigue.

Adam caught hold of her unbandaged left hand. His grip felt warm and protective, not smothering as the senator's often did. The senator. How strange it was, Alyssa reflected, that she consistently thought of her fiancé in terms of his public office rather than by his given name.

"Listen to me," Adam said. "Really listen to what I'm saying, Alyssa, because I'm trying to help you. To be honest, I'm not sure if your amnesia is faked or not. In a way I hope it is. Life might be safer that way for both of us. Because if you genuinely have no memories of your own past, you're at the mercy of whatever lies anyone chooses to tell you. And I'm sure this is a dangerous time for you to be so susceptible to other people's manipulations."

His warning paralleled her own earlier recognition of danger, but she wasn't willing to let him see he'd touched a nerve. "So I need to be wary of everyone in the world except you, right, Adam? You're Mr. Integrity personified, virtue and compassion encased in impeccable pinstripes."

"I'm wearing a positively dashing suit today," he offered, his voice mild, but his eyes gleaming with a hint of self-mockery. "Haven't you noticed the frivolous pattern?"

Alyssa stared at Adam's suit and managed to detect the faintest hint of a dark navy check woven into the fabric. Impossibly, when she looked back up at him, she found herself wanting to smile.

"Clothes tell you more about a man's profession than they do about the man," Adam said softly, holding her gaze. She felt her cheeks growing hot beneath her bandages and she pulled her hand away from his. He leaned back in the chair, his manner returning to its customary briskness.

"Alyssa, I'm the trustee of your estate, and I'm paid to give you good advice whether you want to listen or not. If you're faking amnesia, please ask yourself if this is really the best way to achieve your own safety. You haven't known me for long, so I accept that you have no reason to confide in me. But please go to the authorities with whatever is bothering you. The FBI has its moments of bureaucratic idiocy, but their agents are more efficient than most people credit."

"I'm not faking amnesia," she said tiredly. "For heaven's sake, how many times do I have to tell you I don't remember anything about my past life."

"Then if you have a genuine memory loss, will you start using some of the intelligence God gave you? Don't keep it buried like you usually do beneath the image of mindless young society matron."

"Use it how? For what?"

"Protect yourself. Don't believe everything you're told. Watch the people around you. Listen to what they're saying. Better yet, listen for what they're not saying, or glossing over. Maybe even allow yourself to relax occasionally and trust your gut instincts. I'm sure they're sound."

Alyssa gave an unladylike snort. "Fine advice coming from someone as uptight as you. I'm willing to bet you've never trusted your instincts in your entire life."

"You'd lose," Adam said. "I'm trusting them now, with you."

ALYSSA HAD TWO WEEKS to wait until her bandages came off, two weeks during which little seemed expected of her.

She was impressed by the efficiency of the household, which ran on smooth invisible wheels, providing her with tempting meals, clean laundry, polished furniture and a total absence of responsibility. At first Alyssa tried to take care of simple tasks for herself, but when Shirley, the housekeeper, found her searching for detergent to put in the washing machine, she just laughed, and said, "Lord love us, Alyssa, you never washed your clothes when you were a hundred percent fit. Why are you doing it now when you need all the rest you can get?"

A good question, Alyssa thought, and wondered why her stupid memory continued to provide such unreliable flashes of information. She could have sworn that she had taken care of her own washing in the past, and she had a vivid mental picture of the local dry cleaning store to which she was sure she had always paid frequent visits before the crash. Adam Stryker would probably tell her to trust her memories and doubt the housekeeper, but Alyssa refused to sink to such a level of paranoia. Good grief, her past method of cleaning clothes could not possibly hold any significance.

Barb Mackintosh, the nurse, told her not to worry about apparent inconsistencies. "The mind's a funny old thing," she said, as they sat in the backyard, soaking up the late-fall sunshine. "Don't press it. One day something will set you off, and all your memories will come rushing back, you'll see."

The nurse's words seemed scientifically doubtful, but reassuring nonetheless. In the lethargy of convalescence, Alyssa was content to let such minor mysteries as her laundry habits float away into the accommodating depths of her subconscious.

Neither Adam nor her fiancé neglected her, although they both remained out of town. Adam sent her a typed letter saying he was in New York, pursuing his investigations into the missing trust funds. Matthew sent roses every day, and phoned her each evening from Washington, asking after her health with tender concern and tactfully questioning her about the state of her memory.

Strangely enough, Alyssa began to dread Matthew's solicitous calls, and on a couple of occasions feigned sleep rather than go to the phone. She excused herself for the deceit by telling herself it was only natural to feel strained with somebody she was supposed to love passionately, but actually couldn't remember. She also began to acquire an unreasoning antipathy to roses.

Of all her frustrations, Alyssa found her inability to remember her half sister the worst. She didn't need access to her memory to know that her younger sister was suffering from plenty of teenage problems. Jackie was a sophomore at Woodhouse College, a private day school in the far western suburbs of the city. She drove her own BMW car to school each morning, and rarely returned to the house until late at night.

The ghoul look was obviously acceptable at expensive private schools, because Jackie left the house each day with her face layered in white pancake makeup, her eyelashes spiked with heavy black mascara, and her outrageous—and hideous—clothes decorated with assorted chains and clanking, oversized metal pins. Her contact with anyone inside the Humphrey household seemed minimal, and although she was willing to answer Alyssa's questions, she never initiated any contacts or conversation. It was a sad reflection on their past relationship, Alyssa mused, that Jackie invariably seemed startled when Alyssa tried to make friends.

"Why are you always home so late?" Alyssa asked one day, trying not to sound accusatory, and yet wondering who kept a check on Jackie's activities. Sixteen seemed very young to have complete freedom of movement and unfettered use of a BMW. The rich certainly organized their lives differently from the ordinary run of people, Alyssa reflected.

"Do you belong to after-hours clubs, or something?" she persisted. "Have I forgotten that you're the school's star dramatist, or its ace lacrosse player, or something?"

"I'm nothing. I mean, I'm not into organized activities," Jackie flashed a bright smile that didn't quite cover a hint of bravado. "You don't have to worry about me. I go to my girlfriend's house to do homework after school. It's easier with a friend to help out, you know. You don't mind if I'm not here for dinner, do you, Lyss? Mom never minds one way or the other."

Mom. Jackie's mother, Lena Vincent Humphrey. The elusive second wife of Alyssa's millionaire father, now widowed and according to the housekeeper's gossip dedicated to a life of dispensing charity around the world. Lena had left town two days before the plane crash, en route to a missionary school in South Africa. Unfortunately an emergency operation for appendicitis, followed by a bad bout of flu, had left her too weak to travel home to the States. It wasn't Lena's fault that she'd succumbed to appendicitis in a remote stretch of the African veld, but Alyssa couldn't help thinking that the woman needed to reevaluate her priorities. Jackie at the moment seemed more in need of her mother's guidance than even the most worthy distant charity.

"Well, if your mother thinks your schedule's okay, I guess I can't complain." Alyssa patted her sister's arm. "Remember, if you run into any problems, anything at all, I'm here to help. Algebra homework is my specialty. I'm a whiz at quadratic equations."

Jackie laughed with genuine merriment. "Right. Any time I want a guaranteed *F* I'll come to you, Lyss."

"Why do you say that?"

Jackie looked at her oddly. "Hey, Lyss, you can't have forgotten your math grades were always a family joke. I mean, how can you forget that you don't understand something?"

Alyssa covered a jolt of uneasiness with a cheerful grin. She could have sworn she'd always been terrific at math in school, but obviously this was just another confusion thrown up by her scrambled memory banks. "How about boyfriend problems?" she suggested lightly. "Do I rank better than an *F* on that?"

"Maybe. Although you were divorced at twenty-two."

"Hey, youthful miscalculation. Now I'm engaged to a U.S. senator. With the benefit of my experience, you'll do it right the first time around."

"I guess Matthew Bradford's quite a catch, isn't he? Do you really love him, Lyss?"

"Of course." Alyssa made the reply all the more fervent because she so desperately wanted it to be true.

The friendly laughter in Jackie's eyes died and she turned abruptly. "I'll see you around sometime," she said. "Don't wait up."

In fact, far from waiting up, Alyssa felt tired and went to bed early, leaving the nurse and the housekeeper downstairs in the basement watching Clint Eastwood restore justice to the world at the point of a well-aimed gun. Unfortunately, after a brief nap, Alyssa found sleep elusive. She roamed the bedroom restlessly, searching the shelves and drawers in search of—she wasn't quite sure what. Perhaps a piece of herself that would bring back memories.

She found her diary, but it was full of appointments for lunches and pedicures rather than the outpourings of her heart. She rummaged on. In the bottom drawer, hidden under a pile of lacy lingerie, she discovered a white leather photograph album with the words Our Wedding emblazoned in tarnished silver across one corner.

Alyssa knew that looking into this album was going to be painful for her. The divorce had been finalized eight years ago, but somehow she had this odd feeling that her husband's betrayal was a raw wound, a scar on her soul too fresh to have healed. She opened the album with fingers that shook slightly, and stared at the pictures of her younger, starry-eyed self, and at the young man who had briefly been her husband. He was tall and good-looking in a dark, beefy way. Not the sort of man Alyssa thought she would find appealing nowadays, except that his eyes had a decided twinkle, as if he found the world a humorous place, and in just a couple of the photos he seemed to be looking at her with so much love that Alyssa felt a knife pang of regret for what they had somehow managed to squander.

Tucked into the back of the album was a thin packet of letters. Love letters, she soon realized, skimming them with a burst of sweet nostalgia. Love letters written by a very young man who was full of passion and hope for their future. She turned to the last of the letters and discovered that this had been written by Tony at a much later date, seemingly in response to the announcement of Alyssa's engagement to Senator Matthew Bradford.

The news of your engagement even made it to the *LA Times*. I'm writing this letter instead of calling because I don't want to screw up and say the wrong thing, and we never have been able to talk without fighting. Or making love.

You're making a mistake, Lyss, honey, and I want you to think again, for Bradford's sake as much as for mine. He seems like a decent politician—if that isn't a contradiction in terms—and he deserves a wife who really loves him. You don't love him, Lyss. What we shared last month wasn't just great sex. Hell, we've both had enough sex with enough different people to know that all the technique in the world can't produce the fireworks we felt at the cottage. You're thirty-one years old now, honey. Isn't it time you looked at your life and decided to do what you want, not what your daddy wanted? Richard Humphrey is dead, Lyss, and he died without ever understanding the woman you really are. Don't marry Bradford because that's what you think your father would like you to do.

Alyssa shoved the letter back into the photo album, wishing she hadn't read it. Tony was just a ghost from her past, trying to rekindle a marriage that had been dead for years. She had enough on her mind at the moment without starting to question the basis of her relationship with Matthew.

She bundled the album back into the drawer. When she heard the sound of one of the garage doors rolling open, she felt a surge of relief. This must be Jackie! She tightened her robe and thrust her feet into a pair of slippers, hoping to intercept her sister and invite her to a game of chess, or a plain old chat over a cup of hot chocolate.

Alyssa walked out into the upstairs hallway just as her sister pushed open the swinging kitchen door and entered the downstairs vestibule.

"Hi, Jackie!" Alyssa started down the stairs. "Want to take pity on your totally bored sister and challenge me to a game of chess?"

Jackie didn't reply for a moment. She raised her head rather slowly and looked at Alyssa through wide, solemn eyes. "You don't play chess."

"Sure I do," Alyssa said. "My father taught me when I was barely seven years old." Even as she made the claim, she felt a sickening stab of pain over her left eye, and for a moment she had to cling onto the stair rail for support. Then, as swiftly as the pain had come, it vanished.

"You've never told me that before," Jackie said. "How can you re-mem-ber? You never told me you could play chess. I di'n't know you . . . could . . . play."

She spoke a little too loudly, and it seemed to Alyssa that she articulated the words with excessive care. A dreadful suspicion grabbed her, and she ran down the remaining stairs, forgetting both the chess and her headache in the overwhelming rush of anxiety.

"Have you been drinking?" she demanded the minute she reached her sister's side.

"Of course not." Jackie sounded indignant, almost outraged by the suggestion.

Alyssa snapped her mouth shut. Dumb question, she told herself. You know she's going to lie. They always do.

"Want to come into the kitchen and share a cup of hot chocolate?" she suggested, bending close to see if she could detect the smell of alcohol on Jackie's breath. She'd seen enough drunks to spot them at fifty paces, and she would have staked her life on the fact that sixteen-year-old Jackie was tanked to the eyeballs.

Jackie leaned back against the wall, trying to appear casual. "I'm . . . not . . . thirshty," she mumbled.

Peppermint, Alyssa realized. Jackie smelled of peppermint, not alcohol. The kid must have chowed down two or three rolls of breath mints in her effort to cover up the smell of booze. No wonder she looked ready to throw up at the slightest provocation.

"Jackie, I know you've been drinking," Alyssa said quietly. "What happened? Did some of the kids at school talk you into it?"

"Yeah, that's what happened. It was a party," Jackie mumbled, scuffing the toe of her shoe in the marble tile of the hallway. "Michelle's parents were out and they left the liquor cabinet unlocked. I guess we all got a bit silly pouring liqueurs onto ice cream. It won't happen again, Lyss, I promise. I know drugs and alcohol are only for losers."

A believable excuse and a sincere apology. Too sincere? Too easily given? Alyssa wanted to accept Jackie's explanation at face value, but a tiny voice inside warned her that she couldn't afford to let her sister off lightly. For a kid under the influence of alcohol—supposedly for the first time—Jackie was frighteningly controlled and much too glib.

"Did you drive yourself home?" Alyssa asked.

"You know I did. Why not? I always do."

"Not anymore," Alyssa said. "And never when you've been drinking. Sorry, Jackie, but you need to learn the hard lesson that there are some mistakes we have to pay for. You can have the car back next month, when I'm sure this party was a one-time mistake, not a habit."

"I told you it was a mistake," Jackie said, her voice getting louder. "Mom would never take the car away from me just because a party with my friends got a little exasher . . . esh . . . out of hand."

"I'm sure you're wrong about your mother, but since she's not here, we can't ask her, can we?"

Jackie scowled. "How can I get to school without my car?"

"Juan can take you, and he can pick you up after class as well. He doesn't have much to do in the garden at this time of year."

"Good grief, I'm *sixteen!* I don't want to be driven around like a *baby.*"

"Then perhaps you'd prefer to take the school bus. I'm sure we could make arrangements for you to be added to their usual route."

Alyssa knew that Jackie wanted to protest, to yell and refuse to cooperate. She knew, because she'd dealt with similar scenes so many times before. She could see the precise moment when her sister recognized that she was in no shape to argue. Scowling, Jackie pushed herself upright, away from the support of the wall.

"Boy, you sure have turned into a raunchy old witch since the plane crash."

"Which is it to be?" Alyssa asked, refusing to rise to the bait. "Juan or the school bus?"

"Juan, I guess." Jackie's face muscles spasmed. She clutched her hand over her mouth and hurried in the direction of the downstairs bathroom. "I've gotta go."

Alyssa watched her sister's departure with troubled eyes. Maybe Jackie was telling the truth and this was the first time she'd ever been tempted to drink too much. Alyssa, however, had a depressing suspicion that Jackie was an old hand at the alcohol game, with lots of experience inventing the lies that would protect her habit.

The phone rang. Alyssa picked up the receiver and answered with a quick hello, her mind still on Jackie. From now on, Alyssa decided, she would need to keep a close eye on her not-so-innocent young sister.

"I wish to speak with Mrs. Humphrey, please." The man's voice was hoarse, as if he had a cold, and thick with an accent—a German accent? Alyssa wondered.

"This is Ms. Humphrey."

"Ah, it is good that you are home at last. I have been waiting to hear from you, dear lady. Word of your illness reached me."

"Who is this?"

The man laughed. "Who else but your old friend Kurt? I believe you recognize my accents." His voice softened. "I become impatient, dear lady, for the health of our joint venture. These are fish that cannot be kept on ice forever, and my vendors require their cash before I can ship the produce. Delay is not good for... fish."

Alyssa stared at the phone in astonishment. "I had no idea I dealt in seafood," she said bewildered. "Nobody told me."

Kurt snorted. "Five days," he said. "You have five days and then we must begin the fishing expedition all over again, and the Mediterranean waters are no longer very fruitful. I am sure you have heard of the pollution problem in this sea. We both know you are short of time. Your customers and suppliers are both losing their patience."

"Do I own restaurants, too? Or only stores?"

The man laughed again. "You have not lost your sense of humor, I see. It is always my pleasure to have business with you. I remind you only that you have hungry customers, Ms. Humphrey, and nervous vendors. I need money soon."

"But who do I pa—"

The man hung up the phone before she could complete her sentence. Alyssa frowned. The man had not sounded at all the sort of person she would like to have as a partner in the seafood supply business, or any other business for that matter. She would have to call Matthew tomorrow and ask him what was going on. He ought to know what businesses Alyssa was involved in, so he would tell her what to do.

DOCTOR REINHARD swung Alyssa's chair around so that she faced the big wall mirror. *"Voilà!"* he said, his face wreathed in smiles. "One of my most successful jobs, even though I say it myself."

Alyssa tried to look and found she couldn't. Dr. Reinhard prodded her gently. "It's all right, Alyssa. Go ahead. You can open your eyes now."

Taking a deep breath, she lifted her head, opened her eyes, and saw... a stranger.

The woman in the mirror had big gray eyes, shiny pink skin, and pudgy cheeks. But it was the straggling, thin eyebrows that toppled the image over from the strange to downright plain. Alyssa fingered her misshapen eyebrows sadly. Her hand was now also bandage free, revealing index and middle fingers bent and slightly flattened where the doctors' magic had not quite managed to restore the flexibility of bones and joints mashed to a pulp by falling debris. She was going to have difficulty with writing and signing her name for a few weeks yet.

Alyssa swallowed hard, good manners compelling her to hide her disappointment. "Thank you, Doctor," she said, "I know you had badly damaged bones to work with, and I'm very grateful for your repair efforts."

"Ha!" he said, chuckling. "I detect a definite lack of enthusiasm. Don't worry, Alyssa, my dear. This isn't how you'll look in a week's time, or even a couple of days from now. You have to let the residual swelling go down, and give your new skin a chance to get rid of its shiny glow. And as for your eyebrows, they'll grow back to their former glory in two shakes of the cat's tail, never fear. I guarantee that in a week's time you'll look in the mirror again and see the beautiful Alyssa Humphrey of before the crash."

Alyssa smiled, but in the pit of her stomach a knot of fear that never quite disappeared suddenly tightened. She already had all Alyssa Humphrey's possessions. According to Doctor Reinhard, she would soon have Alyssa's face. Alyssa Humphrey's future beckoned, offering an exciting life as Senator Bradford's wife. But unlike most people, her past didn't lie behind her, safely shrouded in the mists of time. Her past lay ahead of her, waiting to be discovered, an unknown field dotted with land mines.

Alyssa wondered how many people would get hurt when her past finally exploded.

THE HOUSEKEEPER was waiting in the hall when Alyssa returned. "My, my!" she murmured at last. "Well, isn't he a marvelous doctor? Wonderful what they can do these days, isn't it?"

But Alyssa had seen the jolt of surprise Shirley didn't quite manage to conceal. "Is it that bad? Please tell me the truth."

"Bad? Lord no, you don't look bad, Alyssa. To be honest, though, you look—changed. I can see it's still you, of course, but the doctor's fixed your eyes up different. Prettier than before, really. And the shape of your face isn't the same."

"He says my cheeks are still swollen."

"That could be it." Shirley sounded doubtful. "If you ask me, though, it's your chin that's changed the most."

"He didn't touch my chin."

"Amazing. It looks great, mind you, just different. It's as if a new person is looking out of the old Alyssa's face."

Alyssa grimaced. "I am a new person. I was born six weeks ago, when I woke up in that hospital bed with no memories."

Shirley sniffed. "Stop feeling sorry for yourself. There's plenty of folks worse off than you. Which reminds me, you have another heap of mail to open. Good stuff, most of it. Looks like a lot of get-well cards from your friends."

"Thanks." Shedding her jacket, Alyssa walked into the library, which had become her favorite room, although the housekeeper said she'd never used it before the crash. She sat down at the oversized cherrywood desk and started slitting open envelopes.

"Is Jackie home yet?" she asked the housekeeper, who was pottering around the room dusting the shelves.

"Not until five today. Juan's off and she's taking the late bus."

Alyssa laid another beautiful get-well card on top of the pile. She wished she could remember all these people who were showering her with good wishes. She slit the final envelope. "I'm nervous about seeing Jackie," she admitted to Shirley. "Unfortunately she's still young enough to tell me exactly how I look!"

"You look great, so you have nothing to worry about. Maybe Jackie will convince you you're prettier than ever. Well, I'm through with the cleaning in here, so I'll see about dinner. I'm making your favorite tonight, shish kebab and rice pilaf with almonds."

Almonds? Alyssa could have sworn she disliked the flavor of almonds. Good Lord, her taste in food was the one area where her memory had seemed totally reliable. Now even that was suspect. Distracted, she glanced down at the final card, then blinked.

In Deepest Sympathy was printed across the top in flowing silver script. She reached for the discarded envelope, wondering if she had opened someone else's mail by mistake, but her name was typed on the envelope, along with the Maple Street address. She opened the card.

"Our thoughts are with you at this difficult time," read the printed wording. There was no signature, but a slip of paper had been folded inside the card, carrying a typed, unsigned message: "I know you're a fraud, even if you've fooled everyone else. This card is a kindly warning. Disappear. Get out. You are in danger."

Unmoving, Alyssa stared at the card. Finally the power of movement returned to her hands and she snapped the card shut. What did it mean? *You're a fraud.* What kind of fraud? Adam was the only person who doubted her amnesia, but somehow she couldn't believe that he would have stooped to sending an anonymous message. Besides, why would he need to? He'd already told her to her face both that he didn't trust her, and that she was in danger.

Get out. Disappear. With shaking hands, she reached again for the envelope. The card had been mailed three days earlier at Los Angeles airport, but other than that, it told her nothing.

She would have to take it to the police, Alyssa decided. There might be fingerprints that would identify the sender. Or maybe the police labs could even trace the machine the message had been printed on. Detectives on television always seemed to be doing that. Or had that only been in the old days of manual typewriters?

"Alyssa, darling! Shirley said you were in here. My dear, stand up and let me look at you! I've been counting the hours for this moment. How did it go at the doctor's today?"

Alyssa smothered a silent groan. Of all the people she didn't want to deal with right now, her fiancé would have to top the list. "Matthew," she said weakly, pushing back her chair. "What a surprise, I didn't hear you arrive."

"Shirley opened the door before I had time to ring the bell."

Alyssa slipped the sympathy card under a pile of mail. "We weren't expecting you. How did you manage to get away? Rex Clancey told me you were tied up in committee meetings all through the weekend."

Matthew chuckled. "Rex only *thinks* he controls my life," he said. "I always planned to be with you on the day your bandages finally came off." He laid a huge bouquet of roses on the desk and took her into his arms, kissing her on the forehead and then very gently on her closed lips.

He sighed with pleasure as he drew away. "Alyssa, sweetheart, I can't believe how pretty you look. You're every bit as lovely as before."

"Thank you. Thank you for the flowers, too. They're lovely." Shaken by the horrible sympathy card, she tried to inject some enthusiasm into her voice. "My cheeks are still swollen but Doctor Reinhard says they'll be back to normal within a couple of days."

"Darling, your cheeks may be a tiny bit swollen, but compared to all the horrors we were imagining those first few days after the crash, you look like the beauty queen of the century." He sounded so warm and comforting and sincere. So totally unlike Adam, she thought. Of course, she was delighted Matthew was here tonight. It was crazy—disloyal—to think she would have preferred to show that horrible fake sympathy card to Adam rather than to her fiancé. In a minute she would retrieve the card from the bottom of the pile where she had hidden it and show it to Matthew. Maybe after dinner.

"Sweetheart, what is it?" He stroked her swollen cheeks with a tender touch. "Something's bothering you, Alyssa, I can tell. You're not disappointed with Doctor Reinhard's work, are you? And it certainly can't be that silly phone call you had from Kurt."

"Kurt?" she asked, for a moment not remembering. "Oh, Kurt Walther. About the fish." She blinked. "Why would that worry me?"

"I don't know, honey. But Rex said you sounded rather concerned about the whole episode when you called."

"Only because Kurt hung up the phone before I could find out where I was supposed to send the money."

"Well, good. And now you can put that right out of your mind, because Rex has taken care of the bill for you."

"Did he call Adam?"

There was an infinitesimal pause before Matthew replied. "I'm sure he did. I confess, on money matters, I let Rex handle the details. I don't even know who Kurt is myself."

"Don't you think seafood is an odd thing for me to be trading in? And Kurt sounded like such a strange person." She gave an embarrassed laugh. "Honestly, Matthew, the guy talked like the villain in a bad TV movie."

Matthew laughed heartily. "Darling, there must be some better way of celebrating your terrific new looks than talking about Kurt and his load of fish. Let's go and eat Shirley's wonderful dinner, and then we can decide where we're going dancing. A town the size of Denver must have a couple of decent nightclubs."

Alyssa followed her fiancé into the dining room. She ate her shish kebab, minus the almond-flavored rice, and agreed with Matthew's suggestion that Starkey's would be the perfect place to dance. But somehow, between Jackie's arrival home and the pleasure of eating without bandages, she never got around to showing Matthew the sympathy card.

It was three in the morning before Matthew left in his private plane to go back to Washington. Alyssa was exhausted after her first real night out since the plane crash. But she found time to go into the library and read the mysterious card again, before hiding it inside a copy of *Pride and Prejudice*.

She trusted Matthew, of course she did, and respected him too. The only reason she hadn't shown him the card was because he was so busy.

Adam wasn't nearly such a busy man as the senator. Next time he was in town, she'd show Adam the card.

Chapter Six

Adam had worked twelve-hour days for thirteen days straight. Last night, when he'd finally turned off the computer and gone to bed in the New York hotel, neon-green numbers had marched in relentless columns through his dreams. This morning he'd woken in a grouchy mood, rushed to catch the early-morning flight to Denver, and was still definitely not in the mood for confronting Alyssa Humphrey.

The uneventful flight had left him with too much time to brood, and right at this moment Adam wasn't sure whether he felt more irritated by himself or by Alyssa.

He stopped the rental car for a red light, waiting to make a left turn. Okay, he lectured himself. Time to face facts. Dick Humphrey hired you because he thought you were dumb—too dumb to notice that funds were missing from the Humphrey trust. Second fact: you're almost certain Alyssa was in on her brother's schemes right up to her aristocratic and lovely little neck. Third fact: despite two months of hard work, you have only a vague idea what Dick Humphrey's schemes were. Fourth fact: deciphering the cryptic notes left by Jerry Hershel on the computer hadn't helped him as much as he'd hoped.

Adam slowed for an intersection, then made the final turn onto Maple Street. Thirteen days of intensive research had confirmed that Dick Humphrey's financial affairs were in good shape. He had inherited several million dollars and invested the funds wisely. Despite Dick's two expensive ex-wives, Adam couldn't think of a single reason why the man would need to syphon off millions of dollars from his sister's trust fund. No, everything pointed to the fact that Jerry Hershel's notes were correct. Alyssa hadn't stolen the money for herself, or for her brother. She'd stolen it for Matthew Bradford.

Which brought him to the crux of his current problem: had Alyssa genuinely forgotten what she'd been up to before the crash, or was she putting on an act? And if she was putting on an act, how could Adam break down her defenses and find out what she was trying to hide?

He drew the car to a halt in the Humphreys' driveway and parked neatly alongside a bed of brightly colored fall flowers. Damn it all, checking whether or not a person had genuine amnesia shouldn't be too difficult! In the movies the hero fired off a couple of trick questions, and before you knew it, the villain was blurting out a confession. Trouble was, Adam couldn't think of the right trick questions. What's more, despite a lot of evidence to the contrary, he couldn't quite convince himself Alyssa was the villain.

He rang the doorbell and waited only a few seconds before he heard quick, light footsteps walking across the marble foyer. The door opened. Alyssa stood there, silhouetted in the October sun.

Adam drew in a deep, hard breath. Her bandages had been taken off, and she looked even more stunning than he remembered. Her cheekbones seemed higher, and her chin was more clearly defined. Her eyes, which had been slightly protuberant before the crash, now appeared more deeply set and a darker shade of gray. Adam had always felt a reluctant tug of physical attraction toward Alyssa Humphrey. His own unwanted desire was the major reason he had turned her down so brutally when she offered him a night of casual sex the month before the plane crash.

The memories of that evening—Alyssa's naked body and his own callous rejection of it—still had the power to make Adam squirm. He had chosen to humiliate Alyssa with a cruel put-down simply because he had felt so tempted to accept her offer. And in rejecting her, he had pierced her facade of world weary socialite, cutting through to the scared young woman beneath.

Unfortunately none of these insights helped in the least when he tried to decide just how involved Alyssa Humphrey had been in the robbing of her own trust fund. Adam schooled his expression into the careful neutrality he had perfected during the past few years and greeted Alyssa with a remote courtesy that revealed no trace of his inner turmoil.

Alyssa returned his cool greeting with a smile. "This is great, your flight must have landed on time for once." Her vocal chords had been permanently damaged by the toxic fumes she'd inhaled, and her voice always sounded husky, almost sultry. Today she also sounded a little shy. Endearingly shy. Adam cursed himself for being a susceptible fool. Alyssa Humphrey was about as shy as a tarantula preparing to eat its mate.

"Why don't you come in?" she asked. "Would you mind talking in the kitchen? Shirley and I found this old cookbook from the fifties, and we went wild this morning. We made double fudge walnut brownies with chocolate frosting. You gain a pound just by looking, five pounds if you taste one."

Adam didn't move. Worse yet, he responded to the shy woman he sensed rather than the arrogant woman he knew really existed. "You're beautiful," he said. "My God, Alyssa, you look absolutely beautiful."

She blushed, an honest-to-goodness schoolgirl blush. "Thank you. I'm still trying to get used to the new me." She laughed softly, a little breathless. Pleasure, embarrassment, uncertainty—Adam heard all three emotions in her laughter.

"Four days ago, I had eyebrows like a witch and cheeks like a chipmunk, but I guess everything's beginning to look okay now. Although I still stare into the mirror each morning and think *What does Alyssa Humphrey look like to-*

day? And every time there's a different woman for me to get used to.''

The old Alyssa would simply have preened and assumed men found her irresistible, but the new Alyssa seemed anxious for reassurance. To his surprise Adam found he was willing to play along and boost her confidence.

''You look much better than okay, Alyssa. Although I'm alarmed by the stubborn tilt to your chin. Is that Doctor Reinhard's handiwork, or is your true character showing through at last?''

''Probably my character,'' she said with a rueful grin. ''I don't need to bring back any memories to feel sure my natural character is stubborn as an old mule.''

Adam scowled. Damn it, he thought, what is she playing at? The wretched woman had even changed the way she talked. The precrash Alyssa would never in any circumstances have referred to herself as *an old mule.*

''I have some questions to ask you,'' he said, sufficiently annoyed not to care how curt he sounded.

''Okay.'' Her smile contained a hint of challenge. ''But eat a fudge brownie first. Maybe it will sweeten your mood.''

The kitchen smelled of baking and freshly brewed coffee, and Alyssa looked right at home, as if she enjoyed cooking, instead of loathing every aspect of domesticity, which he knew was the truth.

''The housekeeper's in a state of shock,'' she said, echoing his thoughts. ''Apparently in the thirty-one years up until the plane crash, I never so much as put a slice of bread in the toaster. Then the plane crashed and I emerged with this craving to potter around over a hot stove. Do you think when you lose your memory, your personality changes, too?''

''Perhaps. If you want it to change.''

''Do you always give cryptic answers to simple questions? No, don't answer that. Tell me if you take cream and sugar in your coffee.''

''Just black,'' he said.

She handed him a steaming mug of coffee, together with a huge brownie. "Eat up and then tell me what a wonderful cook I am. You can hurl your questions at me afterward."

He took one bite of brownie and said, with perfect truth, "You're a wonderful cook."

"Stick around, you ain't seen nothin' yet. My lasagna with Parmesan butter topping is to die for."

She fell abruptly silent, and he caught the split-second frown that wrinkled her forehead. Of puzzlement? Chagrin? He wasn't sure which. Then the frown disappeared and she sat down on the other side of the kitchen table, cradling her mug of coffee and soaking up the sun, a woman who seemed content with the moment. In the unforgiving light, Adam could see thin scars disappearing into her hairline, and he was struck with renewed admiration for the bravery with which she'd endured weeks of pain.

"Rex Clancey has been calling me all week," he said tersely, determined not to get sidetracked by irrelevant emotions like sympathy or admiration.

"Oh, good. Did he tell you about the check we need for the seafood company?"

"If that's a joke, I missed the punch line."

"You know, Ace Fishing and Supply Company. They called here demanding payment on my latest shipment of fish. Unfortunately I had no idea what they were talking about."

"And I still don't know, Alyssa. Your trust has no investment in any form of fishing company."

"But Rex said I did! As soon as I mentioned Kurt's name, he gave me the name of the company and said it was a very profitable venture for all of us."

Adam felt himself grow still. "Kurt?" he asked as casually as he could. "You don't happen to know his other name, do you?"

"Walther, or something. Adam, what's all the mystery? Kurt sounded really strange on the phone, so did Rex, and now you're sounding almost equally weird."

Surely she wouldn't mention Kurt Walther's name if she was faking her memory loss? Or was she simply testing him?

"It must be a personal investment," Adam said, after a tiny pause. "You can invest your annual income any way you want without consulting the trustees, so it's probably something you went into with the senator."

"I guess so." Alyssa put her coffee mug onto the table. "Anyway, Rex promised to take care of everything for me, so I'm sure he has."

"He's a reliable man for details," Adam agreed. "If you like, I'll double-check with him on your behalf. Make sure the money got paid. If you're involved in a partnership, you don't want to find yourself in default because of an oversight." He smiled blandly, the picture—he hoped—of ignorance.

Alyssa sighed. "Thanks, but there's no need for you to get involved in this. I'll remind Rex myself."

I'll just bet you will baby. Adam watched as she got up and carried her empty mug over to the sink, fighting an absurd rush of sympathy. Damn it, he must be letting hormones take total control of his brain cells if he kept coming back to this crazy belief that Alyssa Humphrey was genuinely lost and suffering.

She spoke over her shoulder. "If Rex wasn't consulting with you about Ace, why did he call you?"

Ace Fishing and Supply. Adam stored the name for future investigation and answered Alyssa's question. "Rex insists that since you have no memories, you're incompetent to handle your affairs. He strongly recommends that I should make all my reports about the missing trust money to the senator, not to you."

Alyssa winced. "Would you like to report direct to Senator Bradford?"

"Not particularly. I don't think your personal financial affairs have anything to do with the senator, at least until you're married. I also believe you're perfectly capable of making rational judgments even though you claim to have no memory of your past."

She picked up on the sting in his words at once, as he'd known she would. "Darn it, Adam, why do you doubt my amnesia? Do you really think anybody could keep up such a difficult pretense over such a long stretch of time? And why the dickens would I want to?"

He shrugged. "You don't have to deceive anyone who knows you very well. With the current budget crisis in Washington, the senator's never here, and your stepmother's in Africa."

"Jackie's here. She's my sister. She believes me." Alyssa picked up his coffee mug and stacked it neatly in the dishwasher. "Adam, why are we wasting time going over and over the same ground? If you aren't convinced about my memory loss by now, nothing I say will convince you, so why don't we talk about something else. Like, did you find out anything useful about the missing money while you were in New York?"

"A couple of things," he said. "There's the interesting fact that your brother flew in person to Zurich, Switzerland, the day after the first million dollars went missing from your trust fund."

She stopped fiddling with the dishes and spun around to face him. "Dick flew to Switzerland? What does that mean? What did he do there?"

"You should know," Adam said coolly, taking a calculated risk. "You went with him."

Alyssa didn't say a word. She looked at him in silence for a second or two, them simply turned and walked out of the kitchen.

Adam caught up with her at the foot of the stairs. "Where are you going?"

"I'm going to my room. Since you seem incapable of accepting the basic truth that I don't remember anything that happened before I got on that plane in Chicago, we obviously have nothing to say to each other. In future please report on the progress of your investigation by mail. I'd like a weekly summation of your activities. Do you need me to show you the way out, Mr. Stryker, or can you find your own way to the front door?''

He gritted his teeth. "Since it's ten feet behind me, I think I can manage to find the door.''

"I couldn't be sure, given your inability to see the obvious. Goodbye, Mr. Stryker. I doubt if we'll be meeting again, which should be a relief to both of us.''

"It should be, but it isn't," Adam said, and there was more truth than he liked in the simple statement. "Damn it, Alyssa, I'm sorry. It's been a hell of a long, hard week, and I'm taking out my bad temper on you. You're right to be mad at me. Could we start over and try again for a reasonable exchange of views?''

"We don't seem to be very good at *reasonable*," she said at last.

"We have a couple of incidents in our past that I guess we'd both rather forget.''

"And that's why we keep snipping at each other?''

"It's part of the reason,'' he said.

"And the other part?''

"I think you know.''

"Tell me, anyway.''

"Because I find you even more desirable since the plane crash than I did before, and you're engaged to marry another man.''

Her expression remained so carefully blank Adam had the impression she was working very hard not to show her surprise. And that surprised him. In the old days Alyssa had never been a woman who struggled to hide what she was feeling.

"You find me desirable,'' she repeated finally. "Do I . . . did I return the compliment?''

"I doubt it,'' he replied, his voice devoid of inflection. The fact that she had once offered him bed privileges didn't mean very much. He suspected that Alyssa Humphrey had shared her sexual charms with a wide range of acquaintances. "Don't worry. I'm not likely to be overcome by a surge of wild, uncontrollable lust.''

She gave the tiniest of smiles. "I don't know. Your defenses look to me as if they're crumbling fast. You're not even wearing pinstripes today. And I swear I can see red dots on your tie."

He hated what she did to him when she smiled. He was too old and much too cynical to be bowled over by a smile. But his voice softened when he said. "It's the weekend. Even lawyers get to shed their uniform on a Saturday."

She wrapped her fingers around the banister, her white knuckles betraying her tension. Then she seemed to reach a decision. "Come into the library for a minute, would you?"

He followed her into the pleasant, oak-paneled room, watching as she removed a copy of *Pride and Prejudice* from the shelves. She took a card out from between the pages and held it out to him. Her hand, Adam noted, was not entirely steady.

"I received this in the mail last week."

He drew the card out of its envelope. A sympathy card, he saw at once. Startled, he read the typed message on the enclosed piece of paper.

"I hope you're planning to show this to the police," he said as soon as he'd finished reading.

She laughed without mirth. "Get real, Adam. Two minutes ago, you damn near accused me of stashing three million stolen dollars in a Swiss bank account. With my murky past, would you really recommend visiting a law enforcement agency?"

Adam read the message again. "I know you're a fraud." In fact, as he had discovered to his cost, there was no way to know for sure that Alyssa's amnesia was a pretense, so the writer of the letter must have intended the accusation either as a threat or as a warning, not as a statement of fact. Which meant that the writer had good reason to know that Alyssa was involved in something dangerous. So far, he and the letter writer were in complete agreement. But did the writer want to push Alyssa into revealing secrets, or was this a genuine effort to alert her to hidden danger? Adam reached for the envelope and flipped it over.

"It was sent from Los Angeles airport," Alyssa said.

"Do you have any idea who might have sent it?"

"None whatsoever."

"Let me keep this card," he said. "My, um, friend in the Chicago police department might be able to tell us something helpful, point us in a direction we aren't thinking of. I don't need to mention your name if that really worries you."

She looked at him for a long, silent moment, then shrugged. "I can't do anything with it so you might as well try. Do whatever you think best."

His heart did *not* give a little skip of pleasure at this mark of trust. He did *not* feel a damnfool urge to tell her he would keep her safe and make sure everything turned out right in the end. There was no denying, however, that he did invite her to drive up with him into the mountains.

"I was listening to the local news as I drove here from the airport," he said. "And the newscaster said the aspen are at the perfect point in their color change. Would you like to take a quick trip into the foothills with me?"

Her eyes lit up. "I'd love that. I've always wanted to see the Rocky Mountains in their fall colors."

She had lived in Denver most of her life. She must have seen the aspens in their autumn glory a dozen times. But he didn't correct her, not wanting to break their fragile harmony. He simply smiled and took her arm.

"Then let's go," he said. "The car is in the driveway."

THE ASPEN SHONE yellow as butter in the October sun, their thin trunks forming dark exclamation points against the surrounding brightness. Alyssa peered through the car window, her cheeks glowing with pleasure.

"This is heavenly," she said to Adam. "Is it your first trip into the mountains at this time of year?"

"Yes, it is. My parents loved to ski, so I came to Colorado a couple of times with them as a kid, but only in snow season."

"Do your parents still ski? Do you?"

"I do, but my parents haven't for the past five years. Dad has arthritis in his knees and my mother is too kindhearted to go without him. They take three weeks in Florida each winter and do a lot of swimming instead."

"They sound happy together. Are they retired?"

"Not for another couple of years. They're teachers in Wichita, Kansas. They met in college thirty-seven years ago. They have five children, four dogs, no money, and they swear they'd do it all again in a minute."

She crossed her arms over her chest. "Is that what you're waiting for, Adam? Somebody you can live with for thirty-seven years and still want to do it over?"

"I've given up believing in miracles," he said flatly.

"Does that mean you've given up on the idea of getting married? Or just on finding the perfect mate?"

Incredibly, God alone knew why, he wanted to tell her about his wife. Since Su-lin died, he'd shared his grief with no one, not even his parents. Yet now, after years of silence, he felt the compulsion to speak. And to a woman he wasn't even sure that he liked.

Fool, he mocked himself. *You want Alyssa Humphrey in your bed so badly that you need to add the illusion of mental intimacy to the ache of physical desire.*

"I found the perfect wife once," he said harshly. He hoped Alyssa would hear the jagged edge of anger in his voice; he hoped she would feel guilty for violating his privacy. "Her name was Su-lin and she was a Vietnamese refugee, an orphan who was brought here from a Cambodian prison camp when she was eleven years old. She was a cellist with a national reputation by the time she was a teenager. We were married on her twentieth birthday."

Alyssa didn't seem to recognize the warning signals, didn't seem to realize she was supposed to back off and leave him alone with his hurt. "What happened?" she asked.

Adam became aware of the fact that Alyssa's hand rested lightly, consolingly, on his knee. For some reason he didn't shake it off.

"Su-lin died," he said, his voice dry as desert dust. "She died very painfully of liver cancer, probably caused by the quantities of Agent Orange she ingested as a child growing up in Vietnam. Poison provided courtesy of the US Government, of course."

Alyssa's eyes darkened with sympathy. "Adam, I'm so sorry. War claims too many innocent victims." She gestured abruptly. "I'm sorry again. That was a trite remark, and I didn't mean for it to sound that way. But at least you have the consolation of knowing for a brief time in your life you gave and received real love. And you made Su-lin happy. That must be worth something."

"My wife never managed to get pregnant, which was her dream, and she died after less than six years of marriage. And you sound envious of me. Alyssa, that's craziness."

"I'm going to marry a man in January that I can't even remember, much less love." She broke off. "Damn! I swore to myself I wasn't going to bring up any of that amnesia stuff. Forget what I just said."

He sure as hell wasn't going to be suckered into offering her sympathy for a memory loss he didn't entirely believe. "Have you considered trying hypnosis again?" he asked.

"I've already tried twice since I left the hospital. The hypnotherapist spent hours with my sister, picking incidents from my past that I have every reason to remember."

"Like what, for example?"

"Like Jackie's birth, when I was fifteen. The therapist tried to guide me back to Rose Memorial Hospital and the first time I saw Jackie in my stepmother's arms."

"You didn't respond?"

Alyssa smiled, but her eyes were troubled. "Not appropriately. I kept saying over and over again in the voice of a three-year-old, 'Mama, isn't *he* a cute baby. Isn't *he* tiny.' So they gave up on Jackie's birth and tried the time I went to Paris with my father."

"What did that produce?"

"Flat denial. I told the therapist I'd never been to Paris. So in desperation they tried the day I graduated from high school. Apparently I started muttering something about Danny Boyd falling down the front steps. At which point I got so agitated, the therapist had to bring me out of the trance." She shrugged. "So much for the wonders of hypnotherapy."

Adam parked in a lookout bay and they both got out of the car. Miraculously for this time of year, they were alone on the graveled overhang with only the mountains and miles of blue sky for company. Despite the sun, the thin air carried a hint of winter snows, and Alyssa shivered. Instinctively Adam put his arms around her waist, drawing her back against his body to shelter inside the cocoon of his overcoat. Her hair blew against his cheek in a tantalizing caress. Her scent, elusive and woodsy, enveloped his senses. With a tiny sigh of contentment, she leaned back against him, her slender body pressed against him from shoulders to knees. Instantly he was fully aroused.

He knew she must be able to feel the effect she'd had on him, but he didn't move away. If anything he pulled her closer, tightening his arms around her waist and splaying out his fingers to the very edge of her breasts. Damn it, he would show her he couldn't be manipulated by sex, however much he wanted her.

He bent low and whispered softly in her ear. "Here's another interesting detail from your past to mull over. You went back to Zurich a second time, the day after the second million dollars disappeared from your trust fund. Think about it, my sweet. Does that little incident ring any bells in your empty memory?"

Her body went rigid, but otherwise she didn't move. "No," she said quietly. "That rings no bells at all."

"You were gone less than twenty-four hours. Hardly a pleasure trip, I imagine. Think business, Alyssa. Think fraud."

This time, she moved. She walked to the railing and stared out at the landscape of jagged mountain ridges. "The Swiss Alps aren't nearly as high as the Rocky Mountains. I read that somewhere." She swung around, looking at him with hard gray eyes. "How did you find out? About all these trips to Zurich, I mean."

"Routine research techniques. I pulled the record on every check written on every Humphrey bank account, then called the travel agent and had her reconstruct your travel schedule for the past six months. After that, it was easy."

The sun shone through the banks of trees, outlining her body in a subtle interplay of golden light and purple shadow. He thought she might just be the most beautiful woman he'd ever seen. She was sure as hell the most desirable woman he'd ever seen. Thrusting his hands into his pockets, he managed to avoid the impulse to run over, grab her and kiss her senseless.

"You sound as if you have investigative experience."

Dangerous ground, this. He shrugged. "Lawyers and investigators have some skills in common."

"Why were your law school grades so mediocre?"

She never asked questions he expected. "Why do you ask?"

"Because you're not dumb and you're not lazy. I don't know what other explanation there could be for your low grades."

There was no reason for him to explain—except that he was such a damned idiot he couldn't bear to have her think he was stupid. "Su-lin was dying," he said. "I was working a full-time job to keep up the medical insurance payments. Hitting the law school books came about number nine hundred and ninety-three on my daily list of things to do."

"Why didn't you take a couple of semesters off? The school would have understood and granted you a leave of absence."

"Su-lin wanted to see me graduate. Her father had been a lawyer before he was killed in a Vietcong ambush."

"My brother didn't know you were married, did he? That's why he didn't understand about your grades. He totally misread your capabilities."

"Dick and I were acquaintances, not friends," he said. "He never met Su-lin."

She persisted. "And so he totally misjudged the person you are, and how smart you are, too."

"Probably."

"Why did he hire you, Adam?"

"The charitable explanation is that he thought the job was easy and knew I needed the money."

"And the other explanation?"

He'd already revealed far too much for lying to be helpful. "That the pair of you planned to steal money from your trust fund and didn't want the theft discovered. So he chose the least competent person he knew."

Alyssa picked up a flat pebble and flung it as hard as she could toward the mountain. It disappeared into the vastness, falling unheard to the ground. When she turned around again, her face looked sad. "I don't think Alyssa Humphrey was a very nice person before the plane crash, do you?"

"People can change, Alyssa. You have the intelligence and the strength of will to become whatever woman you want to be."

She walked back to the car. "I think you're wrong. Do you know, Adam, I've just realized that you can't hide from your own past no matter where you run to, because your past has made you the person you are. So there's nowhere to hide, ever, not from the truth about yourself."

"What are you trying to tell me, Alyssa?"

Her face was deathly white, her gray eyes dark with pain. "Nothing. I'm talking rubbish. Take me home, Adam, I have a terrible headache."

Chapter Seven

Alyssa could feel the memories lurking on the edge of her mind, ducking and weaving as she stretched out to grab them. The more she reached, the faster they pranced away. Trying to catch hold of her past was like trying to see the back of her head without a double mirror. No amount of twisting and turning would do the trick.

Adam, thank God, didn't harass her with questions during the journey back to Denver. They were parked in the driveway before he asked her if she needed to see a doctor. "You're still very pale," he said in his usual cool voice, "and I can see you're in pain."

For once Alyssa was grateful for his detachment. Six weeks of convalescence was enough; she was tired of being hovered over by doctors.

"I'm fine," she said, rummaging for her key. "Except for too many twisting roads on top of three fudge brownies."

He looked at her for a long moment before taking the key and fitting it into the lock. "If you need me tonight, for anything at all, I'm staying at the Westin downtown."

Stepping into the hall, Alyssa dismissed a crazy impulse to beg him to stay. Perhaps she only felt this perverse need for his support because she was so tired, and her head ached. She turned, ready with a polite dismissal, but before she could speak, Jackie's voice greeted her from the top of the stairs.

"Hi, Lyss! I'm going to a party at my girlfriend's house. 'Bye, Lyss! Catch you later."

"Hold on a minute there!" Alyssa managed a smile for her sister, although her headache pounded so fiercely her entire body throbbed with pain. "Where's the party, and who's driving you? Juan isn't working today."

"My date has a car," Jackie explained with an over-bright smile that sent a chill of foreboding down Alyssa's spine. "My friend should arrive any moment, I'm gonna wait outside."

Jackie took her hand off the banister and gestured vaguely in the direction of the front driveway. The lack of support betrayed her. She missed her next step, clutched air in an effort to regain her balance, then skidded to the bottom of the stairs. She was saved from a dangerous landing on the marble-tiled hallway floor only because Adam moved quickly enough to catch her and break her fall.

"You have great reflexes," Alyssa said to Adam, hurrying to her sister's side. Stern-faced, she confronted her sister. "Are you hurt?"

"I'm fine. Thanks for the rescue." Jackie pushed Adam aside and scrambled to her feet, but her movements were clumsy and uncoordinated, and Adam had to keep his arm around her waist to prevent her from falling.

Alyssa drew back from her sister, livid with anger. "You've been drinking again." The words were a flat statement, leaving no room for denial.

Jackie laughed. "Aw, come on, Lyss, don't be shi-silly. Of course I haven't been drinking. Nothing except soda pop, anyway."

At this moment Jackie probably half believed the glib denial herself. Rage funnelled up from the pit of Alyssa's stomach and clutched at her throat, very nearly choking her. She clamped down on her anger, afraid of what might happen if she let her true feelings erupt.

"Don't lie to me," she said through clenched teeth. "My sense of smell didn't disappear in the plane crash. I can smell the booze. I'm an expert at detecting the darn stuff. What have you been drinking? Rum and cola? Bourbon and ginger ale?''

Jackie's expression became sullen. "Get off my back, for Pete's sake, you're not my keeper. You're such a hypocrite, Lyss. I haven't done anything wrong. You're the one who goes out cruising the bars looking for men as soon as you knock back your first martini.''

"I have never picked up a man in a bar in my entire life!'' Alyssa exclaimed. "What's more, I never drink. Someone in our family has to stay sober and hold things together!'' She leaned against the wall, compassion and anger churning with such tumult inside her that she felt dizzy. The pain in her head intensified to a crescendo of agony.

Jackie's laugh was bitter. "It's great losing your memory, isn't it, Lyss? I guess my dear mommy would say all your past sins are forgiven. What's it like being a born-again virgin?''

"That's enough, Jackie," Adam said quietly. "We were talking about you, not your sister.''

The doorbell rang and Jackie stumbled hurriedly to the door. "My ride's here," she said. "See you later, folks.''

But Adam was at the door before her, blocking her exit. "Sorry, Jackie," he said, his voice quiet but entirely commanding. "You're not leaving here tonight. It's not safe, for you or your date. Your judgment's impaired right now, and someone might end up badly hurt. You could easily crash the car.''

The pain inside Alyssa's skull exploded. *Not just hurt, but dead. Like her brother, Bob, was dead.* The grief and rage swelled like a hideous sponge, oozing into the cells of her body, pouring into her mind.

"Do you think I want another trip to the morgue to identify your corpse?'' she demanded of Jackie, although she wasn't really seeing Jackie, she was seeing Bob. Hot tears washed down her cheeks, but she didn't care. "For God's sake, why won't you listen to the warnings before it's too late? Take charge of your life, damn you! Get a grip on yourself.''

She felt the policeman put his arms around her, trying to offer comfort where comfort couldn't be found. The grief at her brother's death couldn't be contained any longer, and she covered her face with her hands, sobbing out the anguish of her loss. The pain washed over her in dark, heavy waves. Frustrated beyond endurance, she sank into the blackness.

The voice came to her from a long way away. "Alyssa, it's all right. Jackie isn't hurt. She's fine, and her boyfriend's left already. They're not going out tonight."

Who was Alyssa? Who was Jackie? And where was Bob? She couldn't see his body anymore. The world was tinged with red, and Suzanne held on to the doorjamb to prevent herself falling onto the icy morgue floor. Except she wasn't standing by the door anymore, she was lying on a sofa. The policeman's arms tightened, giving her the support she so desperately needed, and she turned to him gratefully, letting the scalding tears soak into his shirt.

"Oh, God, he's dead! My own brother. I could have saved him if I'd tried a bit harder, if I'd loved him more."

"No you couldn't. Listen to me, Alyssa. You have nothing to blame yourself for. You couldn't move after the crash. You were trapped, and you were badly wounded. It's a miracle you survived. Nobody blames you for your brother's death and you mustn't blame yourself, not for another minute."

It was true she'd been pinned into place by her seat belt, but why had Bob died when she'd escaped with nothing more than bruises? Suzanne didn't believe in her own innocence. She was nearly three years older than Bob, she should have done a better job of protecting him from their father's alcoholic rages and her mother's timid complicity. And when Bob became a teenager, she should never have let him take his first drink. She should have kept him safe, she should have understood him better, convinced him he was loved. If she'd been better at loving, she would have done something, *anything*, that would have stopped him following the same ruinous path as their father.

"I didn't love him enough," she said wearily. "Maybe Harry was right after all. I'm not very good at loving. That's a funny joke, isn't it. Harry the Snake was right about me all the time."

The policeman had found a wad of tissues and was quietly drying her eyes. His hands—strong, with lean, tanned fingers—felt gentle as he pulled a strand of hair away from her wet, sticky cheek and tucked it behind her ear.

"You did fine," he said. "You were very brave. You helped your brother just by being there."

Lord, how she hoped that was true, Suzanne thought, rubbing her cheek against the policeman's shirt, so that her skin absorbed the warmth and comfort of his strong arms.

Except that this wasn't a policeman. None of the people at the morgue had ever made her feel this safe, this protected.

Suzanne opened her eyes and saw the man who held her. Adam Stryker, she thought, letting her eyelids drift closed again. Adam was holding her, providing this welcome feeling of peace and absolution. She wished Adam would hold her until she fell asleep in his arms.

Dear God, Adam thought she was Alyssa!

In a flash of total awareness, reality tumbled into place. Suzanne remembered her brother had died in a car wreck three years ago. Memories fell into perspective as the white-hot agony of grief cooled into something more bearable.

Suzanne drew in a deep, shuddering breath and felt Adam respond with a slight relaxation of his hold. She was glad when he didn't entirely relinquish her from his arms. Even though she now remembered everything, even though she realized that she was Suzanne Swenson, not Alyssa Humphrey, she still felt shaky and adrift. There were going to be so many explanations and so many legal formalities to complete before the bizarre mix-up could be straightened out. And right now all she wanted was to crawl into bed and sleep for a week. She felt more exhausted than she ever remembered in her entire life. More tired and more . . . lonely.

But reality must be faced. Alyssa Humphrey might waft along on a cloud of irresponsibility, but Suzanne Swenson always prided herself on confronting unpleasant realities. And reality number one was that Adam's shoulder was feeling a darn sight too appealing. Suzanne Swenson would never allow herself to become emotionally dependent on a man. That was why her engagement to Harrison Quentin III had seemed so perfect. Her relationship with Harry had been controlled and civilized. Civilized, that is, until she returned to her apartment and found him making wild, passionate love to Marianne. Her ex-best friend.

No wonder her subconscious hadn't been all that anxious to remember the past, Suzanne thought tiredly. Her life seemed to be in as big a mess as Alyssa Humphrey's, although for different reasons. Sighing, she straightened her spine and firmed her mouth, despising herself for taking so long to regain control of herself. Her memories had flooded back, but her efficiency seemed to be lagging.

She finally managed to work up the energy to extricate herself from Adam's arms at the same time as she flashed him a polite smile. Courtesy and control were two qualities she prided herself on possessing, Suzanne remembered. She had discovered as a teenager that unfailing politeness was one of the very best methods for avoiding intimacy.

"Thanks for the tissues and the loan of your shoulder," she said to Adam. "I'm sorry for the sudden hysterics. I don't know what got into me."

His smile was warm, his eyes too sympathetic. "You're welcome. Anytime. Consoling damsels in distress is one of my specialities."

She should tell him right now about the incredible mistake that had been made, Suzanne thought, and her stomach gave an odd lurch of regret at the prospect. In many ways it was fortunate that Adam, who was a lawyer and the family trustee, should be on hand at the moment she regained her mental faculties. Although even with Adam as the recipient of her news, it was hard to imagine what she should say.

By the way, I'm not Alyssa Humphrey, I'm Suzanne Swenson, an advertising executive from Chicago. That might be a shocking enough statement to jolt even Adam Stryker's cool, she reflected with a touch of unexpected amusement.

Jackie's anxious voice brought Suzanne tumbling back to wider awareness of her surroundings. "Lyss, I won't drink any more, I promise. This time I really mean it. Gosh, you looked so awful just then! Your eyes all rolled up, and you couldn't hear anything even though we were all talking to you."

Lyss. Oh, good Lord, Suzanne thought in silent horror. It's not just Adam I have to tell. This poor, mixed-up kid thinks I'm her *sister.*

She pressed her fingers to the bridge of her nose and closed her eyes, trying to concentrate. How in the world was she going to find the words to say what needed to be said?

"Lyss!" There was no concealing the underlying note of panic in Jackie's voice, or the desperation in the hands that clutched at Suzanne's arm. "Lyss, don't pass out again! Please, I didn't mean to make you sick." Jackie's voice dropped to a husky, embarrassed undertone. "Lyss, you know I love you. I need you, Lyss, to help me get things straight in my life."

"I love you, too," Suzanne said softly, reaching out to touch Jackie's tear-streaked face. Surprisingly the words were true. Over the past few weeks, Jackie's prickly personality had taken firm root in Suzanne's heart. Loneliness responding to loneliness, she reflected wryly.

Suzanne tried to ignore the pain still throbbing inside her skull and the fatigue that deluged her body. She sensed that this was as much a crisis point for Jackie as for herself, and that if the wrong words were spoken, the chance to set Jackie's life on a more worthwhile track might be lost. Suzanne would always believe that she had failed her brother. She didn't want to fail Jackie, too. This certainly didn't seem a good moment to tell the poor kid that the woman standing in front of her was Suzanne Swenson—and that the real

Alyssa Humphrey had presumably died in the crash of flight 127 from Chicago to Denver.

The solution seeped into her consciousness from some buried spot in the depths of her soul.

I could pretend to be Alyssa for a while longer, Suzanne thought. *Suzanne Swenson has been dead for two months. It can't make much difference if I let her stay dead for another few days. I could get Jackie into a good counseling program and talk to the teachers at her school so that I know she's got a support system in place before I tell her the truth.*

Once the idea had formed, it flourished like a weed. Suzanne had no close family, and she doubted if her supposed death was causing anyone much grief. Her fiancé—the handsome, faithless Harrison Quentin III—wasn't likely to have spent the past few weeks weeping over her grave. In fact she would guess Harry and Marianne were pursuing their affair with enthusiasm. Right at this moment her former best friend and former fiancé were probably finalizing arrangements for their wedding as they enjoyed an elegant little nouvelle cuisine dinner in his apartment in Water Tower Place.

Water Tower Place. Each memory triggered a hundred others. Of course, Suzanne thought. Like Senator Matthew Bradford, Harrison Quentin III had an apartment in Water Tower Place. *That* was why she had remembered so much about the general layout of the building, but couldn't visualize the bedroom of Matthew's penthouse where they had supposedly made love for the first time.

Matthew Bradford. "Oh, my God!" she breathed, struggling to get up. "What am I going to say to Matthew? I must call him right away!"

"No need to call, I'm right here," a familiar voice said. "Alyssa, sweetheart, what is going on with you? My dear, you're as pale as a ghost."

The senator was here. She'd forgotten they were scheduled to have dinner tonight and attend church together in the morning. Suzanne wished she could have had a couple of hours to pull herself together before facing Matthew. But perhaps it was fortunate that he'd arrived right at this crucial moment. She would be wading into dangerous legal and emotional waters if she allowed people to continue in their mistaken belief that she was Alyssa Humphrey. Matthew's presence settled the issue in favor of explaining the truth as soon as possible. But not right this second. She couldn't reveal the bizarre facts with Jackie listening, overwrought and still half-intoxicated.

She managed a smile for her supposed fiancé. "It's nothing. I just have a headache."

"I'm so sorry to hear that." Matthew strode toward her, but old political habits obviously died hard. He couldn't enter a room without working the crowd, and his smiling blue eyes quickly swooped over the other two occupants of the room.

"Jackie," he said, detouring to ruffle her spiked hair. "Nice to find you home on a Saturday night for a change. And Adam, too. What brings you to Denver at the weekend?"

Adam rose to his feet. "I needed to discuss a few business matters with Alyssa."

"Are you making any progress in tracing those missing funds?"

"Nothing dramatic, unfortunately."

"Well, keep us posted." Matthew's smile never faded and his voice radiated warmth. But to Suzanne's sensitized ears the warmth barely concealed his displeasure. Matthew, she realized, didn't like to find his "fiancée" nestled on the sofa in Adam Stryker's arms.

If Adam had detected Matthew's displeasure, and Suzanne strongly suspected that he had, he showed no reaction. "You arrived in the nick of time, Senator. I'm afraid Alyssa overtired herself today, and I blame myself. We drove into the foothills and stayed out longer than we should have. She's not feeling too good right now. I expect you're the tonic she needed."

Matthew took Adam's place on the sofa, leaning over to drop a reproachful kiss on his "fiancée's" forehead. "Darling, why do you keep tackling more than you're ready for? You'll never get well again unless you rest."

"I'm fine, really I am," she said, guilt making her squirm in Matthew's embrace. She had no business accepting his kisses now that she knew she wasn't Alyssa. But surely she ought to be alone with him before she blurted out the truth? Quite apart from Jackie's fragile emotional state, the senator himself deserved privacy to absorb such shocking and tragic news.

"Lyss, shall I make you some dinner or something? I want to do something to help you feel better." A contrite Jackie spoke quietly, her words still slurred, but not enough for Matthew to notice.

"Alyssa and I will eat later." Matthew dismissed Jackie's offer with a quick wave of his hand. "What your sister and I would really like are a few minutes alone."

"I'll take care of Jackie," Adam said at once. "She doesn't know it yet, but we're going to check over her math homework." He gave Suzanne one of his rare smiles, and her heart raced forward in double-time. In full possession of her faculties at last, she realized that what she had been feeling toward Adam all these weeks was nothing more mysterious than acute physical desire. Floundering around inside Alyssa Humphrey's ill-fitting skin, she had never recognized the tension snapping between herself and Adam for what it was. And now that she recognized the problem, she had no idea what to do about it. Sighing, Suzanne mentally tossed another complication into her overloaded emotional hopper.

"You'll let me know before you leave for the hotel?" she asked Adam.

"Of course. And don't worry about Jackie. I'll keep her so busy with her math problems that she'll be exhausted and pleading for bed by nine o'clock."

Jackie groaned, but Adam merely clapped a friendly arm on her shoulder. "Come on, kid, let's get to it. This is penance time."

He managed to speak so casually that Matthew would have no reason to suspect Jackie had been drunk, and Suzanne was glad of that.

But she had even bigger problems to tackle at the moment than Jackie's drinking. Suzanne realized she was still stretched out full-length on the sofa. She quickly sat up and found herself staring into the worried blue eyes of the man who *wasn't* her fiancé.

He looked stunningly handsome at these close quarters, with few lines and wrinkles to betray his age, and yet Suzanne's chief reaction was overwhelming relief that she would never have to marry this man. He was a dedicated, hardworking public servant, but for some reason he reminded her of Harry.

Which didn't explain why her second reaction was a frisson of fear at the prospect of telling him Alyssa Humphrey was dead. But that was crazy. What was there to be frightened of, other than the difficulty of finding the right words to explain something so shocking?

"Matthew, I have something...strange...to tell you," she said finally. Hardly cutting straight to the heart of the matter, but it was the best she could manage.

Matthew squeezed her hands, his eyes twinkling. "And I have something *wonderful* to tell you. I know looking after Jackie has been a strain, but your responsibilities are nearly over, honey. Lena is coming home on Wednesday. She called me from London with the news just a couple of hours ago. Isn't that terrific?"

Lena Vincent Humphrey, Jackie's mother, was coming home! Suzanne absorbed the marvelous news in relieved silence. Telling Jackie that Alyssa was missing, presumed dead, wouldn't be nearly such a difficult task if Lena was on hand to offer comfort.

"Honey, what is it? You're so quiet, and I thought you'd be delighted."

"I am delighted, Matthew."

"I hear a *but* in your voice."

"No buts. Except—why didn't you tell Jackie her mother's coming home?"

"Lena's still under doctor's orders. I didn't want to set Jackie's hopes too high in case her mother doesn't make the Wednesday flight. She might not be here until Friday."

"Perhaps we could tell Jackie over dinner? I'm sure she misses her mother a lot."

"Of course, if that's what you want, sweetheart. I'll let you know as soon as Lena gives me final details of her schedule."

Suzanne wondered why Lena was communicating her health and travel plans to Matthew Bradford rather than to her daughter. However, Suzanne reminded herself, she was an intruder inside the Humphrey family circle, with no right to question Lena's actions.

"To be honest," she admitted to Matthew, "this is a great weight off my mind. I've been worried about Jackie. She needs adult guidance and someone to love, maybe more than anyone realized when Lena went off on this trip."

"Lena's a wonderful mother," Matthew said. "Her relationship with Jackie is marvelous to watch. She's so patient and understanding. She used to be a teacher—but of course, you know that."

"No, nobody ever mentioned it."

Matthew looked crestfallen. "Your memories haven't come back, then? I hoped by now there'd be more improvement...."

His voice tailed away into disconsolate silence, and Suzanne wondered why she had the sudden, strange feeling that Matthew really didn't give a damn whether or not her amnesia was ever cured. She pushed the thought aside and walked jerkily toward the window. Her jaw was clenched so tight it was hard to breathe.

"Oh, Lord, Matthew, this is so difficult to say...."

He came to stand behind her, putting his arms around her waist and nuzzling her neck. Sweat broke out over Suzanne's body and clung to her skin in a clammy sheen. If he kissed her again, she was suddenly afraid she might throw up.

"You can tell me anything," he murmured into her ear. "We've known each other for years, so there's nothing you can say that would shock me."

Dear God, if he only knew how wrong he was! What she was about to say would shock him to the core. Suzanne worked up the courage to turn around and face him. He deserved more than the back of her head to look at when he heard the awful truth. Her hands were slick with sweat, but her throat was so dry that her tongue stuck to the roof of her mouth. Drawing in a rattling gulp of air, she looked into Matthew's brilliant blue eyes and forced herself to speak the terrible words with crystal clarity.

"Matthew, I'm not the woman you believe I am. I think the real Alyssa Humphrey must have died when flight 127 crashed at Stapleton airport."

She had no idea what reaction she had been expecting, but she couldn't believe it when Matthew laughed softly.

"Stop it!" she yelled, frightened by the inappropriate response. She grabbed the lapels of his suit jacket and shook him. "Don't you understand?" she demanded wildly. "The woman you planned to marry is dead. *Dead.* Killed in the plane crash."

Gently he disengaged her clutching fingers from his jacket. "Honey, is that what's been worrying you all these weeks? Good Lord, is this what's behind your attack of amnesia? Feelings of guilt about the old Alyssa?"

She shook her head, totally bewildered by his reaction, and he patted her hand, trying to soothe her. "Alyssa, honey, of course you don't feel like the same woman you were before the crash. You've gone through a terrible experience, and you've come out of it stronger and better than you were before." He cupped her face with his hands and brushed his thumbs tenderly down her cheeks, wiping away the remnants of her tears. "You need to concentrate on getting back your health, my dear, and then you'll feel more like your old self again. And I'll be one heck of a lucky man—marrying the best of the old and new Alyssa Humphrey reunited in one woman.''

Was he deliberately refusing to understand her? In her worst nightmares, Suzanne couldn't have imagined this scene going any more disastrously wrong, and she almost welcomed the intrusive sound of Matthew's phone beeper going off. He immediately disengaged himself from her arms, and she watched in numb relief while he dialed his office.

"Sorry to put you on hold, honey, but I'm expecting an important call from Rex," he explained, hand over the mouthpiece. "Hello, Rex? Yes, the plane's on standby." Matthew's eyes gleamed with excitement. "Van Plat's making it official tomorrow? Where is he making the announcement?" He snapped his fingers. "Bingo! Couldn't be better for us. The timing's perfect." He fell silent for a moment, then smiled broadly. "Wonderful, Rex. You've done a great job."

He put down the phone and strode back to Suzanne. "Alyssa, honey, I've got to get back to Washington right away. These are busy times on the Hill, dangerous times, in fact, with the international situation so unstable. I'm sure you understand that when duty calls, I have to play my part in shouldering the burden of making hard decisions."

"Of course," Suzanne murmured, wondering why politicians always seemed to speak in out-of-date clichés. She was beginning to feel more relieved by the minute that the senator wasn't really her fiancé. In all the hours they'd spent alone together, she never felt that she had come close to touching the core of the real Matthew Bradford.

He gave her a quick, absentminded hug. "I promise to clear my calendar for next weekend even if the president himself wants me to come for dinner. Lena will be home this week, and everything will change for the better then, I'm sure of it. Who knows, maybe seeing Lena again will cure your amnesia. Now that would be an excuse for a real celebration dinner, wouldn't it?''

Suzanne nodded, smiling with extra energy to cover her guilt. She knew that what she ought to do was detach the senator from his beeper, lock the library door, and force him to listen until he understood the truth about Alyssa. Her first attempt at explaining had gone awry because she made the mistake of concentrating on the fact that his fiancé was dead. Next time, she would *first* identify herself as Suzanne Swenson and *then* try to explain how the freakish mix-up had occurred.

But she wasn't making any more explanations tonight, Suzanne decided. Jackie certainly shouldn't be told the truth before Lena Humphrey came home, and it would make no difference if Matthew waited a few days before hearing that his wife-to-be was dead. He was flying back to Washington to handle business of national importance. He didn't need to have his mind wandering and his attention distracted over a piece of news that would be exactly the same whether delivered now or next weekend.

Matthew said his goodbyes with his usual generous allocation of charm. He apologized profusely to Shirley for not staying to eat her dinner; he shook Adam's hand in a firm, man-to-man grip; he congratulated Jackie on her pages of completed math homework; and wrapped Suzanne in a tender, farewell hug. Suzanne knew it could only be her own guilty conscience that made her feel so profoundly relieved once the door had finally closed behind the departing senator.

In the end it seemed crazy to waste Shirley's excellent cooking, so Suzanne invited Adam to stay for dinner. Adam agreed quite willingly, and his background as the eldest in a large family was soon apparent in the ease with which he talked to Jackie. In return, Jackie seemed surprisingly friendly toward him, given that he had spent the past hour drilling her in math. All in all, the meal passed off more pleasantly than Suzanne would have believed possible.

Realizing she was still in disgrace, Jackie was smart enough to redeem herself somewhat by volunteering to help the housekeeper clean up the dishes, and Suzanne invited Adam to bring his after-dinner coffee into the family room.

"Perhaps you'd like a brandy or a liqueur," she suggested when they were alone. For some reason the tension between her and Adam was particularly strong tonight, and she circled the family room uneasily.

"I'll have a brandy if you'll join me."

"I don't drink," Suzanne said absently, wondering why she had never before noticed what an incredibly sexy mouth Adam Stryker possessed. She wondered what it would feel like to be kissed by Adam, then hastily dismissed the thought. Good grief, her life was complicated enough right now without adding a bad attack of lust to her list of problems.

Adam put down his coffee cup and shut the family room door. Then he walked over to where Suzanne was standing, crooked his finger under her chin, and tilted her head backward until she was forced to look up at him.

"Come on, Alyssa," he said softly. "You don't need to keep up the pretense with me. We both know you love brandy. It's what you'd been drinking the night you came into my bedroom. I've spent most of today wondering why the hell I ever sent you away."

At least she and Alyssa Humphrey seemed to have one thing in common, Suzanne thought dizzily. They both wanted to make love to Adam Stryker.

She couldn't resist the temptation of sliding her hands under his jacket. "You don't understand," she whispered, her hands coming to rest on the firm, hard muscle of his chest. "I'm telling you the truth. I don't drink anything alcoholic and I never came to your bed."

His head bent slowly toward hers. "Alyssa," he said, his voice husky. "Right at this moment I don't give a damn about the past. If you don't want us to make love, I recommend you get the hell out of here within the next twenty seconds. After that I'm going to take you upstairs, strip off your clothes and find out whether we want each other as much in bed as we do out of it."

She didn't move, she didn't run. But she discovered that she was, of all the crazy things, jealous of his desire for Alyssa. She didn't want him to kiss Alyssa. His mouth was only a breath away from hers when she said the five simple words.

"My name is Suzanne Swenson."

Chapter Eight

Adam felt the shock almost before his brain registered the meaning of what she had said. He jerked his hands away from the stranger he'd been about to kiss and stared at a face that all at once appeared startlingly unfamiliar. Even as he watched, her features seemed to align themselves into a new, unknown pattern.

"You're not Alyssa Humphrey?" The question was too crazy to be asked—and yet it was inevitable, the key that made sense out of weeks of nonsense. Damn it, of course this woman wasn't Alyssa. He would have spotted the truth long ago if the diagnosis of amnesia hadn't confused everything.

She shook her head. "I'm sorry."

"Tell me your real name again."

"Suzanne Swenson." She hesitated for a second, then added, "I'm an account executive with Kensington Bennett advertising agency in Chicago."

Possibly. Then again, maybe this was all part of the setup. "Why hasn't anyone been looking for you? No, don't answer. Dumb question. They think you're dead." He poured himself a stiff brandy, and swallowed it neat. "You look a lot like Alyssa. Height. Hair color. Body build. It's easy to see how the mistake was made."

"Yes, I guess we're very alike. Especially now that Doctor Reinhard's finished with me."

"How old are you?"

"Twenty nine. Alyssa is...was...thirty one, wasn't she?"

"Right." He glanced at her. "You look younger than your age. But then, so did Alyssa."

Her mouth twisted wryly. "I don't feel young. Right now I feel about a thousand years old and aging fast."

Maybe I should give her the benefit of the doubt. "How did such an incredible mistake happen? It's unbelievable that two women who look so alike were flying on the same plane. It's an impossible coincidence."

"Life is full of impossible coincidences. Look, I don't know what you're imagining, Adam, but for the record, I never intended to impersonate Alyssa. This wasn't a deliberate ploy on my part to gain access to the Humphrey millions. It was simply a mistake, a terrible mistake."

"I'm sure it was," Adam said, wondering if he was being paranoid even to consider the possibility that Suzanne was lying. "You were unconscious when Senator Bradford identified you, and semiconscious for several more days, so the mistake was no fault of yours. And when you finally came to, you'd lost your memory."

He hadn't meant to let his skepticism show, but she picked up on it at once, and her chin tilted defiantly. "For your information, my amnesia was genuine. In fact, my memory would have come back a lot sooner if people hadn't insisted I was Alyssa Humphrey. I wasted weeks trying to remember a past that wasn't mine. Imagine what it's like to get memory flashes that don't mesh with the life everyone insists is yours. I thought I was going crazy."

She was either speaking the absolute truth or lying brilliantly. Unfortunately Adam couldn't decide which, and until he could make up his mind, he'd be smart to confide none of his suspicions to her. He spoke brusquely to cover his ambivalence.

"I guess the important thing for us right now is to straighten out the mess, not worry about how it happened."

"I guess so." Her attempt at a smile didn't quite come off. "You and the other lawyers are going to be buried knee-deep in forms and legal documents."

"Lawyers with long forms to fill out are like pigs in a mud wallow. We're in our element. By the way, how long have you known who you really are?"

Her smile vanished. "Not long. Just since we arrived home this afternoon."

"Why did your memory come back today, do you think?"

She poked at an elaborate arrangement of dried flowers. "The scene with Jackie triggered some unpleasant memories."

"About your brother? You mentioned an accident to your brother. At the time I thought you were talking about Dick, of course."

Her eyes misted, but her voice held steady. "My brother's name was Bob. He died in a car crash when he was a college freshman. Usually I could tell when he'd been drinking, but this one night he managed to fool me, and I let him get behind the wheel of my car. Jackie seemed all set to repeat history and that upset me. Enough to break down the mental barriers, I guess."

And enough to make her pass out in the hallway, Adam thought, then take a good five minutes to regain consciousness. He didn't believe the best actress in the world could have faked all the physical changes he'd felt her body undergo while he held her in his arms. Which meant that she was telling him the simple truth: she hadn't remembered she was Suzanne Swenson until a few hours ago. The knowledge that the past six weeks had not been one long, deliberate lie was more pleasing to him than it should have been.

"What about the rest of your family?" he asked. "When are you going to call them with the great news that you're alive?"

"My parents are both dead, and I don't have any close family," she said. "My father died of cirrhosis of the liver, and my mother died of lung cancer. She smoked herself to death in an effort to avoid acknowledging that my father was an alcoholic.''

Her voice was so carefully neutral he knew she hadn't come to terms with her loss. Without thinking, he reached out to caress her cheek. ''I'm sorry,'' he said.

She turned her head, and for a split second she allowed her lips to rest against the palm of his hand. Then she straightened. ''Don't be sorry. They were highly intelligent people who wasted most of their lives drowning in self-pity. That's all the sympathy they deserve.''

She didn't seem to realize that his sympathy was for her, not for her parents. Hearing the pain beneath her harsh words, Adam fought the impulse to draw her deep into his arms and offer her whatever comfort he could provide. Although, heaven knew, it would be a case of the wounded leading the lame. He'd long ago recognized his own irrational feelings of guilt at Su-lin's death, but for the first time, listening to Suzanne, he realized that mere recognition might not be enough. He needed to put aside his grief and start living the rest of his life to the full.

But this was not the moment for personal soul searching. ''Why didn't you tell Senator Bradford who you are?'' he asked, careful this time not to sound aggressive. ''From the way he behaved tonight, I assume he still thinks you're Alyssa.''

''I did tell him, sort of, but he misunderstood what I was trying to say.''

''*My name is Suzanne Swenson, not Alyssa Humphrey.* That's pretty hard to misinterpret.''

''Maybe, but Matthew didn't understand what I was telling him.'' She paced restlessly. ''The fact is I was so glad at the reprieve when Rex Clancey called, I practically pushed Matthew out of the door and onto his darn plane.''

''Why were you glad of a reprieve? Don't you want him to know who you really are?''

''The news is going to devastate him. He loves Alyssa so much. He's counting the days until they can get married—''

"Have *you* fallen in love with him?"

Her eyes opened wide in astonishment. "Good heavens, no!"

"Why not? He's an attractive man, in an exciting, powerful job. Unless—are you married?"

"Not married, not engaged and no plans for either. Intimate relationships interfere with a successful career, and I'm a very career-oriented woman." She smiled brightly. "You're looking at a *happy* workaholic."

"Mmm," he said. "That must be why you're destroying Lena's floral arrangement—because you're so happy."

She looked down at the battered stalk of eucalyptus she had shredded, and her poise collapsed. "Oh, God, Adam, I'm such a coward. I'm so darn scared of emotional scenes that I couldn't even find the courage to tell Matthew in clearcut words that his fiancé is dead."

Adam caught hold of her hand, which was icy cold and none too steady, but he didn't answer for a while. He looked out of the window into the shadow-filled darkness of the Colorado night, debating with himself. How much should he tell Suzanne? He didn't have the right to involve her in his professional problems. On the other hand, fate had already tossed Suzanne Swenson right into the middle of a dangerous situation. Was ignorance really the safest course for her? Adam admitted that he didn't know. With so many imponderables, he couldn't do much more than follow his gut instincts. And his gut instincts all cried out that ignorance was never bliss.

"Are you certain that Alyssa's dead?" he said at last.

"She must be." Suzanne's face went blank with shock. "We'd have heard from her if she was alive. She'd be here in Denver."

"Unless she has reasons of her own for staying out of sight."

"What possible reasons could she have for vanishing?"

"Fear, greed, hate, malice. Love. All the usual human motivators."

Suzanne shook her head. "It's much more likely that she's dead, and her body misidentified after the crash."

"That's possible," he conceded.

She suddenly looked so depressed and weary that Adam cursed himself for an insensitive fool. "Come and sit down on the sofa," he said quietly. "You look about ready to keel over."

"That bad, huh?" She followed him to the couch, sitting down and leaning back against the cushions with a sigh of relief. She gave a hiccup of laughter that choked off perilously close to a sob.

"This has been an amazing few weeks," she said. "I guess there aren't too many people who end up living somebody else's life and genuinely believing it's theirs."

She tried hard to sound possessed and in control, but a little quiver in her voice betrayed her. On the point of reaching out to pull her head down to rest on his shoulder, Adam drew back. Suzanne Swenson was far too attractive, and he wanted her too much. She reminded him of painful emotions like intimacy, sharing and gentleness. Emotions that people in his line of work stayed away from unless they wanted to get hurt.

Adam was damn sure he didn't want to get hurt, so he moved to the other end of the sofa, where he felt safer. Far away from Suzanne, far away from temptation.

She spoke quietly into the space he had made between them. "You could be right. Alyssa may not be dead. If I think back to what happened at the airport before the crash, I feel almost certain she never boarded the plane."

Adam was the one who'd suggested Alyssa might be alive, but his stomach lurched—in shock? In recognition—at Suzanne's agreement. "Why don't you think she was on the plane?" he asked.

"The plane was full, so full that the check-in clerk upgraded me from economy to first-class to get me a seat. He was obviously new at the job and couldn't seem to work the computer very well. In retrospect I think he double-booked me into Alyssa's seat and never changed the plane's manifest. That's why the authorities originally identified me as Alyssa Humphrey. Because I was sitting in her seat, next to her brother, not because I look like her."

Adam sat up straighter, his heart pounding. "Why didn't Alyssa board the plane?" he asked. "Did you talk to Dick at all?"

She nodded, her expression rueful. "Dick and I had a very public argument. He was furious because he suspected me of trying to impersonate Alyssa. Apparently he and Alyssa had already had a bitter argument about her behavior, and he wasn't willing to believe that somebody so like his sister could sit next to him by sheer chance."

"That doesn't necessarily rule out the possibility that Alyssa was seated somewhere else on the plane."

"No, but she'd already disappeared at O'Hare airport before the plane ever took off for Denver. Her brother and one of the flight attendants were both searching for her. Besides, if another woman who looked amazingly like me had boarded the plane, don't you think someone would have noticed?"

"You're right," Adam agreed, his mind racing. "But if Alyssa never caught that plane, where is she?"

"And why hasn't she come home?"

"Either she can't, because she doesn't have freedom of movement. Or she doesn't want to."

"She deliberately gave Dick the slip at O'Hare. That's why he was so angry."

"Then she intended to disappear and presumably doesn't want to resurface."

"Nobody would voluntarily leave their fiancé and family grieving over a nonexistent death for almost two months," Suzanne protested.

"She hasn't left a grieving family," Adam pointed out. "As far as Matthew and Jackie know, they have nothing to be sad about. They have you."

"Alyssa wouldn't know that."

"Why not? The press and television gave prime coverage to your miraculous rescue from the flames. And then, the day you left hospital, you appeared with the senator, live on all major networks.''

Suzanne leaned forward and grabbed his jacket. ''The sympathy card!'' she exclaimed. ''My God, Adam, where did you put that sympathy card?''

He understood at once, and clamped down on a leap of excitement. ''In my briefcase. I'll get it.''

The minute he came back to the family room she snatched the card from him and pulled out the typewritten note.

''Adam, this must be from Alyssa. 'The amnesia is a great trick, but I know you're a fraud, even if you've fooled everyone else.' I thought someone was accusing me of faking amnesia, but what if the person who sent this note is accusing me of being an imposter? And who else could make that accusation except the real Alyssa Humphrey?''

''You're ignoring the second half of the message,'' Adam said grimly, taking the note from her. '''This card is a friendly warning. Disappear. Get out. You are in danger.'''

''Melodrama.'' Suzanne waved her hand in impatient dismissal. ''Alyssa loves everything to be larger than life, and this message is right in keeping with her personality. Besides, she thinks I'm deliberately deceiving Matthew and her family. She *intends* to scare me.''

''And obviously didn't succeed, but she's sure as hell scared me. Suzanne, the smart thing for you to do is to call Matthew and tell him the truth, then take the first flight home to Chicago. You're into something way over your head.''

He had already learned to recognize the stubborn tilt to her chin, a tilt that was one hundred percent Suzanne Swenson and owed nothing at all to Alyssa. ''No,'' she said. ''I'm not telling Jackie who I am until her mother is home and we have her enrolled in a counseling program.''

Frustration roiled in Adam's gut. ''I agree that Jackie needs help. But you don't know what you're risking if you hang around here pretending to be someone you're not. If the real Alyssa has gone into hiding, you can bet she didn't disappear because she wanted to catch some rays on a quiet beach in Tahiti. To run she must have been scared—and Alyssa's not a woman who scares easily.''

Suzanne appeared unimpressed by his dire warnings. ''I'm not planning to spend the rest of my life masquerading as Alyssa, only the next few days. A few days that mean almost nothing to me, but could make a world of difference to Jackie. I blew the chance to help my brother. I'm not blowing this chance to help someone who thinks she's my sister.''

''Someone stole three million dollars from Alyssa's trust fund, then killed Jerry Hershel to cover their tracks. Doesn't that make you a little bit nervous about what the next few days might hold?''

''It would if I didn't think Dick Humphrey was responsible for the theft, and maybe even for what happened to Jerry.'' She rested her hand lightly on his arm. ''Adam, don't worry. I'm not aiming at a short life of noble self-sacrifice. Dick is dead and dead men are no threat.''

''But their associates might be,'' Adam said, not allowing himself to notice that his hand had tightened around Suzanne's.

In her eagerness to convince him, she leaned forward, leaving only a crack of space between their bodies. ''His associates aren't going to come looking for me in the next couple of days,'' she said, smiling. ''Why would they? We haven't seen so much as a glimpse of their whiskers over the past two months.''

Why the hell did she have to wear such seductive perfume? And why the hell couldn't he concentrate on the matter at hand? It was time to thrust some semblance of reality into her obstinate skull. ''You may not have seen any of Dick's associates, but you heard from one. Do you remember Kurt Walther?''

Suzanne looked puzzled. ''The seafood broker?''

Adam snorted. ''If Kurt Walther is a seafood broker, then he has a whole new profession since he last showed up on Interpol's computers. Until he disappeared last year, he was a neo-Nazi thug, who supported himself by drug dealing and anything else unsavory that came along. There are warrants outstanding against him in both France and Holland.''

Suzanne's cheeks paled. "What for?"

"Intimidation. Grievous bodily harm. Murder. Mr. Walther believes in racial purity. He doesn't like immigrants flooding into Europe from Africa and the Middle East, so he beats them up whenever he gets the chance. On at least two occasions, he didn't stop beating until it was too late. The victims died.''

"How do you know all this?''

She looked so worried that Adam realized it would be inhumane of him not to put his arm around her shoulder and offer some comfort. Friendly comfort, of course, without any hint of sexual possessiveness. "Last week I finally managed to break Jerry Hershel's computer code and access his private files. His notes were sparse and pretty cryptic, but everything I just told you about Kurt Walther is quoted directly from Jerry's files. Makes you wonder exactly what Alyssa owed Kurt money for, doesn't it? And it sure as heck makes me wonder why Rex Clancey told you that cock-and-bull story about Kurt Walther being the manager of a fishing company."

She was shaken, Adam could see that, and he expected her to capitulate at once. After all, she seemed like a reasonable person.

Suzanne, unfortunately, had a different definition of reasonable. She turned within the circle of his arms, closing the last smidgen of space he had so carefully left between their bodies.

"We need to find Alyssa," she said. "She'll be able to tell us what's going on. You know her, where do you suggest we start looking?"

"I'm not even going to dignify that question with an answer," Adam said, appalled by Suzanne's casual attitude to her own safety. Her unwillingness to listen to wise advice from people who knew better was infuriating.

"Alyssa disappeared in Chicago," Suzanne said, completely ignoring him. "You could fly there tomorrow and start tracking her right away. I'll join you as soon as Lena Humphrey is home and settled in.''

"You're showing about as much sense as a warthog," Adam retorted, his control snapping.

"I'm considered an *extremely* intelligent woman."

"A totally undeserved reputation," Adam muttered.

He might as well not have spoken. "Do you know if Alyssa has any old friends in Chicago where she might be staying?" Suzanne asked. "Maybe I could call them, pretending to be her. That would throw whoever's hiding her into a state of total confusion."

He gave up the attempt at rational persuasion and did what any sensible man would have done in the circumstances. He tightened his arms around Suzanne's waist, pulled her hard against his body and kissed her into an appropriate state of submission.

WITH A TINGE of regret Matthew rewound the videotape of his appearance on *Face the Nation*. At the last minute he couldn't bring himself to turn off the VCR, and he pressed the Mute button on the remote control but allowed the tape to continue running. Without sound his face dominated the small screen even more completely. Damn, but his profile came over well on TV!

Matthew almost wished Rex hadn't arrived so promptly for their meeting. They had a lot of business to get through, but he would have liked to review the tape in private one last time. There was always room for improvement in a politician's performance, although—modesty aside—that had been one hell of a moving speech he'd delivered today on behalf of South Africa's oppressed minorities. What's more, he'd written every word of it himself, unlike some of the senators who would be reduced to dithering silence if they ever had to come up with their own material. Skill at speech making was all a matter of belief and conviction, Matthew reflected. He genuinely cared about creating health and educational opportunities for deprived children everywhere, and he cared especially about reversing the devastation being visited upon inner-city blacks by insensitive Administration policies. Scowling with frustration, he swung around, acknowledging Rex's presence for the first time.

"When I'm president of the United States, there's sure as *blazes* gonna be a change in the government's priorities. No more tax breaks for corporate fat cats while a third of the children living in single-parent homes don't get proper food."

"Right," Rex said. "We're behind you all the way, Senator. But first we have to get you elected."

Matthew smoothed out his frown and gave Rex a reassuring smile. "You know we're heading in the right direction, Rex. I think we have our timing just right. Governor Rivers is the only candidate who deserves the presidency— apart from me, of course—and Van Plat's killing him in the polls. Rivers has the worst campaign staff I've ever seen."

"True, but Gordon and Minetti are waging good campaigns."

Matthew dismissed both presidential contenders with a snap of his fingers. "Lightweights, Rex, and you know it. They look good on TV, and that's about the extent of their assets. They have no solid achievements behind them, and the two of them together couldn't come up with a worthwhile policy for governing this country. The media will have killed them off by spring, and then it's gonna come down to the two of us. Me and Van Plat."

Rex nodded. A cautious man, given to worrying, for once he looked almost optimistic. "Van Plat's digging himself into a deep hole on civil rights issues. With Daniel Schaak's help, we'll blow him right out of the water."

Matthew chuckled. "Makes me feel good every time I think about how we're using that bastard Schaak." He sobered. "Okay, let's get down to brass tacks, Rex. Have the accounts in Zurich been cleaned out?"

"All taken care of, and Walther's been paid just enough to cover his next delivery. We still have Alyssa's last million left for the final payoff."

"Can we trust Walther to deliver now that his past-due bills have been paid?"

"He'll deliver right on time and no hassles, I guarantee it. Schaak has acknowledged receipt of the first consignment of guns, and the second is already en route. Plus we've laid a paper trail leading to Van Plat that nobody will be able to unravel."

"Walther won't talk?"

Rex laughed. "Senator, are you kidding?"

Matthew felt a spurt of annoyance. "Look, Rex, I'm not being unreasonable in double-checking. You said it would take five years to discover the money from Alyssa's trust fund was missing. Instead, Jerry Hershel took a mere two months, and why he wasn't fired earlier I'll never know."

"But Jerry was taken care of, Senator."

Matthew gave his aide an oblique glance. "You mean we got lucky because Jerry Hershel had a boating accident?"

"Right. Yes, of course that's what I meant."

"Okay, but then what happened? We've been lucky with Jerry, so Dick supposedly buries the theft even deeper—and Adam Stryker uncovers it in three weeks! Good God, he'd hardly read through the damn trust papers before he was squawking! We're talking major inefficiency here, Rex."

"You're right, and I apologize. Dick screwed up. He didn't cover his ass like he promised. However, we're not in any real trouble. Hershel may have suspected Dick stole the money, but the trail stopped right there. Hershel never had an inkling of an idea as to why Dick needed the money."

"I hope you're right," Matthew said.

"We've searched every file, every piece of paper in Hershel's home and in his office. And the same for Dick. We turned up nothing. At least nothing bad. Finding those Zurich account numbers was a gift from the gods. We'd have been totally lost if Dick hadn't written them down."

Matthew winced at the narrowness of their escape. "That plane crash nearly ruined everything, what with Dick dying and Alyssa losing her memory."

"It was a bad few weeks," Rex agreed. "Knowing we had three million dollars sitting in a Zurich bank and no way to access the money."

"Well, it's 'All's well that ends well.'" Matthew smiled, feeling cheerful again. The tape of his interview ended, and he flipped off the TV, staring for a moment at the blank screen. "I think Alyssa's memory is coming back," he said abruptly.

Rex's breath hissed out in surprise. "Damn! That's not good news."

Matthew raised an eyebrow. "How come? Three weeks ago you were frantic for her amnesia to be cured."

"Because we needed those Zurich bank account numbers! Now we've already cleaned out the accounts, and frankly the fewer people who remember they existed, the better I like it." Rex poured himself a bourbon. "What are you going to do about Alyssa?"

"Marry her, what else?" Matthew would have preferred to remain single, but going through a ceremony with Alyssa—and even sleeping with her occasionally—didn't seem like a very big sacrifice to make in pursuit of the presidency. Nobody, he thought proudly, could accuse him of having scrambled priorities. He clapped Rex on the shoulder.

"I don't know why you're getting so uptight about Alyssa. After all, you were the person who told me I need a wife. The campaign consultants agree it's essential. Single men can't get elected president of the United States, not in the nineties."

Rex sighed. "It's true that weddings make for great publicity. On the other hand, funerals play quite well if you do them right, and they have one enormous advantage—dead women can't make indiscreet revelations. Dick was a loose cannon and told his sister way too much."

Matthew shook his head. "We don't know that Alyssa will cause trouble if she regains her memory. She was getting antsy before the plane crash, but that doesn't mean she'll continue to want out of the marriage. Right now she's convinced we're madly in love.''

''I think you need to give your plans for Alyssa some thought,'' Rex advised. ''Personally she makes me nervous. There's something about her since the crash—she's not the same woman she was before. Not the same woman at all.''

''Funny,'' Matthew commented. ''That's exactly what she said.''

Chapter Nine

Adam never made it back to the hotel on Saturday night, although when midnight struck on the hallway grandfather clock and Suzanne was still locked in his arms, she did retain enough sense of self-preservation to direct him to a guest room instead of inviting him into her bed. Battle-scarred after her experience with Harrison Quentin III and the psychological upheavals of the past few weeks, she knew it would be insanity to get involved with a man who was attracted to her chiefly because she looked like another woman.

Hours later, lying wakeful in bed, her body taut with unfulfilled desire, Suzanne congratulated herself on making the sensible decision. Unfortunately, good sense didn't seem to make her rampaging hormones one bit easier to deal with. Drat Adam, anyway, for making her want him.

Jackie woke up on Sunday morning still full of contrition for the previous day's drinking. Her face lit up when Adam suggested that they all three take a trip to the nineteenth century mining town of Central City.

For some reason Jackie chose not to hide behind her usual defensive veneer of world-weary sophistication. Her personality emerged as intelligent and shy, leavened with a bubbly sense of humor. She and Adam were soon involved in one giggle-inducing game after another, and gradually Suzanne found herself drawn into the carefree silliness of it all. Walking down the steep board sidewalks, watching

Adam and Jackie squabble over which fast-food outlet made the best milk shake, her heart contracted in a pang of regret for her own dour childhood. This was what families were supposed to be like, she thought, and this was what she would fight to provide for her little "sister."

Jackie was disconsolate when they dropped Adam off at the airport, so Suzanne suggested a visit to the movies to round out the evening. "Your choice," she said.

Jackie gleefully bought tickets for *Ghouls from the Graveyard IV,* and when Suzanne complained, she chuckled. "Hey, keep an open mind, big sister, and I'm sure you'll love it."

Suzanne, who hadn't seen anything but foreign art films photographed in grainy black and white, since the day she met Harry, munched popcorn, clutched Jackie's arm and screamed happily through an hour and a half of spear-toothed vampires, blood-drenched zombies and headless ghosts. Leaving the movie theater, Jackie awarded the film her highest accolade. It was, she announced, totally, utterly gross.

True, Suzanne reflected, but not nearly as gross as sitting next to Harry and pretending to be fascinated by a Czech neorealist movie with French subtitles. Why in the world had she never admitted to Harry that she liked her movies to come in living color and preferably with happy endings?

Open, honest communication had obviously not been one of her strong points, Suzanne decided the next morning. In precrash days, if she had thought Jackie needed help to overcome her drinking problem, she would simply have gone to Jackie's school and outlined the situation in brisk detail, having taken appropriate legal advice first. The idea of warning Jackie that her privacy was going to be so drastically invaded would never have occurred to the old Suzanne. But her weeks seeing the world through Alyssa's eyes seemed to have increased her supply of wisdom.

She went downstairs early and shared breakfast with Jackie in the kitchen. "I need to talk with you," she said, pouring orange juice for them both. "With your permission, Jackie, I'd like to go to your school later on this morning. I need to have a heart-to-heart chat with your teachers."

The easy rapport of the previous day was immediately broken. Jackie's mouth drew into a hostile line. "What for? You've never bothered to talk to any of them before."

Suzanne recognized the hurt beneath the hostility, and she tamped down on a surge of anger toward the absent Alyssa. "Look, honey, you've gotten yourself into a difficult place in your life, and you probably need professional help to climb out of it." She reached across the table and took Jackie's hand. The warm, human contact felt amazingly good, and she squeezed Jackie's fingers encouragingly.

Frowning, Jackie turned her head away, but Suzanne noticed that she didn't move her hand.

"It's tough being sixteen," Suzanne continued. "I know how tough because when I was sixteen, I made a total mess of my life. And unfortunately nobody took me on one side and told me what a jerk I was becoming."

A ghost of a smile lightened Jackie's expression. "And you're doing the favor of telling me I'm a jerk?"

"You're not a jerk, Jackie, except when you drink."

"My teachers can't help, they're all nerds."

"Maybe, but they spend all day, every day, with young people like you. They'll know the very best places in Denver to find you a support group, or whatever else you need. There are plenty of people out there who know how to help teenagers find their feet in the world, and we'll locate them, Jackie. Because there's one thing I know absolutely for sure. Whatever problems you have, whatever's bothering you right now, you're never going to find a worthwhile solution in a bottle of booze."

Jackie's face closed tight again, and she wouldn't meet Suzanne's gaze. After an endless pause, she gave Suzanne's hand the tiniest answering squeeze. Then she snatched her hand away and stuffed it into her pocket, afraid she might have revealed too much.

"Okay," she said gruffly. "You can talk to Mrs. Derrick. She's my advisor, and she's a million years old, but she's not too bad." In a small voice, she added, "Do you think I'm an alcoholic, Lyss? I don't often drink too much. Just when I feel . . . scared inside."

Probably the worst reason of all for drinking, Suzanne thought. Her heart contracted and she hugged Jackie until the ramrod resistance in the girl's bony shoulders softened into an answering hug. "We'll get you help, honey."

"I'll be late for class," Jackie said after a moment of silence. "Juan must be waiting out front."

Suzanne gave her a swat. "You're right. Go get 'em, kid."

Supervised by Mrs. Derrick, Suzanne spent over three hours in meetings with Jackie's teachers and advisors. Fortunately, since Lena Vincent Humphrey was away from Denver, "Alyssa" qualified as Jackie's guardian and the staff was willing to talk to her. At first Suzanne experienced a few pangs of guilt over her deception, but as they talked she became convinced she was doing the right thing for Jackie, and she left the headmaster's office feeling good about the day's discussions and hopeful for Jackie's future.

The sun shone out of a cloudless blue sky, typical weather for Denver at most times of the year, Suzanne had learned. She was in no hurry to get home, and she strolled around the grounds of the school, stopping for a few moments to watch a team of small boys play enthusiastic lacrosse. The campus was huge, almost as large as a small college, but the layout was easy to follow and she had no difficulty finding a path that cut back past the administrative offices toward the visitors' parking lot where she had left her car.

She was on school grounds, on a sunny afternoon, and the parking lot was in sight. Suzanne didn't give a passing thought to the fact that this particular stretch of campus appeared deserted.

When the denim-covered arm lashed out and dragged her back into a shed full of garden equipment, she didn't immediately grasp what had happened. Her first ridiculous instinct was to apologize for having bumped into someone. A split second too late, she began to struggle. When she started to scream, a broad, meaty hand slapped over her mouth, cutting off her cry, and most of her breath with it. The man yanked her backward, so that his body pressed against her spine from neck to knee.

I'm going to be raped.

Her attacker was taking no chances of being identified. He kept carefully behind her, out of sight. He had almost complete control of her body movements, with one of his arms drawn tight around her breasts, pinning her arms to her sides, and the other holding her head thrust against his cheek, with his hand covering her mouth. She gave a desperate kick to the rear, causing him to grunt and twist away, and for an instant she had enough room to wriggle free of his hold. Out of the corner of her eye she caught a fleeting glimpse of him as she started running. Tall, dark, swarthy, slightly overweight.

The tiny hope of escape vanished as he recaptured her instantly, swinging her around in a single swift movement, pushing her face against the rough wooden wall and clamping his body against the entire length of her back. She was trapped by his weight, skewered in place against the wall.

She heard a click, an odd little swoosh, then cold metal pressed against her neck. "I have a switchblade. Try anything funny and I'll use it. Understand?"

Fear kept her silent, and when she didn't answer he grabbed her hair and shook her head angrily. "Answer me, damn you, and keep your voice down! Why are you here?"

"I'm . . . going to . . . my car. In the parking lot."

"That's not what I meant." His voice was gravelly and breathless with nerves or perhaps anticipation. Suzanne forced back the panic and tried to catalog every identifying detail of her attacker. She might not be able to stop him raping her, but by Heaven she would make sure she could identify him if she was ever given the chance.

At least six foot tall, heavily built, bulging biceps. Wearing jeans, and a sweater under his denim jacket. His hands were tanned, but clean and not callused, and he smelled of after-shave. Expensive after-shave, mingled with sweat. She tried to turn just enough to glimpse his face, and he grabbed her head again, shoving it back toward the wall, screening her view.

"Who are you?" he demanded, "and who's paying you? When did you set this scam up? Before or after the crash?"

His questions made absolutely no sense to her petrified brain. "I . . . don't understand."

"Damn it, who's paying you to impersonate Alyssa? Was she supposed to die in the crash?" The knife blade slid over her skin, but Suzanne didn't even know if she'd been wounded. *He knew Alyssa. He wasn't a mad rapist.* Her body went limp with relief.

He wrapped his hands in her hair and tugged. "Talk, damn you. *Talk!*"

"It was a mistake," she said, her voice emerging flat with fear. "I was wrongly identified after the plane crash. Nobody set up a scam. Has Alyssa sent you?"

"No questions," he growled. "If you admit you're not Alyssa, why are you still at the house? What the hell are you playing at now?"

"It's because of Ja—" She broke off abruptly. Dear God, she'd been about to mention Jackie's name. "I've been too sick to move," she said.

"Does Bradford know who you are, or was this impersonation another of Dick's smart-ass ideas?"

From outside the shed came the sound of voices. "Joe, give me a hand over here, will you? This doggurn spiggot ain't gonna turn off without a spanner."

"Hang on a bit. This hose is heavier than a—"

Suzanne screamed, a primeval scream backed by all the volume her terror could provide. "Help! I'm in the shed. Help me!"

If she'd stopped to think, she would never have screamed. After all, her attacker still had his knife and had threatened to use it.

But for some reason he didn't make good on his threat. Swearing viciously, he jumped away from Suzanne. Then, the instant she turned to run, he slammed his clenched fist against the side of her head.

"Hell, I'm sorry, lady."

Had the man with the knife really apologized? Suzanne swayed on her feet for two or three sickening seconds. Distant voices blurred into a single fuzzy drone. The last sound she heard was the bang of the door as her attacker escaped out of the back entrance to the shed. Blackness took her.

It was almost eight o'clock before Suzanne and Jackie arrived back at the house. The school nurse had insisted on a trip to the hospital emergency room, and the school principal—justly concerned about a violent criminal on the loose in the vicinity of his five hundred students—had insisted on making an official police report.

Suzanne, trying to reassure Jackie that she wasn't hurt and simultaneously answering the barrage of questions pouring in from all sides, had found herself in a dilemma. If she gave an accurate version of what the attacker had said, she would need to reveal that she wasn't Alyssa. In the end she compromised by saying a large man had tried to snatch her purse then gotten scared by the sound of the yard workers' voices and run off.

Everyone accepted her story, but it was a harrowing few hours, not helped by a headache. Jackie, having committed herself to substance-abuse counseling, was also feeling under pressure, and the two of them let out identical sighs of relief as they returned home and entered the kitchen. Shirley, the housekeeper, greeted them with a smile.

"Lord love us, Alyssa, you sure are set on finding trouble these days. No real harm done, Jackie told me when she called."

"Thank goodness, no."

The housekeeper looked worriedly at the square of gauze covering a small scrape on the left side of Suzanne's forehead. "Did the brute who attacked you open up any of your plastic surgery scars? Should I call Barb Mackintosh and ask her to come and help out for a couple of days?''

Suzanne shook her head. ''Thanks, Shirley, but I'm way past the stage of needing a nurse. I'm fine. I scraped my forehead when I fell, that's all.''

''Huh. I suppose that knock on the head didn't do anything useful, like bringing back your memories? That's what always happens in the movies.''

''No such luck,'' Jackie piped up. ''I already asked Lyss about that. She said the only things she remembers about the precrash Alyssa Humphrey are what we've told her.'' She opened a saucepan lid and sniffed appreciatively. ''Mmm-mm, homemade tomato soup. Roast beef in the oven. How did we get so lucky on a Monday night?''

Shirley's eyes twinkled. ''You haven't taken a peek into the living room, yet. This is an eventful day. There's a couple of people you might be interested to see, waiting there for you.''

''Is it Mom?'' Jackie flew along the hallway without waiting for a reply, Suzanne following behind. Jackie flung open the heavy double doors leading into the formal living room.

''Mom, you're home! Oh boy, this is great.''

''Darling!'' A woman of medium height and slender figure rose from the sofa where she had been sitting with Matthew Bradford. She gathered the hurtling Jackie into her arms for a hug, stroking her daughter's mane of dark brown hair with delicate, pink-tipped fingers.

Matthew smiled indulgently and came to stand next to Suzanne. ''Now there's a sight to warm the iciest heart,'' he murmured. ''Their hair is almost the identical shade, isn't it?''

''Yes, they're going to be quite alike when Jackie matures.''

Matthew cupped her face with his hands, his gaze intent as he looked down at her. ''I've missed you, Alyssa. Let's leave them to their own devices for a couple of minutes and concentrate on us for a change.''

She smiled nervously, anxious to avoid any intimate conversation, and even more anxious to avoid his kisses. "You've only been gone thirty-six hours, Matthew."

He rubbed his thumbs over her cheeks in a butterfly caress. "That's about thirty-five hours too long as far as I'm concerned. And what's this dreadful news I hear from the housekeeper about some sneak thief accosting you right on the school grounds this afternoon?" He touched the gauze pad on her left temple. "My poor wounded warrior, fate isn't treating you kindly these days, is it? Are you sure it was just a sneak thief, and you were only a chance victim?"

"What else could it be?" Suzanne asked, searching her conscience to come up with the least deceptive answer possible. Although, now that Lena was home, there was really no reason why Suzanne shouldn't simply announce the truth to the whole world. *After dinner,* she decided. *After dinner, I'll take Matthew somewhere private and tell him who I really am.*

"Alyssa, my dear!" Lena put an end to Suzanne's soul-searching. She crossed the room and enveloped her supposed stepdaughter in a warm, perfumed hug. *She's wearing Poison,* Suzanne thought, concealing a shudder of distaste. Lena couldn't be blamed because she'd chosen the same distinctive scent that Marianne always favored.

Lena clasped Suzanne's hands. "My dear, I wrote to you about poor Dick as soon as the doctors let me hold a pen. I was devastated when I heard the news, but at least we must all thank God you didn't share the same fate as your brother. Sometimes it's so hard to understand God's plan for the world, isn't it? We just have to take a giant leap of faith and pray everything will turn out right in the end." Lena smiled sadly. "Dick will be missed."

"Thank you, Lena. Welcome home."

"How *good* it is to be back again with the family! I've missed you all so much. Now, let me look at you, Alyssa, really look, and see if that doctor did as wonderful a job as Matthew and Jackie said in their letters."

Lena retreated to arm's length, her clear-eyed gaze sweeping over Suzanne in frank appraisal. After a moment's silence she sighed in mock despair. "All I can say is that if I didn't have the disposition of a saint, I'd be green with envy. Alyssa, I swear the surgeon has made you prettier than ever. And younger looking, darn him! Maybe I'd better ask you for his name and phone number."

Suzanne laughed, thinking how wide of the mark she had been in her judgment of Jackie's mother. Lena was as far removed from the stereotype of wicked stepmother as it was possible to get. "My doctor's name is Reinhard, and his offices are right next to University Hospital, but you sure don't need his services, Lena."

"Every woman of my age needs to know a good plastic surgeon. Let's face it, Alyssa, I'm thirty-nine next month. I plan to have a huge party, and then develop an acute attack of amnesia for the next ten years." She stopped abruptly, her rather pale cheeks suffusing with color. "Whoops, that wasn't the most tactful remark to make, was it? Sorry, Alyssa."

"Lyss doesn't mind," Jackie said. "You're kind of used to having no memories by now, aren't you, Lyss?"

"As accustomed as a person can ever be, I guess." Suzanne quickly changed the subject. "So tell us about your trip to Africa, Lena. We were sorry to hear about your pneumonia. I hope your illness didn't ruin all your plans?"

"Oh, no, it was just a silly little virus—"

Matthew interrupted. "Now, Lena, my dear, you know we agreed that you aren't going to tell that lie anymore. The time for sheltering your family is over. You're home now, and Alyssa's regained her strength, thank goodness. Your daughters deserve to hear the truth. Otherwise how are they going to understand why you left them alone for such a long period? Jackie didn't complain, but she must have felt you could have made more of an effort to fly home when she needed you so badly."

Jackie jumped up from the sofa. "Mom, what is it? What happened?"

Lena stroked her daughter's hand and glared reproachfully toward Matthew. "Honestly, my dears, trust a man to make a fuss about nothing. The fact is, by the most horrid coincidence, I had a little car accident on the very same day that Alyssa and Dick suffered that awful plane crash."

"A little car accident!" Matthew exclaimed. "Translation—the lunatic driving her Range Rover crashed head-on with a tour bus. Lena was in traction for four weeks while the doctors decided if she'd ever walk again. And on top of that, she developed a rampaging case of viral pneumonia that they couldn't control with drugs."

Jackie clutched her mother's hand. "Oh, Mom, how awful! No wonder you couldn't write or come to the phone until a couple of weeks ago."

Lena gave her daughter a gentle, reassuring smile. "But everything's fine now," she said. "I've seen specialists in Switzerland and in London and they all assure me I've been put together just like new." Ruffling Jackie's hair, she added teasingly, "Unless the rain's coming in from the north, you won't even hear me creak when I bend over."

Jackie giggled and her air of worry dissipated. "You and Lyss will have to compare hospital horror stories," she said.

Lena flashed Suzanne an amused glance. "There's a treat in store for both of us. Why don't you tell me what's been happening in your life since I left."

Five minutes later they were all chatting comfortably when Shirley came in to announce that dinner was served.

Whatever the root cause of Jackie's problems, Suzanne reflected as the excellent meal progressed from succulent roast beef to a light-as-air lemon soufflé, Lena Vincent Humphrey seemed admirably qualified to take care of her troubled daughter. It was gratifying for Suzanne to realize that by continuing her deception for a mere forty-eight hours, she had provided Jackie with a staunch supporter to lean on while a search for the real Alyssa Humphrey was set in motion.

The tension that she'd often sensed when Jackie mentioned her mother seemed entirely absent tonight. The more

Suzanne saw of Lena, the more she became convinced that Lena was a loving mother, who combined good looks and keen intelligence with a warm, caring personality. And this was the woman she had condemned for abandoning Jackie! Mentally chastising herself for leaping to wild conclusions on the basis of no evidence, Suzanne listened intently as Lena recounted in moving detail the efforts of her church group to establish tutorial centers for high school students in black South African townships.

"The primary education isn't too bad," Lena concluded, "but at the high school level, black kids often run into a vicious cycle. To pass the advanced courses, they need books and equipment. They have no money for the books or the equipment, so they fail the courses. Then the state authorities claim that they can't afford to allocate money to schools with such terrible dropout and failure rates. So the whole pitiful cycle starts over again, and the black population remains largely uneducated."

"It's not only a problem in South Africa," Matthew said. "I could quote you a hundred similar stories from inner-city schools right here in the States. The school districts with the greatest needs usually have the lowest expenditure per pupil." His voice shaking with passion, he banged his fist down onto the table. "Damn it, we're not talking about frills like microscopes and ballet lessons. I know families from the projects in Chicago where brothers and sisters go to school on alternate days because they've only got one pair of shoes between them! And then our political leaders in both parties pretend there's nothing the federal government can do to improve the situation! I'll tell you what would improve the situation—money spent on education instead of on agricultural subsidies for multibillion dollar farming corporations. Money for preschools and day-care centers, instead of space telescopes that don't function. Money so that five-year-old kids from the inner city can spend the day at kindergarten instead of warehoused in front of a TV set watching violent cartoons."

He cut his flow of angry words abruptly, grinning rather sheepishly. "Hey, I'm sorry. You press my buttons on the subject of education, and you're usually guaranteed twenty minutes of nonstop rhetoric."

Matthew spoke with burning sincerity, and Suzanne had rarely liked him as much as she did at that moment. She didn't want to marry him, but she was beginning to hope he'd change his mind and run for president. When she told him she wasn't Alyssa, she'd promise him her vote!

The conversation became less heated, with Matthew and Lena contributing fascinating anecdotes about school systems and educational experiments around the world.

Shirley came in with fresh coffee. "Just saw you on the news, Senator, debating with Governor Van Plat. Them reporters keep asking if you're gonna run for president. They won't take no for an answer, will they?"

Matthew shrugged. "Being pesky is their job, Shirley. I've learned to tolerate the questions."

"Well, they're right about one thing. You should run for president. I'd rather vote for you than any of the candidates they've got running so far, Democrats and Republicans both. Maybe you should think on what those reporters are telling you, Senator."

His deep blue eyes shone with merriment. "Thanks for the compliment, Shirley. If I decide to run, I'll put you in my campaign commercial. Voices from the heartland speak out for Bradford."

The housekeeper tried not to look flattered and failed. "It would be a pleasure to speak on your behalf, Senator, and that's a fact."

Lena smiled affectionately at Shirley's retreating back. "If you can win her approval, Matthew, the other two hundred and fifty million Americans are pushovers." She smothered a yawn. "I'm dead on my feet, folks. If you'll excuse me, I'm going to make this an early night."

"An excellent suggestion," said Matthew. "My day started with a five a.m. briefing, and I'm exhausted." He dropped one of his usual chaste kisses in the air near Suzanne's cheek. "See you tomorrow morning, darling. I don't need to leave for DC until after lunch, so we can have a long chat after breakfast."

Shirley stuck her head around the living room door. "Phone for you, Alyssa. A woman, didn't give her name."

"For me?"

Shirley grinned. "As far as I know, you're Alyssa Humphrey."

Suzanne gave a sickly smile. That did it, she decided. She had spent too much of the past forty-eight hours deceiving these good people. She was tired of feeling lower than a worm's belly. However weary Matthew might be, she would tell him the truth tonight. No more delays. No more excuses.

"Thanks," she said to Shirley. "I'll take the call in the library."

Suzanne walked across the hall, mentally framing the opening words of her explanation. *I'm sorry, Matthew, you must prepare yourself for a dreadful shock.* No, that sounded like a doctor diagnosing a fatal illness. *My memory came back a couple of days ago. I'm not Alyssa Humphrey. My name's Suzanne Swenson.* Yes, that was better.

She picked up the phone. "Hello, sorry to have kept you waiting. This is Alyssa Humphrey."

A bark of angry laughter, then the caller spoke. "What a coincidence. So is this."

Chapter Ten

Suzanne stared blindly at the phone until the buzz of the disconnected call turned into an irritated beep, warning that the handset had been left too long off the receiver. She went back to the living room, but fortunately everyone had gone to bed and she was able to escape upstairs without talking to anyone. She flipped on the lights in her bedroom and sat down in front of her dressing table—no, not *her* room, not *her* dressing table. *Alyssa's* room, and *Alyssa's* dressing table.

A sense of loss drifted up out of nowhere. It wasn't so much that she wanted to continue being Alyssa Humphrey, Suzanne reflected. Rather, she was repelled by the prospect of becoming once again the cautious, uptight, work-obsessed individual Suzanne Swenson had been.

Confused by the welter of emotions besetting her, she realized suddenly that what she wanted to do more than anything else was talk to Adam.

She dialed his number, her fingers tightening around the phone when he answered, "This is Adam Stryker."

Absurd that the sound of his composed, measured tones could make her heart thump violently against her rib cage. Absurd that her tongue should seem too clumsy for any of the casual opening gambits she'd planned. "Alyssa Humphrey just telephoned me," she said. The words came out in anxious lump.

He gave the tiniest hiss of surprise. "So she *is* alive. What did she say?"

"Just that she was Alyssa Humphrey. Then she hung up the phone."

"Disconcerting for you," he said. "After weeks of thinking you were Alyssa, it must have been unnerving to actually hear the voice of your alter ego."

"You have an infuriating habit of putting my half-formed feelings into crisp sentences."

He smiled. She could feel it across a thousand miles of telephone wire. "Confusing that we think so much alike, isn't it? Makes you wonder why we spend such a lot of our time together arguing."

"Because you're an infuriating man."

He laughed, a deep throaty chuckle. "That could be the reason."

Darn it, she would *not* allow herself to tingle just because the wretched man had laughed. What's more, she did *not* wish that Adam was here with her. In fact, there was little point in prolonging this foolish conversation. She would apologize for having disturbed him at this late hour and hang up.

"How soon can you come back to Denver?" she asked. "Adam, I . . . need you."

"Then I'll be there. I'll catch the first plane out tomorrow morning."

"Lena Humphrey came home today," she explained hastily, appalled by the disconnection between her brain and her tongue. A woman had to be a fool to tell a man she needed him, and Suzanne had no intention of being a fool over Adam. "I'm going to explain to Matthew who I am tonight, and I'll tell Jackie tomorrow. I'm sure everyone will have loads of legal questions. Your presence would be very helpful."

"The first flight lands at eight-fifty Denver time. I'll be on it."

"Thank you," she said stiffly. She didn't want to sound too friendly and grateful or Adam might get the wrong idea—especially since they had spent hours on Friday night exchanging the kind of kisses that were guaranteed to create every sort of wrong idea in the male mind.

She had nothing more that needed to be said at this time of night. She really ought to hang up the phone instead of standing here, her breath coming out in tight little puffs of excitement.

It was Adam who broke the lengthening silence. "What are you wearing?" he asked in his usual, cool voice.

Startled, she glanced into the mirror. "Tweed skirt, paisley turtle neck, discreet sweater." She realized, without much pleasure, that the reflection was much more Suzanne Swenson than Alyssa Humphrey. "I look very color coordinated and neat."

"Pity," he said. "I was imagining you in a slippery black silk robe and nothing underneath." He paused for a split second and continued in the same even voice, exactly as if he were discussing the weather. "I've discovered over the past two nights that a vivid imagination makes sleep hellishly difficult."

Suzanne uncurled her fingers that had somehow become knotted in the twists of the phone cord. She didn't have to wonder any more how Adam would look if his astonishing self-control ever snapped. She knew exactly how he would look. Like her. Because they were two of a kind; people whose passions ran so deep and so fierce they needed to keep those passions under the tightest of lock and key. But if either of them ever chose to unlock the gates... Suzanne found that she was trembling.

"Good night, Suzanne. I'll see you tomorrow. Nine-thirty at the house, or close to it." He hung up the phone with a soft click.

Suzanne stared into space until the chime of the grandfather clock striking eleven brought her back to an awareness of her surroundings. Hurriedly running a comb through her hair and rinsing her hands in cold water, she found that she was finally anxious to confront Matthew with the truth about who she was. The time had come for an official search to be set in motion for the real Alyssa. It was certainly time to start tackling the problems in Suzanne's own life.

She walked swiftly across the hallway to the largest of the guest bedrooms and knocked on the door. She was answered by silence.

Bother! She hadn't bargained on Matthew falling asleep so quickly. Despite all that seemed to have happened, it was less than an hour since she'd been summoned from the dining room to take Alyssa's phone call. Should she go back to her room and wait until morning to tell Matthew who she was? No, she had delayed giving him this news long enough. He needed to know the truth. Suzanne tapped on the door, louder this time.

She was answered by a rustle of bedclothes and Matthew's groggy voice. "Who is it?"

"It's me." She didn't want to lie by claiming to be Alyssa. "Matthew, I'm sorry, but I need to speak with you. Urgently."

The house dated back from the twenties and was solidly built, but she heard the faint squish of bedsprings and the patter of Matthew's footsteps crossing the carpeted floor. He pulled open the door and peered around it, modestly concealing the lower half of his torso. His hair was tousled and his complexion flushed.

"Alyssa, my dear, I've taken a sleeping pill. Unless you're sick and need me to call the doctor, this is a rotten time for us to talk."

"I'm not sick, but it is rather important. Very important, in fact—"

He opened the door an inch or so wider, and leaned his upper body toward her, brushing one of his hit-or-miss kisses into the air above her left eyebrow. "Honey, my brain is barely functioning. Tomorrow morning, I promise, you will be number one on my agenda."

Suzanne recoiled in shock from his kiss. Dear God, was she leaping to conclusions again? She could hardly believe the evidence of her own senses. Matthew Bradford, honorable United States senator, and supposedly her loving fiancé, smelled strongly of perfume. Poison perfume. As worn earlier this evening by Lena Vincent Humphrey.

If she had been capable of movement, Suzanne would probably have pushed the guest room door wide open to look for Lena. As it was, she did no more than blink when Matthew repeated his good-nights and firmly shut the door.

The click of the latch closing restored Suzanne's power of bodily movement. Telling herself she was overreacting, that her experience with Harry and Marianne had left her mean spirited and suspicious, she nevertheless crept along the corridor, stopping only when she reached the master bedroom suite. Lena's rooms.

She didn't knock. Of course she ought to have done so, but she was afraid Matthew might hear the sound, even though the guest room where he slept—if he was sleeping—lay at the far end of the corridor. Very quietly she turned the handle and pushed open the door.

Lena had left a bathroom light on, and it cast a dim, uneven glow of light throughout the suite. Not much light, but enough to see that the small sitting room was empty. So was the oak-paneled dressing room, originally intended for the master of the house. The bathroom was empty, too. And so was the bedroom. Lena, who had left the dinner table claiming exhaustion, had not even turned back the covers on her bed.

But perhaps she had gone downstairs to fix herself a nightcap or a mug of warm milk. Traveling long distances often caused insomnia, and Suzanne was determined not to leap to conclusions. She went downstairs and methodically searched every room, even the basement laundry, pantry and TV room. Jackie was sleeping restlessly, but she was not being watched over by Lena.

Suzanne returned to her room and sat on her bed. The conclusion was inescapable. Unless Lena was spending the night in the housekeeper's tiny apartment over the garage, there was only one room where she could be. Matthew's room. Lying in Matthew's bed, in his arms, permeating his skin with the unmistakable scent of Poison perfume.

Several long minutes passed before Suzanne could overcome her reluctance to investigate further. Eventually she kicked off her shoes and crept along the hallway toward the guest room. Spying on Matthew and Lena was repugnant to her, but many important decisions hung in the balance, and she couldn't afford to condemn them for a betrayal they hadn't committed. Drawing in a deep breath, she switched off the overhead lamps, plunging the hallway into darkness. Now no telltale light would shine into the guest room, warning of her presence.

She stopped outside the guest room, stomach churning in revulsion. Discovering Harry and Marianne making love had been a horrible accident, but if she opened this door, she would be deliberately setting out to spy on Matthew and Lena. Her hand reached out the doorknob four or five times before she finally grasped it and turned. Praying there would be no squeaks, she inched the door open.

Thank God, there were no squeaks. Better yet, there was no need for her to look into the room. She could hear the unmistakable sounds of two sexually active people, together with the low murmur of Lena's voice and Matthew's answering rumble. She closed the door.

"What are you doing?"

Suzanne whirled around, cheeks flaming with guilt. *Dear God, it was Jackie.* Her mind raced and her heart did its best to leap into her throat. All she could think of was hiding from Jackie the truth of what was happening in Matthew's bedroom. The poor child didn't need to know what her mother was doing at this precise moment.

Suzanne gave her best imitation of an embarrassed chuckle. Heaven knew, sounding embarrassed wasn't difficult. The chuckle cost her almost everything she possessed.

"Well, sweetheart, Matthew and I are both adults, and we're engaged, remember."

Jackie looked at her suspiciously. "You looked like you were listening to something."

Somewhere the fates had to be laughing at their own sick joke. The only way she could stop Jackie suspecting the truth was to convince the child that she and Matthew had been making love. She spoke sharply because she didn't know how else to handle the situation.

"Jackie, I don't think my sexual relationship with Matthew is really any of your business, do you?"

"I thought I heard Mom leave her room."

"No, no! I'm sure you didn't. You must have heard me." Smoothing the edge of panic from her voice, Suzanne added. "Come on, you've been asleep, you know, and probably dreaming. Let me tuck you up in bed. It'll be like old times."

"We used to have fun, didn't we?" Jackie sounded wistful. "In the old days, before you divorced Tony and Dad got so angry and you started having all those geeky boyfriends." With the inconsequential logic of a teenager, she added, "I liked Tony. He always knew the best places to eat pizza."

Suzanne fluffed up Jackie's pillows. "I'm gonna let you into a big, grown-up secret. It takes more than good pizza to make a marriage work. Hard to believe, but true."

Jackie smiled, then hastily changed her expression to a frown.

"Into bed, kid," Suzanne said. "You'll never be up in time for school tomorrow."

Jackie climbed under the covers, her shoulders still hunched to show that all was not yet forgiven. Suzanne ignored the signal. She sat on the edge of the bed, gently stroking Jackie's hair. There was still enough of the child left in Jackie that her eyelids started to droop.

"Wouldn't it be nice if Mom was always friendly like tonight?" she asked sleepily.

Shaking with rage, Suzanne managed to control her voice. "It would be super," she agreed.

Jackie's eyes closed. "Don't marry Matthew," she mumbled. "It won't work out for you, Lyss, I know it won't."

"We'll see. We'll talk about it later."

"'Night, Lyss."

"'Night, Jackie. I love you."

Suzanne returned to her room. She sat on the edge of her bed, letting tears of rage roll unchecked down her cheeks. After a little while she regained enough calm to ask herself why she was so angry. She herself was deceiving Matthew, so did she have any right to complain if he was sexually unfaithful?

Yes, she thought, with a renewed flare of disgust. Yes, she darn well had every right. Some of her rage, admittedly, was left over from her own experience of betrayal with Harry. The rest of it, however, was compounded of equal parts sympathy toward Jackie and the missing Alyssa. She loathed the sickening hypocrisy of Matthew and Lena. How could the pair of them indulge in their sordid affair right under the noses of Lena's teenaged daughter and the woman Matthew insisted he loved and wanted to marry? A woman, moreover, who was especially vulnerable, since, as far as Matthew and Lena knew, "Alyssa" still suffered from amnesia.

As the heat of her temper faded, Suzanne began to consider some of the wider implications of her discovery. Lena had seemed a concerned mother tonight, and a friendly stepmother to "Alyssa." Appearances, obviously, were deceptive. The hard fact was that after a two-month absence from the United States, Lena was ignoring her daughter's problems and spending her first night at home in her lover's bed.

In fact, come to think of it, was this really Lena's first night back in the States? Lena and Matthew had flown into Denver today from Washington, DC. How long had Lena spent in Washington before she came home?

Suzanne remembered the phone call from Rex Clancey that Matthew had taken on Saturday. With sudden cold certainty she knew what that phone call had been about. Rex had called to announce Lena's return to the States. To Washington, DC. And Matthew had immediately left his "fiancée's" side, barely able to restrain his impatience to return to Washington—and his mistress's arms.

The only minor mystery was why Matthew had ever come to Denver on Saturday night. Hadn't he known Lena was on her way back to the States? Perhaps the doctors withheld approval for Lena to catch the flight until the very last moment. Although, come to think of it, Lena didn't look like a woman so frail and convalescent that she needed medical permission to fly. Suzanne had the oddest feeling that if she could understand this seemingly minor mystery, a lot of far bigger puzzles would be cleared up.

She got off the bed, tugging off her clothes, and stepped thoughtfully into the shower. Tomorrow she and Adam would discuss the best and quickest way to find out where the real Alyssa Humphrey was hiding. She would make sure that Jackie attended her first session at the addiction counseling center. And she would definitely *not* tell Matthew Bradford and Lena Humphrey that she was Suzanne Swenson. She would save that little revelation for a moment when it was guaranteed to cause the pair of them maximum embarrassment.

She stepped out of the shower and wrapped herself in a soft, fluffy towel. The new Suzanne Swenson, she discovered, had a healthy appetite for revenge. Strangely enough, her desire for vengeance didn't extend to Harry and Marianne. They had each other. That, she thought with a touch of amusement, was punishment enough. She would save all her active vengeance for Matthew and Lena, a pair of hypocrites on the truly grand scale.

THANKFULLY, Suzanne wasn't constrained to watch Lena being saccharine sweet over breakfast. By the time she came downstairs at nine o'clock, only Matthew was left in the breakfast nook, sipping orange juice and reading the *Economist,* a British journal much favored by Washington's in crowd.

"Hi, where's everyone?" she asked, taking care not to get within touching range of Matthew. She wasn't sure she could tolerate being on the receiving end of one of his kisses, however platonic. She sat down at the far end of the table and poured herself coffee.

"Morning, darling." Matthew gave her a loving smile, and Suzanne choked into her coffee. "Jackie's left for school, of course, and Lena had a breakfast date with the head of United for Children. That's the charitable organization that funded her work in South Africa."

"I see. Where's Shirley?"

"Gone to call the cleaning company for extra help, I believe."

"Oh, good, I meant to suggest that she should."

"Naturally, Lena already gave the order. My dear, you don't have to trouble your pretty head with these household duties anymore. Lena's home."

"She is indeed." Suzanne spread cream cheese on a bagel and stared out of the window at the view of Pike's Peak. Short of telling him that he was a louse with the morals of a tomcat, she couldn't think of anything to say to Matthew.

It took him a good five minutes to realize that their conversation had ceased. "You're very quiet this morning," he said jovially.

"I guess I'm not a morning person."

"But you had something urgent you needed to discuss with me, darling. You said so last night. Wouldn't this be a good time, when we finally have a few precious moments of privacy?"

"Right," she said, wondering what in the world she could tell him. A demon of mischief planted the idea, and she spoke without giving herself time for second thoughts. She put down the bagel and wiped her fingers on a napkin with exaggerated care. "I want to end our engagement," she said. "I've decided we're not suited."

She was looking closely at Matthew, and for a moment she was sure that his beautiful blue eyes looked murderous. Then his features relaxed into the familiar, patented, thousand-watt smile. "Alyssa, my dear, what nonsense is this? We've been passionately in love for months—"

"I haven't seen much passion." Or love, either, she thought. If she'd really been Alyssa, hothouse roses every day would never have compensated for the fact that Matthew was rarely around.

His smile widened. Now that she was looking with unblinkered eyes, she saw the condescension in his smile. "Oh, I see. Honey, is lack of passion the problem? Alyssa, I've only been waiting for you to say the word. Darling, I've been out of my mind with wanting you for weeks now." He got up from his chair and walked around the table, clearly intending to kiss her. And not one of his up-in-the-air kisses, either.

Suzanne jumped up so quickly that her chair fell over. "No, Matthew, that's not what I want." She hurried to put the width of the breakfast table between them. "The fact is," she said, trying to sound ingenuous, "I've realized I don't want to be a senator's wife."

"This is a hell of a time to decide that," Matthew snapped. He recovered his poise and started moving toward her again. She retreated, and he lifted his arms in an expansive gesture, half plea, half resignation. "Alyssa, honey, you've gone through a hellish couple of months, and you still don't remember everything we once meant to each other—" He broke off and cocked an inquiring eye toward her. "That is, I presume you haven't remembered anything?"

"Oh, no," she said. "Not a thing. Alyssa Humphrey's life before the crash is a completely closed book to me. It might as well have happened to another person."

"Well, then," he said, as if that settled everything. "We owe it to each other to give ourselves more time."

"How much more time?" Suzanne asked with genuine interest. During the night she had begun to wonder why Matthew Bradford was so keen to marry Alyssa. After all, the widowed Lena Humphrey would have seemed an equally suitable political choice—more suitable, in fact, since she was closer to him in age—and the senator's personal preference was obviously for Lena. So why was he intent on getting himself married to Alyssa, a woman for whom he felt, at best, massive indifference?

Matthew arranged his features into an intent, considering expression. "Dearest, you know I'd like the wedding to take place tomorrow, but I'm not going to impose artificial time limits. I want to give you all the time you need to feel really happy about your decision."

She had to give him high marks for mouthing the right platitudes. "But what about you, Matthew? Your feelings count. I can't leave you dangling forever."

"My feelings haven't changed since the day you agreed to marry me, except to get deeper." He walked around the table, but halted tactfully a few inches away from her when he saw her flinch. "That's why I'm willing to wait, my darling. True love always wants what's best for the other person, and I want what's best for you."

She wondered how she had ever been taken in by him, even when she was genuinely amnesiac and functioning on only half of her brain power. She gazed deep into his beautiful, lying blue eyes. "Thank you, Matthew. You're such a . . . you're such a . . ."

"Good guy?" he suggested with a modest chuckle.

"That wasn't quite the word I was searching for, but it will do."

"Alyssa." His gaze fastened on her lips in a marvelous imitation of helpless yearning. "I do have one favor to ask."

"What's that, Matthew?"

"Meet me in Chicago on Saturday. It's the most important fund-raiser of the year for me, black tie, a thousand dollars a plate. I need you there at my side, Alyssa. Could you do that for me?"

"Matthew, I can't!" Her panicked refusal was entirely genuine.

"Really, darling, that doesn't seem too much to ask."

"It isn't. I didn't mean . . ." She gulped, swallowing over the lump of fear lodged high in her throat. "I can't get on a plane," she said tightly. "I just can't."

"Oh, my poor dear, I never thought!" Matthew was all compassion. Then his face lit up. "But that's no problem, honey, you can take the train! Amtrak goes from Denver to Chicago, I'm sure it does. Say that you'll come, Alyssa. Lena will be there, so you won't lack for a friend."

"Lena's going?" Suzanne murmured, her equilibrium reasserting itself in a flash.

"She wouldn't miss it for the world."

"Then neither must I. But maybe I could ask Jackie to come with me? The experience would be very broadening for her."

Matthew grimaced. "If that'll make the train journey less tedious for you, my dear, then by all means invite her to come. But please make sure that she doesn't turn up at the dinner looking like a scarecrow. The press latches on to these family problems so quickly."

Suzanne smiled tautly. "I'll see she looks like your PR man's dream of a teenager."

Shirley stuck her head around the door. "Mr. Stryker's arrived. I put him in the library, Alyssa. Senator, are you going to be staying another night, or can I send the cleaning crew into the guest room?"

"Sadly, duty calls, and I must get back to Washington. I'll go upstairs and pack my overnight bag right away. That'll make it easier for your cleaning ladies to do their jobs, won't it?"

"Sure will, Senator." Shirley watched him go with a fond smile. "Such a gentleman," she remarked to Suzanne. "The old-fashioned kind you don't see anymore. Thinks of other people before himself every time."

Suzanne muttered something noncommittal and refilled her coffee cup, feeling suddenly tired. Whoever claimed that you couldn't fool all of the people all of the time hadn't met Matthew Bradford, she thought. The way things were going, she wouldn't be surprised if he managed to fool the voters all the way into the presidency of the United States.

And that, she couldn't help thinking, would be a disaster of major proportions.

Chapter Eleven

Adam stood by the library window, a sheaf of papers in his hand. His face was in shadows, but he turned at the sound of her arrival, and Suzanne's heart began its familiar erratic thumping.

She closed the door carefully behind her. "You're punctual," she said, relieved that her unruly tongue hadn't gushed out with something mortifying like: *You look sexy as hell.*

"Punctuality is the courtesy of kings. And lawyers." His gaze flicked over her. "So what happened when you told the senator who you really are?"

"Um . . . actually, I haven't told him. I'm glad you didn't blow it with Shirley by asking for me by my real name. I was counting on you to be discreet."

"Perhaps I shouldn't have been so damn discreet." Adam's expression hardened. "This masquerade had gone on long enough, Suzanne. Too long, in fact."

"I have a good reason for the delay," she protested. "I discovered something last night that made me decide we need to continue the pretense for a few more days. Just a few more days, Adam."

"A bad decision," he said. "And one I can't allow to stand."

"I hate it when you sound pompous," she said crossly.

"No, my dear, you hate it when you know I'm right."

My dear. He'd never called her that before and she rather liked the sound. She scowled, annoyed by her need for Adam's approval. "You don't know what I found out last night, so you can't make judgments."

"Whatever you discovered, Matthew and Jackie need to be told the truth about who you are. The two issues aren't related, Suzanne."

"Shh! Don't call me that!" She glanced nervously over her shoulder, expecting to see Matthew come bursting through the doorway demanding an explanation of what he'd just overheard.

"We need to talk somewhere more private than this," she said to Adam. "Can I buy you a cappuccino or something?"

Twenty minutes later, seated in the bay window of a pseudo-French café, Adam stirred sugar into his cup of espresso. "All right," he said quietly. "Tell me what's happened since we talked last night."

"I discovered that Matthew Bradford is having an affair with Lena Humphrey."

She should have known better than to expect Adam to show surprise, but he did at least stop stirring his coffee. "Well," he said softly. "That explains rather a lot."

"I'm glad you think so! Personally, I think it's bizarre. If he's attracted to Lena, why propose marriage to Alyssa?"

"That's easy," Adam said. "Alyssa has ten million dollars."

"But Lena has lots of money, too."

"She can lead a luxurious life by most people's reckoning, but she's a pauper in comparison to Alyssa. What's more important from Matthew's point of view, Lena loses her entire income if she marries again."

"And you think Matthew wants money badly enough to marry a woman he doesn't love?"

"Surely you're not surprised? Politics is an expensive business. Matthew won't be the last ambitious man to propose marriage to a woman he doesn't love, and Alyssa won't be the last woman to accept."

Suzanne pushed away her uneaten croissant, her second unsuccessful attempt at breakfast. She was so damned self-righteous in her condemnation of the senator, but her motives for getting engaged to Harrison Quentin III were no better. She'd wanted stability, a dignified family life, in-laws who played polo instead of getting sloshed on cheap whiskey. What was that if not the ultimate marriage of convenience? Matthew might be a hypocrite, but then, so was she.

She couldn't change her own past actions, only resolve not to repeat them in the future. She cut to the core of what had been troubling her since she discovered the truth about Matthew's relationship with Lena. "Adam, do you still think Matthew's going to run for the presidency next year?"

"I'm sure of it. His campaign team's in place and his PR machine has been operating full blast for weeks. The fact that he hasn't made an official declaration is irrelevant. He has squads of volunteers all over the country making sure that his name is entered into the necessary primaries. Every legal necessity in every state has been complied with. I don't know when Matthew is going to make his candidacy official, but I can guarantee he has some scenario worked out that he plans to play to maximum advantage."

"I don't think he'd make a very good president."

"Because you discovered him in bed with Lena last night?" Adam sounded amused.

"No, I'm not that naive. If we cleared the Congress of every politician who'd ever been sexually unfaithful, the buildings would probably be half-empty. But you know that trite old saying about scales falling from your eyes? That's what happened to me last night, and I finally saw Matthew for the man he is. I realized he's such a convincing liar because he's totally unconcerned by the need for truth. He has no center to his soul, Adam. He's hollow in the middle where his integrity ought to be."

"He's a passionate, hardworking advocate of civil rights," Adam pointed out. "That doesn't sound like a man with no soul."

"That's odd, isn't it, but people can be full of contradictions, don't you think? Why shouldn't Matthew truly believe in equal opportunity for all citizens at the same time as he's utterly cynical in his manipulation of the democratic processes of government? People are only totally good or totally evil in comic books, not in real life. I didn't say that he was devoid of worthwhile convictions, only that he has mush where his personal integrity ought to be. Matthew believes that the end always justifies the means, and that's not a good characteristic for a president with his finger on the nuclear hot button."

Adam leaned back in his chair. "I agree, but nothing you've said explains why you didn't confront him this morning with the fact that you're Suzanne Swenson, and not his fiancée."

Her hands curled around her empty coffee cup. "I want to find Alyssa before I leave Jackie alone in that nest of vipers. Good grief, Adam, Lena doesn't care a plugged nickel what happens to that poor kid. Somebody has to be around to take care of her, and Alyssa's the only available candidate."

"You're not being honest with yourself," Adam said. "Jackie's well-being may be part of what's motivating you, but you also want to humble Matthew Bradford. You discovered him in bed with Lena and wham! You've gone from aching with sympathy for the man to being ready to knife him in a dark alley."

"He deserves to be humbled," she said fiercely. "I've had personal experience with a man like Matthew, and I despise these good-looking Lotharios who can't keep their pants zippered. He's using Alyssa and betraying her at the same time."

"*Betray* is a loaded word. The real Alyssa Humphrey may not have quite the same attitude toward sexual fidelity as you."

"Maybe not. But she's scared enough to have run away, and to have stayed hidden for over two months. I've lived her life all that time, Adam. I owe her something for the loan of her life."

"Yes, you do," he agreed. "You owe her a willingness to hand back her life now your amnesia is cured."

"I am willing, of course I am, but not today. I'd like the general public to understand precisely what sort of man Matthew Bradford is before I call it quits. Whatever Lena and Dick were up to, Matthew was involved in their schemes."

"How do you reach that conclusion?"

"Rex Clancey, for one. He deliberately lied to me about Kurt Walther."

"That implicates Rex Clancey, not Matthew Bradford."

Frustrated, Suzanne scrunched her napkin into a tight ball. "Dick probably stole three million dollars of his sister's money, Alyssa has run away, Rex Clancey is lying through his teeth, Lena is flying secretly around the world making contact with a notorious foreign thug, and you expect me to believe that Matthew is the innocent guy at the center of the storm? Come on, Adam, you're a lawyer. Haven't you ever noticed that when a person is surrounded by crooks and sleazes, he tends to be a crook or a sleaze himself?"

Adam's eyes gleamed with humor. "Yes," he admitted. "My job has taught me that."

"There you are, then." Suzanne leaned back in her seat. "You must agree I need to continue the pretense a bit longer. I want people to know how sleazy Matthew's morals are, and then maybe they won't reelect him to the Senate. I've had this unique chance to see behind the scenes in the life of an important public figure, and I have a responsibility to see that he doesn't continue to hide behind his phony facade."

"Disabuse yourself of that crazy notion," Adam said harshly. "You're a private citizen in a more dangerous situation than you're willing to accept, Suzanne. Being a stand-in for Alyssa Humphrey is not a healthy choice of lifestyle at this point in time."

His mention of danger reminded her of the attack at Jackie's school the previous afternoon. She told him about it, and he listened in grim silence, his expression becoming more withdrawn as she spoke. Nevertheless she plunged ahead until she got to the end, sharing with him her growing conviction that her attacker had never really intended to hurt her.

"Adam, when those yard workers turned up and he punched me, I swear he apologized. And he never used the switchblade he kept brandishing under my nose. I don't think he was a would-be rapist, or even a thief."

"What was he, then? An overexcited student hoping for a date?"

She drew in a deep breath, ignoring Adam's sarcasm. "I think he might be Alyssa's ex-husband. I caught just the briefest glimpse of him, and he looked familiar, from the photos in Alyssa's room, you know? I think he was trying to get information from me to help Alyssa."

"That does it," Adam said, getting to his feet and carefully tucking a ten-dollar bill beneath his saucer. The waitress probably saw nothing except a man who had finished eating and was ready to leave. Suzanne knew that his icy demeanor and swift, controlled movements masked barely contained rage. He clamped his hand around her wrist.

"Come with me," he said. "I've decided it's time you realized exactly what you've gotten yourself into."

He was driving the car west on the Sixth Avenue expressway, breaking all speed limits, before she ventured to speak. "Where are we going?"

"To my office."

"Your office is in Chicago."

"I have a branch office here in Denver."

Suzanne hadn't realized Adam's law firm was so successful, and she said as much. He smiled without a trace of mirth. "My Chicago office isn't supposed to look successful."

Wasn't *supposed* to look successful? Suzanne's stomach lurched sickly. Fear, she discovered, could come in many forms. "Adam, stop talking in riddles. You're frightening me."

"Good. At last I'm doing something right." He exited off Federal Boulevard, in the north-western suburbs of the city, and drove into the parking lot of a sprawling office building complex. He headed for a side door on the left of the main building and stopped the car on a double yellow line, totally ignoring a giant-sized No Parking sign. As far as Suzanne could tell, he hadn't even bothered to look for a vacant parking spot.

With the inevitability of sunrise, a paunch-bellied motorcycle cop materialized from the service alley at the back of the building. He stopped his bike in front of their car and walked with ponderous self-importance toward the driver's seat.

"Good morning, sir. Can't you read? The sign says Tow Away Zone, and it means what it says."

Adam already had the door on his side open, and he scarcely awarded the policeman a glance. "Out of the car," he said to Suzanne at the same time as he reached into his jacket pocket and withdrew a small leather wallet. It said something for Suzanne's state of mind that she was relieved he wasn't reaching for a gun. Adam flipped the wallet in the direction of the policeman, displaying some sort of badge.

"Excuse me, Officer. This is a major emergency." Striding around the car, he frog marched Suzanne into the building without a backward glance.

"That's a nifty badge," Suzanne said, choking back a bubble of hysteria. "I could use one in downtown Chicago traffic. What in the world does it say?"

"I'll show you when we're inside the office," Adam replied curtly. He nodded toward a middle-aged woman seated at a reception desk. "Morning, Luanne. I need a temporary pass for this lady, please. I'd prefer her name to be off the record, so I'll sign her in on my own recognizance."

"Yes, sir."

Suzanne was beyond surprise, or she would long since have been squeaking with astonishment. Clipping a plastic-coated visitor's pass to her jacket, Adam propelled her through a maze of gray-carpeted corridors into a glass-walled office marked *D*—Security Level One. The windows looked out onto a succession of small cubicles, at least half of which seemed empty, and the other occupied by people working at computers.

"Sit down," he said, pointing to a chrome and plastic office chair. "We can talk here. It's soundproofed and swept for bugs."

"Adam, when I said we needed to talk somewhere private, I didn't mean we should storm the local offices of the Pentagon."

"This isn't the Pentagon." Adam sat behind the desk and depressed the switch on an intercom. "Darlene, this is Adam Stryker. Bring me the Humphrey/Zurich file, would you please? I'm in Conference Room *D*."

"Hi, Adam. File coming up. What are you doing back in Denver? The Chief said you'd be spending this week in Chicago."

"Even the Chief can be wrong sometimes."

"Don't tell him that, for Pete's sake. He thinks he's infallible." The intercom clicked off and less than a minute later a pretty young woman came into the conference room, carrying a file. She looked with some curiosity toward Suzanne, but didn't seem surprised when Adam offered no introductions. "The timer is set for thirty minutes," she said, putting the file in the center of the desk. "Is that long enough? Too long?"

"Should be about right," Adam said. "Thanks, Darlene."

Darlene left with obvious reluctance. Another victim of Adam's fatal charm, Suzanne thought bleakly. Maybe she should just take a number and stand in line. She was a fool to have imagined that there was some special bond of feeling growing between herself and Adam. Since she clearly didn't have the faintest idea who or what the real Adam Stryker might be, how could she . . . care . . . about him?

"Have you quite finished with all the dramatics?" she asked frostily, determined not to let him see how exposed and vulnerable she felt. Why was she always so bad at judging men? First Harry, then Matthew and now Adam. She seemed to have no capacity for seeing behind the male facade to the person beneath. "If I'm supposed to be impressed and astonished, you've succeeded. I'm stunned. Where am I? And what in the world does your badge say to have such a devastating effect on a traffic cop?"

Silently he pushed the leather wallet across the desk. She opened it up, annoyed to see that her fingers were shaking as they traced the raised letters on the heavy metal badge. FBI. And on the laminated card underneath, she read, Adam Stryker, Special Agent.

She closed the flap and swallowed hard. "Very impressive."

"Not to a traffic cop," he said wryly. "I'll bet we go out there and find a ticket on the windshield. The best I can hope for is that he doesn't order the car towed."

She spread her fingers over the cold metal of the desk. "Adam, what does all this mean? Why are you pretending to be a lawyer? And why does the FBI have a file on Dick Humphrey?"

"I'm not pretending to be a lawyer," Adam said quietly. "I am a lawyer, with a lot of experience in handling trust funds. Almost every FBI agent has a graduate degree in some subject. More than half of us have law degrees. Suzanne, trust me, everything I've told you about myself is true."

She smiled sadly. "I guess it's what you haven't told me that's important."

"I'm working undercover on a complex case with major national and international implications," he said. "Until recently you were a prime suspect in my case. What the blazes did you expect me to tell you about my job?"

"Nothing, I suppose. Why did you suddenly decide you could trust me with the truth?"

"Because you're in danger, and you need to be given a realistic picture of what you're up against."

"You have complete control over my actions. You know who I really am, so my fate is in your hands. You can end this masquerade anytime you want simply by telling Matthew Bradford that I'm not Alyssa Humphrey."

"You're absolutely correct," Adam said, and only the faint twitch of a jaw muscle betrayed that his impassive demeanor was costing him considerable effort. "I could end this masquerade. But the truth is, from the point of view of my investigation, it's better if I don't reveal who you are."

She looked at him quizzically. "So the end sometimes justifies the means after all, Agent Stryker?"

"Sometimes." He ran his fingers over the polished surface of his badge. "Personal feelings don't mix very well with the demands of this job, Suzanne. That's something which hasn't mattered much to me since Su-lin died, at least not until now."

Adam was not a man who would ever confess personal involvement easily. Suzanne's instinctive reaction was to reach out and take his hand, the one that rested in a tense curve over his badge. Her second reaction, conditioned by a lifetime of protecting herself from the pain of intimacy, was to lean back, away from the desk, away from the danger of emotional exposure.

Adam smiled ruefully. "I'm not sure six inches of extra space is going to help us," he said. "I know exactly what you're feeling, Suzanne, because I feel the same way."

She didn't doubt him for a second. "It's crazy, isn't it, what we do to each other?" She looked up, letting him glimpse for one brief moment the passion she usually kept so deeply buried. "You're not in the least the sort of man I want to be attracted to. We're too much alike, too used to dominating the other people in our life. With you I'm not in control, and that terrifies me."

He drew in a sharp, hard breath. "You're not the only one who's terrified. If we ever do go to bed with each other, I hope we're both ready for the consequences."

Suzanne closed her eyes, summoning up a sudden vivid image of a love-mussed bed and Adam straddling her naked body. The image was too real, too pleasing, too *exciting* to be tolerated, and she quickly pushed it away. Adam made her believe that the myth of everlasting love and overwhelming desire might be real. And she wasn't ready for that. Determinedly she dragged her thoughts back to the business at hand.

"We need to talk about the reason you brought me here," she said. "What do you have in that file, Adam?"

"Pictures," he said, matching her briskness after an infinitesimal hesitation. He opened up the file Darlene had brought and removed a set of black-and-white photos from a plastic cover. He pushed them across the desk toward Suzanne.

"Look at these. I think you'll be interested."

She picked up a photo from the top of the pile. It showed a flight of shallow marble steps leading up to metal doors of polished steel, set into a facade of weathered gray stone. The picture was so clear she could easily make out the face of the woman walking down the marble steps toward the camera. Lena Humphrey. Almost equally clear was the name blazoned into a small, but shiny brass plaque at the side of the door: Die Internationale Bank von Zurich.

Suzanne put down the photo and reached for another. This one showed Lena Humphrey, seated at a table in a restaurant, deep in conversation with a middle-aged man. Blond-haired, thick-necked, casually dressed in a turtlenecked sweater and denim jacket, the man was a complete stranger to Suzanne.

"Who is he?" she asked Adam.

"Kurt Walther."

"Kurt Walther? My God!" Suzanne dropped the picture. "You mean this is the man all those European policemen are searching for on charges of murder? The man who called Alyssa on the phone and I answered?"

"That's the one. But he didn't call Alyssa, by the way, at least I don't believe so. He asked for *Mrs.* Humphrey, but

Lena was away from home, whereas you were there. In the circumstances, Shirley assumed he wanted to speak with *Ms.* Humphrey, in other words, with Alyssa. The mistake was easily made. His accent is quite strong, I believe.''

''Yes, it was. Is.'' Suzanne shook her head. ''Are you trying to tell me Lena is hiring an international hit man to commit a murder, or something? Because if so, Adam, I'm sorry, I won't believe you.''

''Why? Because she's a woman, and women don't do things like that?''

''No, of course not because she's a woman...'' Her indignant protest faded away under Adam's ironic gaze. She blushed. ''Well, maybe a little bit because of that. What business could Lena possibly have with a man like Kurt Walther? Who could she want to kill?''

''I've been asking myself the same question for several weeks now,'' Adam said. ''I haven't come up with any good answers. Look at the rest of the pictures.''

Six of the remaining photos showed Lena Humphrey in conversation with various women. Three more showed her with an extremely good-looking man in his late thirties. Suzanne recognized the man immediately, although she had met him only once.

''Dick Humphrey,'' she said, pointing to him. ''But who are these women? More international assassins?''

''Not quite.'' Adam grinned. ''Actually, they're officials from several very respectable charities.'' He indicated an elderly woman wearing gloves and a pillbox hat. ''This lady, for example, is the European coordinator for the International Red Cross. A formidable organizing genius despite her dozy appearance.''

''I don't understand. Is Lena using her charitable activities as a cover for something else?''

''Seems likely, don't you think? But wait, I saved the best until last.'' Adam extracted a final picture from inside the file folder and set it in front of Suzanne. She swallowed a little gasp of astonishment. For a split second she thought she had seen herself.

"It's Alyssa," she said, her heart sinking. Somehow, until this moment, she'd managed to cherish the hope that Alyssa hadn't been involved in stealing money, or silencing Jerry Hershel. Having lived Alyssa's life for so many weeks, Suzanne really wanted to like the woman. She studied the picture sadly. "I guess this settles it, then. Alyssa's there in Switzerland with Dick and Lena. She must be part of whatever weird thing they're plotting."

Surprisingly, Adam didn't agree. "I'm not sure of that," he said. "True, she's standing right next to the table where Lena and Dick are sitting, but do you see the odd way she's positioned behind that greenery?"

Suzanne looked again at the photo. "Good grief! You're right, she's all hunched up. Do you think she's trying to keep out of sight?"

"That would be my guess. In which case, we got really lucky with this shot. What we have here may be a picture of Alyssa lurking behind an oversized potted plant, trying to hear what her brother and stepmother are saying to each other."

Frustrated, Suzanne pushed the photos away. "Nothing makes any sense. Not just Alyssa's behavior, but why was someone taking these photos in the first place? Presumably FBI photographers don't hang around with a telephoto lens hoping something interesting will happen across the street."

"Those pictures were taken at my request," Adam said. "I ordered photo surveillance on Dick Humphrey as soon as I knew he was going to Zurich last July. The first batch of pictures included that shot showing him with Lena. Since Lena at the time had announced to all her friends and relatives that she was relaxing at a health sap in New Mexico, I added her to the surveillance order."

"And these photos were all taken in the summer?" Suzanne picked up the picture of Lena and Kurt Walther. "Some of the people in this picture seem to be wearing winter clothes."

"They are," Adam agreed. "That photo was taken three weeks ago, at the end of September."

"But three weeks ago, Lena was supposed to be too deathly ill to leave South Africa!" Suzanne protested. "Supposedly she could still barely hold a pen to write Jackie a letter."

"I know. Interesting, isn't it?"

"Not interesting. Sickening." Suzanne shuffled through the pictures. "Let me get this straight. You're suggesting that Lena and Dick Humphrey stole three million dollars from Alyssa's trust fund, without Alyssa's help or agreement."

"They stole the money, yes. I'm not sure how much Alyssa knew about the transaction."

"Well, either with or without Alyssa's knowledge, they approached Kurt Walther. Why? Is Lena going to pay Kurt three million dollars to kill someone?"

"I don't think so. In the first place contract murders don't carry that high a price tag, unless you want to take out a head of state. Second of all, Lena is too smart to make such a dumb move. Kurt isn't a highly trained assassin—he's a lowlife racist thug with a short temper and a reputation for dirty trading. A few weeks of research would turn up a hundred names of better hit men than Kurt."

"Then what does she want him for?"

"His reputation is as an efficient middleman when you want to broker something dirty."

"That would fit in with his call to me," Suzanne said slowly. "Looking back on it, he was really telling me that he had a shipment of something dangerous waiting for consignment, and he wanted payment before he made delivery."

"I agree. But what was Lena shipping?"

"Drugs?"

"That would be an obvious guess. But, damn it, we've had every customs agent on the lookout for weeks, and we can't trace a single gram of heroin coming within twenty miles of Kurt, or Rex, or Lena. And Lena hasn't made any effort to establish a dealer network here in the States, or even to make contact with any of the drug lords."

Suzanne felt an idea niggle at the edges of her thoughts, but she couldn't quite capture it. "Maybe the phone call was misleading. Perhaps Lena doesn't need to hire Kurt as a broker. Maybe she needs to hire him because he's a racist thug."

Adam's gaze sharpened. "What for?"

Suzanne's fuzzy idea took on shape. "To stir up trouble by exploiting inner-city tensions?" she suggested.

"How would that benefit her?"

"If Matthew is really running for president, he could increase his stature by provoking riots and then going out to calm them. He's one of the few politicians in this country who has the respect of inner-city dropouts *and* middle-class Americans."

"Interesting that you should think of that," Adam said. "That was my guess, too. But we can't turn up any evidence that Kurt is in touch with neo-Nazi groups here in the States, or with Skinheads, or even with the fringe rabble attached to respectable politicians.

"Besides, why would Lena be willing to spend three million dollars on such an uncertain enterprise? She must expect more for her money than inciting right-wing bigots to provoke a riot."

The idea Suzanne was trying to force into shape dissolved back into misty vagueness. She gave up and tried a different tack. "If the bureau has been tracking Lena, do you know if she really went to South Africa?"

"Tracking is a relative term," Adam explained. "We don't have agents in raincoats dogging her footsteps. We track her by computer. And to answer your question, it seems likely Lena was in South Africa at least some of the time she claimed to be there."

"How likely?"

"Airport records show her leaving New York on August 2, and South African Immigration shows her arriving the same day in Johannesburg. So far, despite a lot of legwork, we can't find any hospital in South Africa that claims to have treated her, or any hotel that registered her after August 5. She vanishes from sight until she turns up in London, four weeks ago.''

''Then she went to Zurich, right?''

''Yes. We managed to photograph her there with Kurt Walther. That picture was a real breakthrough for us, of course.''

Somehow it was Lena's trip to South Africa that kept gnawing at Suzanne. Johannesburg was too far from New York for Lena to have gone there without a reason, but what that reason might be, Suzanne couldn't imagine. Matthew was a staunch advocate of civil rights; he had spoken out over and over again about the South African government's failure to abolish the remnants of apartheid. Besides, foreign policy rarely decided US elections. How could Lena do anything in such a faraway country to influence the voters in Matthew's favor?

She gave up on a puzzle that seemed without solutions. ''I don't even understand why you were investigating Dick Humphrey in the first place,'' she said to Adam. ''Did you become suspicious of him for some reason and then persuade him to take you on as executor of Alyssa's trust fund?''

''The opposite. I didn't persuade him—he approached me about the job, which seemed perfectly legitimate.''

''Then why did you accept? FBI agents don't work as trustees for law-abiding citizens, and you just said you had no reason to suspect Dick of being a crook.''

''As a matter of fact, undercover agents take on all sorts of routine jobs. When Dick approached me about becoming Alyssa's trustee, I accepted because I needed genuine clients to maintain my cover. I'm supposed to be a not-too-successful lawyer, still struggling to establish a practice, six years out of law school. I need enough legitimate clients to generate some income, but I can't take on any case that looks as if it would be too demanding. The Humphrey Family Trust was supposed to be a straightforward client that wouldn't take time away from my undercover investigations.''

"But it didn't turn out that way."

"It sure didn't. Two weeks after I'd started work as trustee, I told Dick I needed to resolve some discrepancies in the accounts with Jerry Hershel. The day before we were supposed to meet, Jerry Hershel died."

"It could have been coincidence."

"Not likely. Then in July, Dick Humphrey told me he was going to Zurich, and I arranged for the photo surveillance. You know the rest."

Suzanne nodded. "The police dug a little deeper into Jerry's death and decided it was murder. You told Alyssa and explained about the money missing from her trust fund."

"Right, and it was obvious she knew a lot more than she was willing to share. Then the plane crashed, killing Dick and leaving you without any memories. All in all," Adam concluded dryly, "this had not been one of my most successful cases."

"Why don't you arrest Lena Humphrey?"

"On what grounds? Suspicion of not being sick when she claimed to be?"

"How about—stealing three million dollars of Alyssa's money?"

"Every penny of that money was transferred electronically. Either Dick or Jerry Hershel's authorization code is appended to each transaction. Every follow-up piece of paper is signed by one of the two of them. There is no way in the world to prove that money was transferred out of Alyssa's account by anyone other than Jerry or Dick. And with Jerry and Dick both dead, there's no way to prove that either of them was deliberately robbing Alyssa's trust fund."

Suzanne looked at Adam. "It's so amazingly convenient for someone that both Dick and Jerry are dead. Are you absolutely sure the plane crash that killed Dick was an accident?"

"The FAA swears it was. Deadly wind shear and a lightning bolt that struck one of the engines at just the wrong time. Acts of God, as they term it, without even contributory negligence on the part of the crew or the control tower."

"It's a relief to know Lena isn't willing to wipe out a couple of hundred random victims in pursuit of whatever she's pursuing."

Adam leaned forward, his gaze intent. "But I wouldn't like to wager a dime on how willing she'd be to murder Alyssa Humphrey, would you?"

Suzanne realized at once how neatly she'd walked into Adam's trap. "Am I any safer if I become Suzanne Swenson again? Isn't Lena going to worry about how much I know?"

"I'm afraid so. Otherwise, believe me, I'd have blown the whistle on you long before this."

A buzzer sounded. Adam depressed the intercom. "Ten more minutes, please, Darlene."

"Okay, boss, you've got it."

"What was that?" Suzanne asked, startled.

"Security precautions," Adam explained. "Darlene checked this file out to me for thirty minutes. I just requested an extension on the loan."

That small, practical detail somehow brought home to Suzanne more vividly the reality of her situation. "Do you really believe that Lena might try to harm me?" she asked.

"If Lena's plans are threatened, I believe she's perfectly capable of taking whatever action is needed to protect herself. Jerry Hershel is proof of that."

Suzanne shivered, and Adam walked around the desk pulling her to her feet and twisting her around to face him. He was careful to make sure that only their hands touched. "Suzanne, I'd insist on you going home to Chicago right now, except for the fact you just brought up. I'm afraid you might be at greater risk telling people you're Suzanne Swenson than you would be remaining as Alyssa Humphrey."

"I think I might be," Suzanne agreed. "Lena and Matthew both believe that Alyssa has amnesia, and a woman with amnesia is no risk to anyone, because she doesn't remember any secrets.''

''Right. Suzanne Swenson, on the other hand, is a much riskier proposition. She has her memories back, and she's been observing the Humphrey household from the inside out. Lena and Matthew may begin to wonder just what she's found out during the past couple of months. The hell of it is, Suzanne, I'm not sure you can feel safe right now whether you play the role of Alyssa or return to your old life as Suzanne.''

''Then the choice is easy,'' Suzanne said. ''Jackie needs me to be Alyssa, and so does Alyssa. We have to find her, Adam, before Lena and company realize that she's missing. I wouldn't give much for her chances of survival if they find her first.''

''I agree. But there are two hundred and fifty million people in this country, and Alyssa's in hiding. Where in hell do we start looking?''

Suzanne grinned. ''Actually,'' she said, ''I have a suggestion to make. I think you should set your bloodhounds to tracking down the whereabouts of her ex-husband.''

''You mentioned him before. Why in the world would you suggest him?''

''Because when I still thought I was Alyssa, I read a letter from Tony. It's obvious from the letter that they'd been seeing each other, Adam. And Tony admits he's still in love with her.''

''I suppose this letter didn't have anything helpful on it like a return address? A phone number?''

''Neither of those. But he mentions LA a couple of times. That's where they lived when they were married, and I think Tony's still there.''

''Great. I now only need to set the computers to checking twenty million people. Should be a real breeze.''

''How do you set out to trace someone?''

''It's not as easy as you'd think. That's why criminals on the run sometimes manage to hide for so long. The FBI has computers in DC that can run Delano's name through their various data bases at high speed to try to dredge up an address. We can also send out a request to all the drivers' license bureaus, credit companies and so on. But unless he's come into contact with the law, he might not be as easy to find as you'd expect.''

''I have Alyssa's address book and diary. There might be something in there that helps.''

Adam's patrician features broke into a huge grin. ''Suzanne, my sweet, have I ever told you that you're a wonderful woman?''

''No,'' she said, answering his smile. ''But feel free to tell me anytime.''

''You're a wonderful woman.'' His voice caught on a little breath of surprise. ''And I think I'm falling in love with you.''

Her laughter died away on a rush of emotion so powerful it left her breathless. She swayed toward him. ''Adam?''

He lowered his mouth to hers, claiming her lips with all the force and passion he'd held in check for too long. Need and longing twisted painfully inside her and she melted into his arms. She was burning up with the fever of wanting him, shaking with the desire to know how it would feel to make love to him.

''Not here,'' he muttered against her mouth. ''We can't, Suzanne, not here. But soon. It has to be soon.''

''Sorry to interrupt,'' said a chirpy voice. ''But your extra ten minutes is up. Adam, could I please have the Humphrey/Zurich file? And the Chief wants to see you. Pronto.''

Chapter Twelve

Bill Macguire, otherwise known as the Chief, shared none of Adam's doubts about whether Suzanne should continue her impersonation of Alyssa Humphrey. An old-time agent left over from the glory days of J. Edgar Hoover, he usually considered civilians too unreliable to be trusted with tying their own sneakers, let alone participating in an official investigation. But in Suzanne's case he was prepared to make an exception.

"Holy bananas," he said, staring at her when they were introduced. "Never seen two women as much alike as you and the Humphrey woman, except for twins. Great piece of luck for us that you were on that plane!"

Nobody had ever accused the Chief of suffering from divided loyalties, and he obviously viewed the plane crash and Suzanne's memory loss as the good Lord's personal intervention in a difficult case. In all fairness Suzanne had to admit that he didn't totally brush aside the question of her personal safety, but he considered most of Adam's fears exaggerated.

"Dunno what's the matter with you, Stryker. What are you so darn pantywaisted about? Suzanne seems like a nice, smart girl and we're not dealing with homicidal maniacs, here, or fanatic terrorists."

"Kurt Walther isn't exactly an Eagle Scout."

"He's in Zurich, under surveillance, and he isn't going to leave there without being arrested. Holy potatoes, Adam, he's wanted by the police in three countries, and they're not going to let him get away.''

"I don't see what Suzanne can do inside the Humphrey household that we can't do just as well without her.''

"She can buy us time to find the real Alyssa Humphrey,'' the Chief said. "That's what she can do.''

"At the cost of her own personal safety?'' Adam growled.

"Saints preserve us!'' Bill looked at Adam as if he'd just discovered a rancid odor under his nose. "Holy tomatoes, I hate it when you young agents can't find anything better to do with your time than fall in love!''

"I am not young and I have not fallen in love!'' Adam yelled. "And if I have, it's none of your business!''

"Then quit acting like a fool,'' the Chief yelled right back. "According to the little lady here, the senator's planning a major fund-raiser in Chicago next weekend, and he wants her to be there. Today's Monday. She'll have to leave on Thursday's train to get there by Friday. That gives her three days to snoop around the Humphrey household and see what she can find out now that she's got her eyes and ears properly open. You can meet her at the fund-raiser and reevaluate the situation. If you have any real reason to believe she's at risk, tell the senator that Suzanne's memory miraculously returned when she saw her hometown of Chicago, and that'll be the end of it.'' Ignoring Adam, the Chief turned to Suzanne. "Does that plan suit you, young lady?''

"It sounds reasonable to me,'' Suzanne agreed, amused rather than offended by Bill's determination to sound like a character from a 1950s movie. She let her hand rest for a moment on Adam's arm. "Really, Adam, this is what I want to do.''

The Chief grunted before Adam had a chance to speak. "That's settled then. As for you, Stryker, you can get your tail down to Washington and get those computers programmed to find the real Alyssa. We need her.''

Adam gave a resigned sigh. "Arguing with you two is like trying to reason with a pair of Mack trucks. But, Suzanne, listen to me—if I agree to let you keep up this impersonation, promise me there'll be no heroics, okay?''

She ought to have been furious at his arrogant assumption that he had the right to decide her actions, but nobody had ever worried about her before, and Suzanne discovered there was an insidious pleasure in being cosseted. ''Adam, don't worry,'' she said, taking his hand. ''The Cowardly Lion is brave in comparison to me.''

DESPITE HER NEW perspective on people and events in the Humphrey household, Suzanne didn't uncover much over the next few days that she considered worth reporting. She took Alyssa's address book and appointment diary to a print shop and photocopied all the entries, then express-mailed the results to Adam in Washington. Alyssa had listed some of the phone numbers by initials rather than by a complete name, but Suzanne couldn't find an entry for any combination of initials that might have been Tony Delano's.

Adam called on Wednesday to say that the bureau's computers were humming, but he had nothing concrete to report, and that he was looking forward to seeing her in Chicago on Saturday morning. After she hung up the phone, Suzanne delivered herself a stern, one-hour lecture on the stupidity of females who reached the ripe old age of twenty-nine and still found themselves quivering with desire at the mere sound of a man's voice turning husky. The lecture, unfortunately, was a total waste of time.

Jackie's pleasure at having her mother home in Denver quickly faded into sullen moodiness, and she turned often to Suzanne for support. Lena always greeted Jackie with warmth and affection. She asked all the right questions, listened patiently to the answers and made helpful, motherly comments. It took very careful watching on Suzanne's part before she realized that Lena's interest in Jackie didn't extend one minute beyond the time her daughter was in sight. Lena was all superficial concern and virtually no genuine interest. All of which, Suzanne reflected, might explain why Jackie seemed so lonely and confused.

In a small way she tried to make up for Lena's shortcomings by taking Jackie to the best hairdresser in town for a complete make-over, and was rewarded by the discovery that Jackie's hair was beautiful when cut properly and allowed to fall in natural curls. She also helped her to choose a "grown-up" evening dress for Matthew's fund-raiser. Suzanne figured she had become a truly successful older sister when she managed to persuade Jackie to take home a simple dress in soft rose silk, rather than an off-the-shoulder, split-to-the-thigh nightmare in stiff black satin.

Lena took up the threads of her old life with amazing speed. Her days were crammed from breakfast until the cocktail hour with the business of charity. Socialites from all over the state perked up, now that the doyenne of charitable functions was back in town.

Lena's attitude toward her "stepdaughter" was much the same as her attitude toward Jackie: superficial friendliness and a total lack of genuine caring. Curious to get a better idea of what made Lena tick, Suzanne accepted an invitation to a luncheon where Lena and three needle-thin, hollow-cheeked matrons were planning a gala benefit for the Colorado Opera.

The three ladies were vocal in their delight at seeing "poor dear Alyssa" back in harness again. "Your surgeon's done a marvelous job, darling," gushed a blond woman called Muffy. "You look as good as new, doesn't she, Helen?"

"Better than before." Helen stirred artificial sweetener into her iced tea with hands so thin they were clawlike. "I swear, Alyssa, dearest, I don't know how you survived all that surgery and managed to come out of the hospital looking so—healthy."

Suzanne was amused. For *healthy* no doubt she was supposed to hear *fat*. These women obviously believed skeletons had the ideal female figure. "Didn't I look healthy before?" she inquired mildly.

"Oh, Alyssa, it's so sad to hear you ask a question like that!" Muffy wailed. "Fancy not knowing how you used to look! Don't you remember anything, you poor dear?"

"Not a blessed thing," Suzanne said cheerfully. "As far as I'm concerned, Alyssa Humphrey's past might have happened to another woman. In fact, I'm almost resigned to never recovering any memories before the crash." She gave a sad little smile, composed—she hoped—of equal parts nobility and regret. "Perhaps in some ways I'm lucky to have amnesia. How many thirty-year-old women can truthfully say they have no regrets about their past?"

"Thirty-one," Lena said, crumbling a bread stick. None of the women at the table had actually eaten any of their shrimp-stuffed avocado. "You're thirty-one, Alyssa, dear. Thirty-two on the twentieth of next month."

Suzanne gave a merry little laugh. "Now that's one reminder I could have done without, Lena. Except—yes, why not? I've just had a wonderful idea! Why don't I suggest to Matthew that we should get married on my birthday? I've been waiting for my memory to come back before agreeing to set a date, but if we wait for my amnesia to be cured, it looks as if we could wait forever." Suzanne gave her stepmother an extrawide smile. "I'm beginning to be impatient to claim Matthew for myself! You will be matron of honor at the wedding, won't you, Lena? And Jackie can be bridesmaid, so it'll be a real family affair."

Lena's eyes went blank with fury, and for a moment she couldn't speak. Her poise returned quickly, however, and she accepted the invitation with a warm hug and a flurry of excited exclamations.

With a final bright smile, Lena turned the conversation to business and kept it there, impressing Suzanne with her efficiency as she assigned tasks and assembled schedules for her three cochairwomen. Clearly Lena had acquired her reputation as an organizing genius the old-fashioned way—she'd earned it.

Which meant, Suzanne reflected bleakly, that whatever mayhem Lena had been planning for the past few months was all too likely to succeed.

THE TRAIN JOURNEY from Denver to Chicago went off without a hitch. Suzanne was surprised to find herself perched on the edge of her seat as they chugged into Union Station. After so many weeks in Colorado, she felt a sense of homecoming, a reclaiming of her roots, as they emerged into the blustery winds of a typical October day in Chicago. Waiting outside for the limo, she stretched her arms wide, drew in a lungful of moist, Lake Michigan air and laughed out loud for no reason at all except that it was great to be alive, to know who she was and to be back on her home territory.

Jackie blushed and clutched at Suzanne's sleeve. "Hey, Lyss, what's with you? Cool it, for heaven's sake. People are staring at you."

"Let them stare! Isn't it great to be here? Look at that fabulous skyline. Chicago has the most interesting architecture in North America, you know."

"Lyss, stop swinging your arms around! That man over there is looking at you as if you're a performing poodle or something."

"Shall I sit up and beg?" Suzanne asked, laughing. She glanced in the direction of Jackie's gaze, and suddenly she wasn't laughing anymore. Voices, the hum of traffic, the rattle of luggage carts, all faded into silence as she saw the tall, handsome man standing on the other side of the road. Dear God, it was Harry!

Harrison Quentin III, her ex-fiancé, appeared as transfixed as she was, staring at her as if he couldn't believe his eyes. Which he probably couldn't since he wasn't the sort of man to believe in ghosts. Suzanne found that her lungs were suddenly having trouble drawing in enough air.

Not now, she thought. *Not here.* This wasn't the place for a confrontation with her past. She shouldn't be surprised to see him, though. Harry was a creature of habit, and every Friday night he caught the commuter train to Winnetka and had dinner with his parents. Her skittering brain wasted a second or two wondering why Marianne wasn't with him.

How in the world was she to avoid an encounter with Harry? She glanced at her watch without seeing the dial. "Goodness, the limo's late. We'd better catch a cab. We don't have time to be hanging around here."

Jackie gave her a curious glance. "It's only five o'clock, what's the rush? Anyway, here's our limo. See, it's got Matthew's special license plates. Oh, look. Rex Clancey's come to meet us in person. I wonder why?"

Who cared why, so long as the limo was here. Harry was crossing the street, breaking into a run.

"Get into the car," Suzanne ordered. She grabbed a handful of Jackie's coat, pulled open the door of the Lincoln and literally stuffed Jackie inside. The limo still hadn't come to a full halt when she followed suit.

"Hello, Rex, good to see you. Can you ask the driver to hurry up with the luggage?"

Rex—what else had she expected?—was talking on the car phone. He adjusted his face into one of its most self-important expressions and flapped unintelligible hand signals at her. But the chauffeur, thank Heaven, was too well trained to need instructions. Within seconds he'd left the car to see to their luggage.

Suzanne craned forward, searching the crowds. *Dear God, where was Harry? I can't see him anymore.* Sweat ran down her back and trickled between her breasts. You're overreacting, she told herself. Harry was a man ruled by the conventions. He would never burst into a closed limo to demand of a woman if she was really his ex-fiancé returned from the grave.

But why couldn't she see him? He ought to have crossed in front of the limo if he was on his way to the commuter train and dinner with Mr. and Mrs. Harrison Quentin II.

She registered—just barely—that Rex had finished his phone call. He and Jackie were talking. Now Rex was talking to her. She must concentrate. What had he asked her?

"How was the journey, Alyssa?"

"Fine, thank you. I had no idea there was still so much empty land in the States." A reasonably intelligent answer, given the gibbering incoherence of her brain.

She could hear the chauffeur talking to someone. A man. Oh, God, who was he talking to?

"...and Matthew will look forward to seeing you at lunch tomorrow."

"Great. Isn't the chauffeur taking a long time to load three suitcases into the trunk?"

Rex looked at her in surprise. "Alyssa, we haven't been here more than a couple of minutes. Besides, here he is! What's your rush, anyway?"

"That's what I want to know?" Jackie agreed. "All we have to look forward to is a heavy date with a TV set."

The limo drew away from the curb. Smothering a profound sigh of relief, Suzanne settled back against the leather cushions. "I'm feeling restless," she said. "I guess I'm just anxious to get to the hotel and have a shower."

The glass partition separating them from the driver slid open. "'Scuse me. Somethin' happened just now that you might want to know about, Rex. A man came up to me while I was loading the suitcase in the trunk."

"A man? What did he want, Wes?"

Suzanne closed her eyes. Her heart was hammering so loudly she wondered how Rex and Jackie could hear what the chauffeur was saying over the noise.

Wes cleared his throat. "He wanted to know who you was, Miss Humphrey. I didn't give your name, or nothin'. Just said you was Senator Matthew Bradford's fiancée and told him to buzz off."

"You did the right thing, Wes. Probably it was some reporter after a story."

"I don't think so, Rex. Looked like a businessman, if you know what I mean. Dark suit and tie, carrying a briefcase and one of them fold-up umbrellas. Gave me his business card, too. Here it is." The chauffeur stretched backward over his shoulder and extended a small white card. "Said if the young lady wanted to get in touch with him, he'd be waiting for her call."

Jackie took the card. "'Harrison Quentin III,'" she read. "'Vice President, Chicago City Bank.' That's cool, Lyss. It must be the man who was staring at you." She chuckled. "You made a conquest with one glance from your fiery violet eyes."

"I have gray eyes," Suzanne said mechanically.

Rex spoke firmly. "I'll take that card, Jackie. Maybe we'd better get one of Matthew's security people to run a check on this guy. Bank vice president or not, he could be a homicidal maniac for all we know."

Suzanne bit off an instinctive protest. Better not to say anything to make this incident stick in peoples' minds more than it already had. Adam was obviously about to get his wish. Her masquerade was ending, collapsing under the weight of its own lies. Adam might have at most two or three more days to locate the real Alyssa Humphrey. Suzanne hoped it would be enough.

THE PHONE RANG with the distinctive sound that marked a call on his confidential line. Matthew, snoozing comfortably on Lena's breasts, came awake instantly. He'd been waiting for this call. He untwined one of his arms, rolled over onto his back and picked up the receiver. "Yes?"

"Our packages left Zurich on time, by the route we arranged. No interceptions."

Matthew smiled into the darkness. "Good. Arrival time in South Africa?"

"The seventh, which is what we promised Schaak. Lena's transportation plans seem excellent. No hitches or glitches so far."

Matthew patted Lena's flat stomach in absentminded approval. Damn, but she was the best lover he'd ever had, and had a razor-keen mind. If only she had money, she'd make a perfect wife. Unfortunately Alyssa was the woman with the money, and the damn woman was actually talking about ending their engagement. He sighed. "Daniel Schaak's been notified?" he asked.

"Sure has. He's primed and waiting. We'll give him a few days to get the product moving through distribution channels then we'll denounce him to the South African police."

"You're sure the paper trail is in place? Rex, that was Dick's part of the deal, and I'm afraid he screwed it."

"Don't worry, Senator. Everything's in place and leading right back to Van Plat. Like I told you, even Kurt Walther and Daniel Schaak think Van Plat's funding the purchase."

Matthew grunted. "Okay. How's the background check coming on Stryker? I don't trust that guy, Rex. Dick promised me that he was hiring someone dumb, and Stryker isn't dumb. What's more, there's something going on between him and Alyssa. I can smell it. If they aren't lovers already, they will be soon."

"Your instincts are letting you down this time, Senator. Alyssa's behavior has been purer than Snow White's since the plane crash, and I've had Adam Stryker checked out by one of our best investigative guys. Stryker's just what he seems—a not-too-bright lawyer struggling to make it in Chicago's competitive legal market. Every detail on him checks out."

"Well, that eases my mind. You seem to have done a great job, Rex, as always. Lena and I will fly into Chicago tomorrow. Separate planes in case there are any reporters watching."

"Great. There is just one thing, Senator. It's rather odd, in fact."

Matthew sat up so quickly Lena nearly fell out of bed. "What is it?"

"A man approached Wes at the train station this afternoon. Wes was putting Jackie's and Alyssa's bags into the trunk of the limo when this guy came barreling up and demanded to know Alyssa's name."

"So he was a reporter or some other media person on the scrounge."

"No. He gave Wes his business card, which said he was a vice president at Chicago City Bank. The card said his name was Harrison Quentin III."

Matthew searched his memory. "Doesn't mean a thing to me. Probably a phony card."

"To be on the safe side, I had our investigators run a quick check. Seems there really is a VP by that name working at Chicago City Bank."

"Then what's the problem?"

"Jake, our investigator, has a computer program that scans past issues of the Chicago *Tribune* for mentions of a specific name. Mr. Quentin's name appeared in the *Tribune* twice, once last April when he was quoted in a financial page article on the Savings and Loan crisis, and again back in August, this time on the front page. Our investigator called in some favors down at the paper and got someone to pull up the August article. It seems Mr. Quentin was interviewed by a *Tribune* reporter when he came down to O'Hare in search of information about the crash of flight 127."

Lena was stroking Matthew's stomach. Impatiently he pushed her hand away. "Why was Mr. Quentin interviewed about the crash?"

"His fiancée was on the flight."

Matthew discovered he was sweating. He wiped his hands on the sheet. "What was her name? The fiancée."

"The article doesn't say."

"Then you'd better have Jake find out. And pretty damn fast."

"We're working on it, Senator. Don't worry. I'm taking every precaution, but I can't believe there's anything here that needs to worry us."

"That's why I'm a senator and you're my assistant, because I know when to worry. Damn it, Rex, I want that woman's name."

"You'll have it, Senator. By Monday. That's a guarantee."

Matthew hung up the phone. He rolled over and pinned Lena to the bed in a savage embrace. "Damn it, I hate unsolved mysteries, and Alyssa isn't behaving right these days."

"She isn't smart enough to cause us any problems," Lena said. Her body arched provocatively against his. "Oh, yes, do that again, Matthew."

He obliged, and Lena seemed satisfied, but Matthew had suddenly remembered a scene from the previous weekend with Alyssa in the library of her Denver home. What had she said then? Something about not feeling like the same woman since the plane crash?

Beneath him, Lena's body spasmed with pleasure. Matthew scowled, his desire dissipating. Damn Alyssa! He was beginning to think it was a great pity that she had survived the plane crash. Dead women were guaranteed to reveal no secrets.

There was a lot to be said in favor of dead women.

Chapter Thirteen

"Ladies and gentlemen, I give you our favorite senator from Illinois, the honorable Matthew Bradford, and his lovely bride-to-be, the brave survivor from flight 127, Miss Alyssa Humphrey!"

Applause and cheers echoed from the vaulted ceiling of the ballroom. Matthew strode out from the tiny side room onto the dais, radiating warmth and confidence. In the glare of the spotlight he looked younger than his forty-four years and yet gifted with power and experience that older men might envy. With a wave to the audience, he turned and extended his hand, welcoming Alyssa to his side.

The forest-green satin of her dress rustled around her ankles as Suzanne walked out into the blazing circle of lights. Dazed by the thunderous applause, she stood uncertainly at Matthew's side. Slowly he bowed and, with love written in every line of his body, carried her hand to his lips. Gazing deeply into her eyes, he brushed a tender kiss over her knuckles. "Thank you for being so beautiful," he whispered, just loud enough for the microphones to pick up the husky murmur. "And thank you for being here with me tonight, Alyssa."

Matthew's supporters—all of them rich and enthusiastic enough to have paid a thousand dollars each to eat tenderloin tips and reheated carrots julienne—went wild.

For one crazy second Suzanne responded to the adulation of the crowd. For an instant, smiling into rows of invisible faces, basking in the roars of approval, she understood how the craving for power and popularity could become a need that squeezed out more noble ambitions.

Matthew finally managed to quiet the crowd, and Suzanne's reason returned. Cringing at the effectiveness of his technique, she watched Matthew establish contact with the audience just by smiling.

"Thank you, ladies and gentlemen, for our splendid welcome. My fiancée . . ." He paused for another kiss on Suzanne's fingertips and another round of cheering. "My fiancée and I are most grateful to you for being here with us tonight. I hope after dinner to make an announcement that will be exciting enough to compensate for the time you've set aside from your busy lives to come here and support my campaign for new honesty in politics. In the meantime please enjoy your dinners and fortify yourselves for the speeches." He grinned. "You're being warned—we have a lot of speechifying ahead of us."

The audience groaned on cue. With a chuckle of irresistible charm, Matthew turned back to the mike. "At least we aren't serving you chicken, and the cellar man assures me the wine is America's finest. My friends, eat, drink and be merry, for in an hour the speeches will start."

To a ripple of laughter and more applause, Suzanne and Matthew were escorted off the platform to the flower-smothered table of honor in the center of the ballroom. Suzanne managed to spot Jackie and Adam seated at a table shunted to the left side of the room, then her attention was claimed by a dapper, middle-aged man who was standing behind her chair waiting to push it in.

"My name's Skerensky," he said, shaking hands with her. "I've been a supporter of the senator ever since he was elected to Congress. It's a pleasure to meet you, Miss Humphrey."

Suzanne acknowledged the introduction and listened politely while Mr. Skerensky told her, at great length, how rich and powerful he was and how much money he was willing to pour into Matthew's campaign. "I have the word from

Rex Clancey," he concluded ponderously. "Tonight's the night. The senator's going to make his declaration. About time, too, because Thomas Van Plat is still running away from him in the polls. How do you feel about becoming the wife of a presidential candidate, Miss Humphrey?"

So Adam had been right all along. Matthew planned to campaign for the presidency, despite all his assertions to the contrary. Suzanne managed a smile. "I'm a well-trained political fiancée, Mr. Skerensky. You can't expect me to say anything except that I support Matthew's decision."

A wine waiter interrupted them at that moment, and she turned with some relief to the stout, elderly gentleman seated on her right. She held out her hand. "I'm Alyssa Humphrey."

He took her hand in both of his. "Understand you've been having some memory problems since the crash," he said gruffly. "My name's George Dixon, and I'm a friend of your father's from way back. I started selling steel the same time he started selling cookies, and I guess we both managed to make a few honest bucks. I've known you since you were a toddler."

"It's a pleasure to meet you again, Mr. Dixon."

"George, please. We go too far back for formality." He frowned. "I was a friend of Bruno's, too, and I was real sorry when he passed away last spring. Tony was pleased you went to the funeral. It meant a lot to him."

Suzanne's attention leapt onto full alert at the mention of Tony's name. "I'm afraid I've no idea who Bruno was."

"Your former father-in-law," George Dixon said brusquely. "Even if you have amnesia, I'd have thought you'd remember Bruno. He was one of life's unforgettable characters. Louder and larger than everyone around him."

"A few details from the past come back every day," Suzanne said cautiously. "But I still have a huge number of blanks. If Bruno was an old friend, why didn't my father want me to marry Tony?"

George Dixon snorted. "Bruno was my friend, not your father's, and even smart men like your dad can sometimes behave foolishly. Your father had perfect instinct where his employees were concerned. It sometimes seemed like he could walk into a factory, sniff the air and tell if the manager was doing a decent job. But for some reason he had lousy judgment where his family relationships were concerned. Tony was a much better man than your father ever believed.''

George Dixon speared a chilled jumbo shrimp and chomped down on it as if he wished it were the late Richard Humphrey. He looked sideways at Suzanne. ''I'll tell you something else, Alyssa, because I'm so old, I've reached the stage where I'm allowed to be rude. You're a much smarter woman than your father ever knew, and you could have made Tony a damn good wife if the pair of you had been left alone.''

''You sound as if you're sorry I divorced him.''

George Dixon put down his fork. ''These pesky shrimp taste like ice cubes flavored with ketchup. Lord, I don't know why I put myself through the horrors of these political shindigs. The food gives me indigestion, and so do the politicians, so why the hell am I here?''

''You haven't answered my question, George.''

He sipped his wine. ''This isn't the right time for asking that question Alyssa. You're on the brink of marrying Senator Bradford. Besides, I'm prejudiced. I've know the Piffheim family for years.''

Suzanne looked up blankly. ''Which family?''

George gave a sad little bark of laughter. ''Land sakes, girl, don't you even remember that?''

''I told you, there's a lot I don't remember—''

He patted her hand. ''I'm sorry, Alyssa, I'm a tactless old fool. The Piffheims were your in-laws.''

''My in-laws! But Tony's name is Delano! That's what it says on our marriage certificate, I saw it. I've seen it since the crash!''

''Honey, Delano was Tony's middle name, and his mother's maiden name, too. He was planning a career as a movie star when he married you. If you wanted to be a movie star, would you go by the name of Anthony Piffheim, when you could legally call yourself Tony Delano? He never made any secret of what his birth name was, but he didn't use it very often in those days. Now he's a bit older and wiser, he uses it all the time.''

Anthony Piffheim, Suzanne thought feverishly. *AP!* She remembered seeing those initials in Alyssa's personal phone book, because she'd thought the initials stood for Associated Press, and she'd wondered why Alyssa had bothered to record the phone number of a news-gathering agency. No wonder the bureau's fancy computers hadn't been able to find Tony's current address. They'd been tracking the wrong name.

It was suddenly impossible to remain at the table, pretending to eat the tasteless shrimp, when Tony Delano—and Alyssa—might be no more than a phone call away. ''Will you excuse me for a moment?'' she murmured to George Dixon. She turned to Mr. Skerensky. ''I'm sorry to abandon you, I'll be right back.''

Matthew paused in his conversation with the two diamond-encrusted ladies seated on either side. ''Where are you going, darling?'' he asked.

''Darling, what a tactless question! I'm going to powder my nose, of course.'' Suzanne smiled prettily, twirled on her heel and just managed to prevent herself from running full tilt for the nearest door. Thank goodness Jackie was sitting with Adam, which would provide her with an excuse to approach him. She could circle around the foyer and come in the door right by his table, slipping a message to him under guise of checking up on Jackie. She walked briskly through the empty foyer, as if heading for the ladies' room.

''Suzanne! Oh my God, Suzanne, is it really you?''

Harry. She froze, even though she knew that a woman called Alyssa doesn't respond when somebody says *Suzanne.* It was too late now for evasive action. Without giving herself any more time to think, she swung around and faced her past.

"Do you want to speak to me?" She was amazed at how little emotion darkened the question, even more amazed at how little emotion she felt.

Harrison Quentin III, a man who was never at a loss for words, rubbed his chin awkwardly. "I'm sorry," he muttered at last. "From a distance you looked like someone I know. I can see the differences, now."

She smiled coolly. "Don't apologize. Everyone's supposed to have a double somewhere in the world." She turned away.

"Don't go!" The pain in his voice stopped her in her tracks. Why did he sound so miserable? Harry wasn't supposed to be suffering. He was the villain, the man who had promised to love her, then carried on an affair with her best friend. She stopped, but she didn't turn around to look at him.

"My fiancée was killed in a plane crash," Harry said, the words tumbling over each other. "Flight 127 from Chicago to Denver. The same plane you were on."

She had twisted the gold link strap of her purse so tightly around her wrist that it began to hurt. "I'm sorry," she said, staring at the welts without really seeing them. "Too many good people lost their lives that night. I know how lucky I am to have survived."

Her voice might still sound cool, but she no longer felt cool inside. Emotions, suppressed ever since the day of the crash, seethed and bubbled inside her. Her brief moment of sympathy for Harry gave way to anger, and the anger roiled like acid in her stomach. She finally brought herself to look at him again, wondering how he dared to appear so distraught about her death, when a few hours before the crash he'd been making love to Marianne—and in Suzanne's bed, to add insult to injury.

Maybe her anger showed. After one quick glance at her, he dropped his gaze and shuffled his feet. "You look very like her," he mumbled. "Like my fiancée, I mean. Amazingly like her." His face crumpled and he covered his eyes with his hand. "Oh, damn, I'm sorry. There's no reason for you to stay here and listen to this, Ms. Humphrey. You're the guest of honor. Excuse me, I guess I'd better leave."

In her wildest fantasies of revenge, she had never expected to see Harry so unsure of himself, so clearly lost in pain. The fourth-generation heir to a family of prosperous bankers, Harry had breezed through prep school and Princeton without experiencing a single moment of self-doubt. Watching him shuffle away, hunched and defeated, Suzanne discovered that of all the emotions she felt toward Harry, the strongest one at this moment was pity.

She hurried to catch up with him. "Come on," she said, taking his hand and leading him to a secluded alcove where there was a table flanked by two small padded banquettes. "I think you need someone to talk to. Tell me about your fiancée."

The old Harry would no more have talked about his feelings to a stranger than he would have stripped naked and strolled down Michigan Avenue. But this new, uncertain Harry seemed eager to talk.

"Her name was Suzanne," he said. "She was beautiful and bright and successful, one of these golden people that everything goes right for, you know the kind? They sort of float through life on a haze of success."

Suzanne wondered if her eyes would pop out of their sockets. "No," she said dryly. "I can't say that I've come into contact with many people like that. Success and hard work seem closely related to me."

"Oh, Suzanne worked hard, but she was totally together if you know what I mean. She came from a rough family, but somehow she'd overcome all those disadvantages and won a scholarship to Princeton. That's where we met, at a Princeton alumni dinner."

"Sounds like a paragon," Suzanne said, unable to restrain her sarcasm. "But success isn't everything. Was she kind? Did she reach out and grab life with both hands? Did she make people happy, just because she was around?"

"She was kind, but she was...elusive," Harry said. "Somewhere right at the heart of her there was a—need—I could never quite touch." He turned brick red, and his voice thickened. "She made me feel inferior, and I resented that. In the end, I hurt her terribly."

Suzanne discovered that she was trembling. "How did you hurt her, Harry?"

His name came out before she could stop it. He didn't seem to notice, or perhaps he assumed she'd read his name tag. "I had an affair with her roommate," he said after a long pause.

Suzanne swallowed hard. "That must have been pretty devastating for her. It doesn't sound to me as if you cared about her too much, Harry."

"It was a dumb, despicable thing to do," he said. "Worst of all, I didn't give a damn about the roommate, I just wanted to hurt Suzanne. The day she found out about the affair, she left for Denver. The plane crashed and I never saw her again." His face was white, and his hands shook. He hid them under the table. "Oh, God, I've wanted to tell her I'm sorry so many times."

The afternoon she found Harry in bed with Marianne, Suzanne would have given five years of her life to see him humbled and choking back tears as he apologized for betraying her. But reality didn't tally too well with her fantasies of revenge. She discovered that her hatred hadn't survived the plane crash and two months of living another woman's life. She didn't love Harry—she never had loved him as a woman ought to love the man she marries—but she no longer had any desire to see him suffer.

"Harry," she said softly. "It's time to put all the guilt behind you and get on with the rest of your life. I don't hold any grudges, although I think Marianne and I both deserved better treatment from you. You say you don't care about Marianne. Does she feel the same way about you? If she doesn't love you, why did she agree to sleep with you? She wasn't the sort of woman to go to bed with a man casually."

Harry's hands shook as he lowered them from his face. "How do you know Marianne's name?" he asked hoarsely. "My God, Suzanne, is it you?"

"I guess it is," she said, her voice catching.

"My God, you're alive. I didn't really believe it, even though I only came here tonight because I saw you getting into the limo at Union Station and I wanted to pretend you were her."

She smiled wryly. "You sound confused, Harry, although I can't say I blame you."

Harry shook his head in bewilderment. "But what are you doing pretending to be Alyssa Humphrey? When are you coming back to Chicago so we can be married?"

"We aren't going to be married," Suzanne said gently. "Harry, you don't really want us to spend the rest of our lives together. Think about what you said a few minutes ago."

"What did I say?"

"That you resented me, and that I was a woman whose deepest needs always seemed elusive."

"I also said I loved you."

She took his hand and held it between hers. "Can you love someone if you don't understand what makes them tick? Superficially our lives meshed well, Harry, but deep inside, at the level where it really counts, we never touched each other."

He looked at her sadly. "You've fallen in love with someone else," he said. "Really in love. Is it the senator?"

She shook her head. "Harry, I'm sorry, we can't talk about this. I have to go."

He gave a crack of laughter. "That's insane, Suzanne. We were in love—we were going to be married. Your plane crashed and I thought you were dead. Now I find you again, and you say, 'Sorry but I have to run.' This whole scene is totally unreal!"

"On the contrary, it's very real, and I shouldn't be here. I need to speak to someone urgently."

His gaze narrowed. "Tell me one thing. Does the senator know who you are?"

"No, he doesn't, and you mustn't tell him, Harry. It's important for him to think I'm Alyssa. Sometime quite soon I'll explain what's been happening to me over the past few weeks, but right now, I can't talk about it. The FBI knows my real identity, and I swear I'm only pretending to be Alyssa Humphrey in order to prevent a crime. Now I need you to swear that you won't tell *anyone* what's going on. Not for a week, at least."

"I don't know what's going on," he said. "How can I tell what I don't know?"

"Come on, Harry, that's not a promise and you know it. Please, Harry. I think you owe me one."

"Maybe I do," he agreed slowly. He stood up and held out his hand. "Okay, you have my word, Suzanne. But I want to hear the whole story soon."

"Thank you, and you will." She carried his hand to her cheek and held it there for a moment. "I realized these past few weeks that I don't have nearly enough friends, Harry. Would you be my friend when this crazy masquerade is all over?"

He looked down at her, then laughed with a touch of self-mockery. "You know, in all the time we were engaged, sex was the only thing between us that didn't work. Now you're offering to be my friend and I want you like hell." She started to speak, but he cut her off. "Don't worry, I'm an adult, I can handle being only your friend. Just don't ever invite me to a cozy dinner for two in your apartment."

She squeezed his hand, then let it go as they walked back across the foyer. "It's a deal. And take my advice, Harry, give Marianne a call. You two are made for each other."

They had reached one of the doors that led back into the ballroom. Harry politely held it open. "Why do you say that?" he asked.

Suzanne laughed. "She genuinely adores Czech movies with French subtitles."

THE MAN IN THE UNIFORM of a hotel security guard dialed a number on his cellular phone. It rang only once before being picked up. "This is Rex."

"Chuck here, Zenith Investigations. Thought you would like to know Ms. Humphrey just finished a long, intimate conversation with a good-looking man of about thirty. Lots of touching and holding hands."

Rex grunted. "What did they say to each other?"

"There was no way for me to get close without being spotted. I heard what she said when they parted company, though."

"Yes?"

"'She genuinely adores Czech movies with French subtitles.'"

"That makes no sense," Rex muttered. "Unless it's a code. Did you get the man's name?"

"I got a quick look at his name tag. It said Harrison Quentin III."

Rex was quiet for so long the security guard wondered if the connection had been broken. "Mr. Clancey, are you still there?"

"I'm here. Call into your main office right now and patch through to Jake. Tell him I want an upgrade on our background check of Mr. Quentin. Priority one. I want to know everything about him. Who his women are, how much money he owes, what brand of shampoo he uses. And photographs. I want photos of all the people in his immediate circle. Most of all, I want a name and picture of his fiancée, the one who got killed on flight 127. Fax any photos— no, correction—have Jake personally bring any photos to my room here at the Palmer House. I want some concrete information on Mr. Quentin before we fly out of here tomorrow."

"Yes, sir. It's gonna be expensive, Mr. Clancey."

"The money doesn't matter, not on this one. And put a tail on Quentin. I want to know if that guy so much as sneezes."

Rex returned the phone to the pocket of his dinner jacket. He could have been downstairs mingling with the crowd of celebrities, but he preferred to stay in the shadows, keeping an eye on the overall picture. From his vantage point he could see the entire, glittering banquet. The senator looking so handsome it made Rex's heart ache just to see him. He was going to make the finest president this country had seen in fifty years.

To the right of the senator, Lena Vincent Humphrey hosted a table of twelve dignitaries, including the governor, and the chairman of the important House Finance Committee. A good woman, Lena, a damn good woman. Rex saw Alyssa return to the senator's table and his expression hardened. Now Alyssa was not a good woman. In fact she was a damn nuisance. Except for her lovely money, of course.

Rex watched Alyssa exert her charm over Illinois's three richest industrialists. Every one of them looked smitten. Old men could be just as big fools as younger ones, he thought sourly.

Rex added a note to his mental agenda. Before the night was over, he planned to have a word with Harrison Quentin.

Chapter Fourteen

Jackie was flying high, totally without the benefit of alcohol. Her dinner partner, David, a freshman at the University of Chicago, had danced with her twice and written down her phone number. Jackie, twirling around the bedroom clutching a pillow, had decided she was in love.

"Did you notice how sensitive his eyes are?" she demanded of Suzanne. "And his smile? He's in premed, you know, so he must be incredibly smart."

"He seemed very nice," Suzanne agreed. "Hey, kid, do an old woman a favor. I've just finished an hour and a half of talking nonsense to reporters and PR men. It's two in the morning. Do you think you could scrape yourself off the ceiling long enough for us to get some sleep?"

"Two in the morning is early! You're not even undressed yet. Besides, aren't you excited about Matthew's announcement? All those people really cheered when he said he was running for president, didn't they? Maybe he isn't such a bad guy for you to marry. It would be kinda neat if you became first lady. Would that make me first sister? You know, like Millie was first dog?" Jackie giggled and gave another twirl before collapsing onto one of the beds.

"David liked my dress," she said, yawning. "Thank you for helping me choose it. I like the name David, don't you?"

"It's a great name."

"I'm glad you're my sister and you look wonderful in forest green. David said so." She closed her eyes, content to let the magnificent David have the last word.

Suzanne bent down and kissed her. "I'm glad you're my sister, too." *I wish you were my sister.*

Jackie mumbled through another yawn, and Suzanne went into the bathroom to clean her teeth. When she came out, Jackie was sound asleep, spread-eagled on her back and snoring slightly.

It took Suzanne less than three minutes to change out of her formal evening dress and into a pair of jeans, topped by a comfortable sweater. Shoving a room key into her pocket, she slipped out of the suite into the hotel corridor. Matthew, thank goodness, was spending the night at his apartment in Water Tower Place. He hadn't suggested that she should join him, and Suzanne certainly hadn't volunteered. In fact, the pretense that they enjoyed each other's company was wearing thinner every moment they spent together.

Adam's room was three floors down. Anxious to find out what the FBI computers had churned out about Tony Delano, a.k.a. Anthony Piffheim, Suzanne walked quickly toward the bank of elevators. She was less than twenty feet from the lobby when a ping signaled the arrival of an elevator. The doors glided open and Rex Clancey, still in evening dress, walked out. There was nowhere to hide in the brightly lit corridor, and Suzanne had no choice except to greet him.

"Hi, Rex," she said chirpily, although her heart was slamming hard against her rib cage. "What are you doing up and about at this hour of night?"

"I just got back from the senator's apartment. What about you, Alyssa? Going somewhere special?"

"Very special. I'm looking for a soda machine," she said, appalled at how good she'd become at thinking up quick lies. "The sign pointed in this direction for ice and soda."

"Isn't there a minibar in your suite?"

"Jackie drank all the Diet Coke," she said, forcing herself to smile as she strolled toward Rex. "What's Matthew thinking about, keeping you up so late?"

"It's just as late for you."

She laughed merrily. "Who can sleep after listening to Matthew's speech tonight? Wasn't he great?"

"He's the best orator in Congress today. Perhaps the best orator of this generation. This is my room." Rex pointed to a door. "And I believe you'll find the soda machine through there."

"Thanks. Will I see you tomorrow, Rex?"

"Yes. The senator asked me to drive you to lunch at his apartment."

"Great. See you, then. Good night."

"Good night."

Suzanne pressed some buttons on the soda machine, cranked out a few ice cubes and generally rattled around in the little vending area. She had no money with her, so she couldn't actually buy herself a soda. After a couple of minutes she emerged. Rex was still standing outside the door of his room.

Her stomach lurched, but she smiled widely as she held up her empty hands. "Hey, what do you know? There's no Diet Coke in that machine, either. Must be a run on it, I guess. I should instruct my broker to buy stock in Coca-Cola."

He didn't return her smile. "You can't fool me, Alyssa," he said, and his voice was thick with dislike. "I know you're planning something with Harrison Quentin. And I'll find out what it is quite soon."

"You're being ridiculous," she snapped. "It's too late at night for silly conversations. Good night, Rex." She turned and practically fled back along the corridor toward her room. Could she rely on Harry to keep her secrets at least for a couple of days? Dear God, she hoped so.

Suzanne glanced at her watch. Two-thirty. She'd wait fifteen minutes and then try the elevators again. Surely Rex wasn't suspicious enough to sit up all night waiting to see what she did next? She fished in her pocket for her room key.

The hand came up and clamped over her mouth before she could draw breath, let alone scream. Like a hated nightmare, she felt herself pulled backward against a man's hard body and dragged, kicking and wriggling, across the carpeted corridor.

It was the same man who'd attacked her at Jackie's school, Suzanne was sure of it. She recognized the pudgy, oversized strength of his hand and the faint smell of his cologne. He was nervous, she realized, and sweating. That was why the whiff of cologne was so strong. This time, however, her captor didn't try to make her talk. Instead, he shoved up her sweater sleeve and she felt the prick of a needle in her arm. She bit down into the flesh at the base of his thumb, hoping he would drop his hand long enough for her to draw breath and scream before the drug took effect.

She must have hurt him, but he didn't relax his hold by a millimeter. "I'm sorry," he said gruffly, "but this seems like the only way to deal with the problem. I've been waiting all night to get you alone."

Her arms and legs were turning into rubber bands. "I'll talk to you," she said. "You're Tony Delano, aren't you?"

He didn't seem to hear, or perhaps she hadn't spoken aloud. The walls and floor spun into a sickening blur of color. She closed her eyes so that she wouldn't throw up.

"Alyssa! Oh my God, leave her alone! Don't hurt her!"

Jackie's voice. Jackie screaming. And screaming again. Doors opening.

Her attacker cursed. The arms holding Suzanne relaxed and her rubber legs splayed across the floor. Carpet fibers tickled her nose, but there was no pain. She hadn't fallen, her attacker had laid her down.

Another door banged. Running footsteps. Jackie bending over her. Suzanne tried to make her mouth speak.

"Get Adam," she said. "Only Adam. Just Adam." She had no idea whether she actually managed to say the words out loud. "Don't tell Rex."

The lights in the world went black.

HER HEAD was quite definitely going to explode. The only question was how soon detonation would occur. Suzanne cracked one eyelid and quickly shut it again. A strange man hovered over her. Her attacker? No, he wasn't big enough, or young enough.

She cracked the other eyelid. Adam and Jackie swam into her field of vision. Adam, dressed in jeans and a T-shirt, looked rumpled, unshaven and altogether good enough to eat. Jackie looked as if she'd been crying. With a supreme effort, Suzanne managed to open both eyes.

"What happened?" she croaked.

"Ah, you're coming around," said the man hovering over her, sounding delighted with his ability to state the obvious. "I'm Doctor Chisholm. I think whoever attacked you gave you a shot of phenobarbital. Not too strong a dose. From what Adam tells me, you've been out for less than an hour."

"Adam?"

"I'm here." He walked over to her side, mouth clenched into the stern, uncompromising line that indicated he was worried to death and trying not to show it. Ignoring the doctor and Jackie, he sat down on the bed, placing his arms on either side of her body and staring straight into her eyes.

"This is it," he said tautly. "The end of the road for you, *Alyssa*. You can have ten minutes to tell Jackie the truth, then I'm taking you into protective custody."

Her skull was expanding and contracting. Her brain was expanding and contracting, too. Unfortunately her brain seemed to expand at the precise moment her skull contracted. The pain was acute, and talking was difficult, so she kept it to essentials.

"Have you traced Tony's address and phone number?" she asked, wincing as she struggled to sit up. "We have to see him right away, Adam."

He relaxed his hold enough to ease her upright against the pillows. Then he crooked his finger under her chin and looked down at her, his gaze fierce. "You seem to have developed a slight hearing problem, my sweet. Doctor Chisholm and I are removing you from this hotel and taking you somewhere safe. Tony's whereabouts are no longer of any interest to you."

"Yes, they are. They're of major interest, in fact. I'm sure he's the person who attacked me in the corridor just now."

Adam didn't even blink. "You now have eight minutes left for your talk with Jackie."

His eyes were full of tenderness despite his effort to appear stern, and his mouth was irresistibly close. The need to kiss him was suddenly so intense that Suzanne felt breathless. She leaned forward, closing the tiny gap between them, and kissed him full on the lips. She had intended no more than a quick, almost teasing kiss, and the immediate flare of passion shocked her. For a moment he returned her kiss with satisfying fervor, then he stiffened and pushed her away.

"Tell Jackie," he growled. "And you now have seven minutes. I'll pack your cases while you talk."

"What about Doctor Chisholm?" she asked.

"He's from the bureau, and never asks awkward questions. Doctor, would you get your car and wait for us by the fire exit downstairs? We'd appreciate a ride to Schaumburg."

"Sure thing. I'll see you all in a few minutes." The doctor left the room, and Jackie walked over to stand at the end of Suzanne's bed.

"What do you have to tell me?" she asked, her voice hostile. "And what's going on between you and Adam? You're engaged to Matthew Bradford, remember, or is your amnesia giving you problems again?"

Suzanne drew in a deep breath. "Not exactly," she said. "Look, Jackie, I have something very—strange—to tell you. Come around here and look at me. Look at me really closely."

Jackie sat down on the bed, fidgeting nervously. "Okay, so I'm looking at you. What next?"

"What do you see?"

"I see you. My sister. Lyss, knock this off, please."

"Do you see that I love you, Jackie?"

Jackie drew wavy lines on the bed cover. "Lyss, stop it. You're being weird."

"Only because I'm feeling scared." That was an understatement. Suzanne felt as if she were wading into a whirlpool without benefit of a tow chain. Teenagers were easily hurt, and Jackie was more fragile than most. She looked around for Adam, but he had gone to pack their cases, leaving her with no one to rely on but herself. She forced herself to meet Jackie's accusing gaze head on.

"My name isn't Alyssa Humphrey," she said. "It's Suzanne Swenson. I was wrongly identified after the plane crash. I'm not your sister."

Jackie's head jerked back as if she'd been struck. Her face paled and she sprang off the bed. "What do you mean? That's crazy talk. You have to be Alyssa. You look just like her. Everyone knows you're Alyssa."

"But everyone has made a mistake, honey."

"Don't call me that! How could they make such a terrible mistake? Lyss, this isn't funny!"

"I'm not Alyssa, I'm Suzanne Swenson. The two of us were very alike to begin with, then Doctor Reinhard made the similarities even more striking because he reconstructed my cheekbones to match pictures of how Alyssa looked. I wish you and I were sisters, honey, but we're not." She didn't dare risk touching Jackie, although the urge to hug her was almost overwhelming. "Of course, I'd be thrilled to adopt you as my honorary sister if you'd let me."

"Yuk, never! Oh, God, Lyss is dead and you've been tricking me all this time! I hate you. *I hate you!*"

Suzanne got up and, by dint of hanging on to the headboard, managed to remain standing. "Adam and I don't believe Alyssa is dead. We think she's alive. We're going to find Alyssa and bring her back to you very soon."

Jackie stopped her pacing. "How can Alyssa be alive? Everyone on that plane was killed except you and some children and a few men."

"We don't think Alyssa ever boarded the plane," Suzanne said. Jackie's hand was visibly trembling, and this time she couldn't resist reaching out to offer comfort.

"Don't touch me!" Jackie sprang out of reach. She tucked her hands across her chest. "Why should I believe you? You've been deceiving me on purpose." She dashed her hand across her eyes. "If Alyssa is alive, why hasn't she come home?"

"I don't want to scare you, Jackie, but we think she's hiding."

"*Hiding?* Why?"

"Because she's frightened."

"What of?" Jackie asked, sounding angry. "Alyssa's never scared of anything. She's a great sister, not mean and deceitful like you!"

Adam came back into the bedroom, snapping the locks on a suitcase. "All done," he said, deliberately breaking the moment of tension. He crossed to the bed. "Jackie, this has been a terrible shock for you, and I'm really impressed by how brave and smart you've been about handling the news."

"You've been lying to me, too." Her glance grazed sideways. "Like her."

"We both care about you, Jackie, that's not a lie. And you're right about your sister, she isn't a woman who scares easily. So if Alyssa's run away, we can guess that she must be in danger."

"Then we have to tell the police to start searching for her."

"I am the police," Adam said quietly. "And we're already searching." He reached into the pocket of his jeans and drew out his badge. He flipped the cover open, holding it out for Jackie's inspection.

She stared in silence for several seconds. "You're an FBI special agent," she said finally.

"Yes. I'm working on a very difficult case, and Suzanne's been helping me. Just for these past few days since her amnesia was cured."

"Nothing makes sense any more." Jackie curled up in a chair and covered her face with her hands. Suzanne's heart ached when she saw tears trickling through Jackie's fingers. She knelt beside the chair, wishing she had the right to grab Jackie and hug her until all the pain went away.

"Hey, sweetheart, you've been so brave, don't give up now when we've nearly found your sister."

Jackie gulped back a sob. "You made me like you," she said. "You made our house in Denver feel safe and friendly, like it was before Daddy died, and all the time you were lying to me."

"I never lied about my feelings for you," Suzanne said. She sniffed. "Does Matthew know the truth?"

"No, he doesn't."

"And he mustn't find out," Adam interjected. "That's why I'm asking you to do something very difficult, Jackie. You have to come away with us for a couple of days so that we can put you somewhere safe while Suzanne and I look for Alyssa."

"I could tell my mother. She'll keep me safe—"

"No," Adam said firmly. "We have to be sure that nobody starts looking for Alyssa except us. That's the best way to keep your sister safe, Jackie."

It said something sad about Jackie's relationship with her mother that she didn't protest too much. "But where will you take me? What about school? My mother will be so worried when she finds out I'm missing."

"We'll leave a note for her and Matthew."

"We can't just leave Mom a note, she'll be furious! She'll think I've been kidnapped."

"We'll say that Alyssa has decided to break her engagement to Matthew and she's taken you to the Bahamas for a vacation while she plans for her future. That's the sort of thing your real sister would do, isn't it?"

Jackie rubbed her eyes tiredly. "Maybe. I can't think straight. Nothing is what it seems in my life. My mother—" She broke off abruptly.

Suzanne swallowed over the lump in her throat. "Action's the best cure for the blues," she said. "Let's write those notes for Lena and Matthew and get out of here. The sooner we start searching for your sister, the sooner she'll be home."

"But why is she scared?" Jackie insisted. "I still don't understand why she's hiding."

Adam bent down so that he could put his arm around her shoulders. "You remember I told you about the money that was stolen from Alyssa?"

"From her trust fund? Yes, I remember."

"We think Alyssa may have discovered who the thieves were, and that puts her at risk until she can tell us who they are and we can lock them up."

"Oh, I see. Like the Mafia, or something."

"Sort of," Adam agreed.

Jackie was normally too bright for her own good, but tonight—mercifully—she didn't seem to spot the gaping holes in Adam's explanation. She rubbed her eyes again, looking more sad and weary than any sixteen-year-old ever should. "I wish she hadn't run off without telling me," she said.

Suzanne spoke with far more confidence than she felt. "I'm sure Alyssa had a good reason for behaving the way she did. When she's home again, she'll explain why she ran, and you can straighten everything out between the two of you."

"Right," Jackie agreed, with such total lack of hope that Suzanne vowed she would do something to make the relationship between Jackie and Alyssa come right even if she personally had to drag the pair of them to counseling sessions.

Living the life of another woman, she was discovering, came with its own emotional price tags.

SHORTLY AFTER five a.m., Doctor Chisholm delivered them to an FBI safe house in the northwestern suburb of Schaumburg. Jackie didn't say much during the short journey and, fortified by a breakfast of two Egg McMuffins and a container of orange juice, she willingly retired to one of the bedrooms to play poker with the agent assigned to guard duty. An hour later Fred came out of the bedroom and reported that Jackie was sound asleep. "Although I think she'd have beaten me if she could have kept her eyes open," he added.

Suzanne was gritty eyed with fatigue, and still woozy from the phenobarbital, but she was determined not to go to bed. She knew that if she fell asleep, Adam would leave the house and she would see no more of him until the Humphrey case was closed.

At seven in the morning Adam was still adamant in his refusal to give Suzanne a phone number or an address where she could contact Tony Delano.

"Please try to be reasonable," Suzanne said for what seemed like the hundredth time. She was so tired that even her teeth ached with fatigue. "How are you going to find Alyssa without my help? Even if Tony knows where Alyssa is, do you think he has her sitting around in the living room of his house, waiting for the FBI to come and knock on his door? Obviously if she's scared enough to hide, she's lying very low. They must have come up with a bolt hole that nobody is likely to find. If you turn up without me, Tony's going to be put on his guard, and Alyssa's simply going to burrow deeper under cover."

"The FBI doesn't consist entirely of blundering oafs, you know. I understand how threatened Tony feels."

"It's not that you're clumsy, it's that Tony is *scared*. My way is quicker and probably safer, too. I call Tony and offer to meet him alone, someplace where he feels secure. I'll meet him all wired for sound like they do on those cop shows on TV—"

"Even on TV they're smart enough to know that the wires never work at the crucial moment. I don't have time to argue with you anymore, Suzanne. The plane's leaving for LA and I have to be on it."

"Take me with you."

"No."

"You're not being rational about this, Adam."

"Damn right, I'm not," he yelled. "I love you, and I'm not willing to risk losing you!"

They stared at each other in shocked silence, neither of them able to believe what he'd just said. Suzanne sat down with a bump and Adam—cool, imperturbable, patrician Adam—flushed beetroot red from his neck right up to the roots of his hair. He shifted his weight awkwardly from one foot to the other. After a very long time, he cleared his throat. "I'm sorry," he muttered. "I had no idea I was going to say that."

"Don't apologize." The shock faded, and Suzanne felt warmth ripple along her veins, until her whole body seemed to fizz with happiness. She realized that sometime over the past few weeks the ice, wrapped around her heart ever since her brother died, had melted. She got up and crossed the room to stand behind Adam.

Like her, he was not a person to whom declarations of love came easily, and he stared out of the window as if the words had never been spoken. Another man would surely have tried to sweep her off her feet and into his arms, kissing her into submission. But Adam would never take the easy route of using her sexual desire to manipulate her emotions. And that knowledge made her love him all the more.

"Adam," she said, and her voice contained a lilt of laughter as well as joy. "Adam, do you think you could bring yourself to turn around and look at me? It's awfully difficult for a woman to tell a man's back that she's madly, totally and crazily in love with him."

He spun around, eyes blazing. "You mean . . . ?"

She nodded. "Mmm . . . I do."

"Oh, God," he murmured. "I do, too." He wrapped his arms around her waist and his mouth came down on hers, hard, demanding and full of love. Suzanne had barely time to think how wonderful his kiss felt when a knock came on the kitchen door. International conspiracies and romance, she thought wryly, didn't mix very well together.

Breathing hard, Adam moved a few inches away from her. "Yeah, Fred, what is it?"

"The Chief, Denver station, is calling you on line three. Secured phone. He seems awful het up about something." Fred tactfully refrained from mentioning that Adam and Suzanne looked pretty het up about something, too.

"Thanks, Fred." Adam selected the red phone from a bank of phones on the counter. "Stryker, here."

Staccato bursts of sound cracked out of the receiver, and Suzanne's heartbeat slowly returned to normal as she strained to hear the muffled diatribe. The Chief, she thought in silent amusement, was awful mad for a Sunday morning. Adam listened without attempting to interrupt, the line of his mouth becoming tighter as the Chief's explosive comments continued.

Finally, he spoke. "I appreciate that we'll have to tackle this from another angle. I'll need agents to keep watch on Lena Humphrey, Matthew Bradford and Rex Clancey."

He listened again. "We'll find her, sir. Don't worry. I understand the urgency." He hung up the phone.

"What happened?" Suzanne asked, amusement fading. She had never seen Adam look so weary.

"They lost him," Adam said, not attempting to mask his anger. "Those damn bunglers in Zurich lost Kurt Walther. The computer picked him up under one of his aliases when he landed in Bulgaria, and that's the last we know of him." He slammed his fist into his hand. "I can't believe we've spent all this time watching him, and we don't know a damn thing except that he's been paid three million dollars of Alyssa's money to create trouble somewhere. Damn, we really have to find Alyssa now, and fast. She's our only hope."

"You're right," Suzanne said calmly. "So let me call Tony's number and set up a meeting. Adam, I'm the best chance you have of finding Alyssa and putting a spoke in Matthew Bradford's plans. If you love me, you have to trust me, not try to keep me locked away from every hint of danger." Greatly daring, she added, "I'm not Su-lin, Adam. I'm not going to die."

"You're right," he said. "Not when I'm in charge of your safety. Besides, if Tony is the man who attacked you, he may still be here in Chicago. Maybe we could catch him at the airport. The first flight for LA leaves at seven and then there's one every ten minutes so until eight—"

"Intercepting him at the airport is the last thing you should do unless you want to guarantee spooking Alyssa. Adam, let me call Tony and set up a meeting in LA."

He let out a long sigh. "You're not thinking straight, Suzanne. When are you going to set this meeting for?"

"I could try for tonight. The sooner the better with Kurt Walther running loose in Europe."

"Do you realize what you're suggesting?" Adam asked quietly. "If you're going to meet with Tony tonight in LA, you'll have to fly two thousand miles across country. Four hours in a plane from takeoff to landing."

All the pleasant, fizzy warmth in Suzanne's veins turned instantly to ice. In her mind's eye she saw orange flames leap from the plane's engine to the tip of the wing, then whirl off into the sky. She heard the scream of metal tearing into tarmac and the more awful screams of terrified children. But from somewhere deep inside her soul she dredged up the courage to say the words. "Yes, I'm ready to fly. When do we leave?"

Adam took her into his arms and held her head cradled against his chest, his fingers combing softly through her hair. "I'll be sitting right next to you," he said. "It won't be so bad, you'll see."

With Adam beside her, it was just possible that she wouldn't die of fright before the plane landed. Possible, but not altogether likely. She tried to smile and was rather proud that she managed to stop her body convulsing in great heaving shudders of fear.

"Which phone can I use?" she asked. "I need to call Tony's number and leave a message on his answering machine. I hope he has an answering machine."

Adam reached for his briefcase and pulled out a folder. He opened the file and extracted a computerized sheet of phone numbers and addresses. "Tony owns a dozen very successful restaurants, and he has a small property development company, also quite successful. The house in Malibu is listed as his principal residence."

"I'll call his home first. It's four-thirty a.m. California time, so there's not much point in calling a restaurant. None of them are twenty-four-hour diners, are they?"

"No, they're all upscale, fancy Italian."

She dialed the number for Tony Delano's Malibu home. As she'd hoped, the call was answered on the first ring by the click of a machine. A throaty male voice spoke.

"If you're selling something, hang up. If you're a friend, leave a message and I'll get back to you."

Suzanne waited for the beep. "My name is Alyssa Humphrey and I'm a very good friend of yours, Tony. I'm not selling anything, but I've got something valuable that I'm willing to trade. Information. My information for yours. Are you interested in making a deal? On Sunday evening 7:30, I'll be at La Pergola, your restaurant located at 5525 Ocean Front Avenue. I'm coming alone, Tony, and it's your home territory. Meet me there. We need to talk. Hope you hear this message in time to make the date, if not, I'll keep calling once I'm in California."

When she hung up the phone, Adam gave her no time to think, no time to regret that she had agreed to spend four hours trapped in a metal coffin in the sky.

"Come on," he said. "We have to hurry if we're going to make our plane."

Chapter Fifteen

When their plane finally landed in Los Angeles, Suzanne couldn't get out of her seat. She had sat so tense and rigid for the entire flight that her body was literally numb. Adam patiently massaged her calves and ankles, and eventually, with his arm tight around her waist, she managed to stumble along the walkway into the airport terminal.

"I'm sorry," she said, humiliated by this glaring proof of her cowardice. She was a sensible woman, after all, and she knew that, statistically, flying was a safe way to travel. Somehow, though, up there above the clouds, statistics hadn't helped to obliterate the dread.

Adam guided her to a water fountain, and she drank greedily, gradually reasserting control over her hammering heart and shaky limbs. "I wish I could say I'll behave better on the way back," she said. "But I'm not sure I will."

Adam hugged her tight. "I certainly can't imagine why you're making such a fuss," he said. "God knows, just because you were trapped in the burning wreckage of a plane crash that killed several hundred people, I can't *imagine* why you would be nervous about flying."

She found that she could actually laugh. "Have I done permanent damage to your hand?"

He held it out in a twisted claw. "Oh, nothing that a dozen years of intensive therapy won't cure. Don't give it another thought."

When they arrived at the baggage carousels, Suzanne was enough in control to look at the clock and actually register the time. "Four o'clock. What are we going to do until seven-thirty?"

"We're going to check into a motel, and you're going to take a hot shower and try to get an hour's rest."

"What about you?"

"I need to make sure that the field office here has all the arrangements under control. It's no good wiring you up, unless we have agents around keeping you covered."

"So you'll work your tail off and I'll sleep?"

"I'm trained to keep going for long stretches of time when the need arises."

Suzanne sniffed. "Have I ever mentioned that I despise macho men, particularly macho FBI men?"

He grinned. "No, you never have. Some time soon, baby, we must find a dark room with a big bed, then I'll show you how macho I am, and you can show me how much you despise me. I'm looking forward to the demonstration."

Her insides melted into liquid fire, but all she said was, "I don't even speak to men who call me baby."

He leaned close and whispered in her ear. "When I'm through making love to you, baby, you won't have any breath left to waste on speaking."

Suzanne walked over to the conveyor belt and picked up a suitcase. It wasn't hers, so she had to put it down again and apologize to the irate owner. But at least she'd avoided the shame of being arrested for making sexual advances to a man on civic property.

She spent the thirty-minute cab ride enjoying a splendid fantasy of how she would seduce Adam as soon as they arrived at the motel. She could have saved her energy. The motel room door had scarcely closed behind them before a belligerent face, daubed with shaving cream, peered out of the bathroom.

"So you finally got here," said Bill Macguire. "Kurt Walther's left Bulgaria and the nincompoops still have no idea where he's gone. Those goons over in Eastern Europe haven't the faintest idea how to track somebody now that they aren't Communists anymore.''

"Their snooping apparatus has been dismantled," Adam said mildly. "That's what it means to be a democracy. People can leave the country without reporting to the Secret Police."

"They could still run efficient border checks with passport control, couldn't they? Now, thanks to their lousy computer systems, we have no idea where Walther has taken himself off to. Could be Timbuktu or the Antarctic for all we know." The Chief got soap in his eyes and groped blindly.

Adam handed him a towel. "If we make contact with Alyssa, she may be able to tell us where Kurt is headed."

The Chief grunted. "She'd damn well better know something, or we're up the creek without even a broken paddle." Wiping foam from his chin, he came out of the bathroom and unlocked the door connecting their room with the one next to it. Staring over Adam's shoulder, Suzanne saw that every available surface supported some electronic gadget or other.

The Chief waved his hands. "The marvels of modern machines. Tracking equipment. Listening devices. We got a wiretap authorized on Delano's phones, and we're monitoring it here. We're trying to make sure you don't face any unnecessary risks when you go to meet him, Suzanne."

"Could you show me the mike I'll be wearing?"

The Chief opened a small box. "One of our newest and best. The transmitter will send a signal to a distance of about half a mile. The mike will pick up a pin dropping at ten feet. They cost a thousand bucks each, so we'd be grateful if you didn't lose them. Tuck 'em into your bra and Delano won't spot 'em even if he frisks you."

"Should I do that now?"

"No. Right now, the best thing you can do is to rest for an hour. We can't risk having your reactions blurred by fatigue."

Suzanne left the men to play with the electronic toys and went to take a shower. She felt a lot better after standing for ten minutes under a hot, pounding spray. Wrapping herself in the skimpy motel towel, she lay down on the bed, just to stretch the kinks out of her body. Despite Bill Macguire's advice, she didn't want to sleep, because she knew she'd wake up feeling groggy.

She was more exhausted than she'd realized. It seemed that no sooner had she pulled the covers over her, her eyes drifted closed and sleep came. Then the dream started.

In her dream Adam came to lie beside her, teasing and tormenting her with tiny kisses until she reached up and clasped her hands behind his head, holding his mouth still so that she could kiss him as long and hard as she wanted. He was outside the covers, and she was underneath, but she could feel the stubble of his beard rasp against her cheek, and the warmth of his breath against her lips. Desire uncoiled like a living being in the deepest reaches of her soul.

"Oh, God, Suzanne, sweetheart, I only came to wake you up. We can't do this. Bill Macguire's in the next room with at least three technicians. They could come bursting in at any moment."

She was asleep, so she could say whatever she pleased. "Lock the door. I want you too much to wait." Her voice sounded so husky, so full of desire, that she couldn't help smiling. This dream was three dimensional and in Technicolor and—and she hoped she wasn't going to wake up for a long, long time.

Bedsprings creaked. In this dream everything was authentic, right down to the sagging motel bed and lumpy pillows. She heard the key turn in the lock, and then a draft of cool air swept over her body as Adam slowly pulled back the blankets. Because it was a dream, she didn't need to feel shy. She didn't reach for the sheet to cover her nakedness.

"God, Suzanne, you're so beautiful it hurts."

She was glad he thought so, glad that the plane crash had left her body unscarred. She smiled again, wriggling on the bed in catlike pleasure. The old clichés never went out of style, she thought. Every woman wanted to hear them, even if only in a dream. She stretched out her arms, knowing that Adam would come to her, knowing that he had been waiting for just that gesture of welcome.

She was right, which was the way of dreams. His body felt hard and muscled and strong, and he held her with all the latent power she had always sensed lying behind the pin-striped suits and the button-down shirts. Her hands reached up to touch his face, and his lips pressed urgent kisses against her fingertips.

He caressed her breasts with tender skill, and his voice murmured against her throat, husky with need. "Open your eyes, my darling. Look at me. I want to see you when we make love for the first time."

She opened her eyes.

Adam was there beside her, and of course he wasn't a dream. She had known all along that no dream could ever be this intense, this passionate, this arousing. His eyes were a familiar wintry gray, but their expression bore no trace of his usual cool irony. Instead they burned with a desire strong enough to scorch her. For a moment, faced with the reality of such consuming passion, Suzanne doubted that she was ready to explore all the places Adam might take her. She was willing to share her body, but she wasn't quite ready to make love with a man who demanded the right to touch her soul.

With his infallible instinct for reading her innermost thoughts, Adam gathered her close, banking the fire of his need for a few crucial moments. "This is just the beginning," he told her softly. "We have the rest of our lives to discover how much we mean to each other. I can wait, Suzanne."

The doubt passed, vanishing in the warm security of his embrace. "Don't wait," she whispered. "Don't hold back."

She kissed him then, opening her mouth to the thrust of his tongue, and her body to the ardor of his touch. Unconstrained, his fire leapt out to seize her.

Then there was no more warmth, no more safety. There was only heat and darkness, passion and shared desire. In the end, in the last blinding flash of ecstasy, he took and she surrendered. But in surrendering, Suzanne knew that she had captured him forever.

THE TRANSMITTER was the size and thickness of a dime. The mike was equally small, but a little thicker. Adam showed her how to tape the wires around the edge of her bra so that they were virtually undetectable. She found a light wool dress in her suitcase that didn't look out of place for a mild California night and was loose enough to provide an extra layer of concealment.

Adam handed her the car keys and the directions to Tony's restaurant. The Chief, demonstrating amazing tact, pretended fascination with the night sky while Adam kissed her long and hard through the car's open window.

"Remember, we have a tracer on the car as well as on you," he said. "If Tony suggests driving anywhere, make him take this car."

"I understand. Adam, I'm going to a public restaurant. Nothing will happen to me."

For a moment, looking at the starkness of his face, she knew he was thinking of all the deaths, crimes, assaults and rapes that had occurred in places every bit as public as Tony's restaurant. "Adam," she said quietly. "It's time for me to go."

He stepped away from the car. He had worked undercover for seven years, and he had lots of experience in separating personal emotions from professional need. Suzanne could almost see the lover retreating and the agent taking over.

"We'll follow at about a quarter of a mile," he said. "Good luck, Suzanne."

She edged carefully into the stream of fast-moving traffic. In her rearview mirror, she saw the supposed telephone repair van, crammed full of bureau technicians and equipment, move out behind her. The trouble with modern life, she reflected wryly, was that it too often seemed like a pale imitation of a TV movie. In a movie she would be worrying about masked gunmen leaping out to capture her at every stoplight. But she was much more worried about getting lost or getting her car totaled by one of the crazy Los Angeles drivers who all seemed determined to launch their suicide attempts in front of her car.

The motel had been chosen because it was less than a ten-minute drive from La Pergola. Suzanne drew up at the canopied entrance to the restaurant, and a courteous valet offered to park the car. Giving him the keys, she walked through a vestibule overflowing with plants to the reception desk.

"Good evening. Welcome to La Pergola," the hostess said.

Suzanne hoped she didn't look as nervous as she felt. "My name is Alyssa Humphrey. I have a seven-thirty appointment with Tony Delano."

The hostess didn't so much as blink. "Of course. Please follow me. Mr. Delano arrived just five minutes ago. He's in his office and he's expecting you, Miss Humphrey." The hostess knocked on a paneled door, then pushed it open without waiting for an answer. "Tony, your visitor is here."

The room was all glass and chrome, intimidatingly modern. The man seated behind the tubular steel desk rose to his feet. Suzanne swallowed hard, her nervousness turning for a split second into real fear. It was the same man who'd attacked her, she was sure of it. Tall, dark, handsome, a little bit overweight, he looked at her in unfriendly appraisal. "Thanks, Isabelle. See that we're not disturbed, will you?"

"Of course." The hostess left the room, closing the door behind her. Suzanne brought her fear back under control. She'd survived the flight from Chicago. Nothing that happened here tonight could be as terrifying as sitting for four hours on a jet plane.

Tony Delano closed the file on his desk with a snap. "Long time no see, Alyssa. What can I do for you?"

Whatever else she'd been expecting from this meeting, Suzanne hadn't anticipated this bland acceptance of her fake identity. "Mr. Delano, I don't have time to waste playing games," she said. "We both know I'm not Alyssa Humphrey, and we both know you've attacked me twice in an effort to find out who I am and what I'm doing masquerading as your ex-wife. I'm here tonight because I'm quite willing to tell you. All I want in exchange is for you to tell me the whereabouts of Alyssa."

"What's all this *Mr. Delano* nonsense? Alyssa, honey, you get weirder as the years pass and frankly, I'm not interested in your problems anymore. I grew up, honey, and it's time you did the same."

"Very convincing, Mr. Delano, except I happen to know you still love Alyssa. I've read your letters to her, you see."

He shrugged, saying nothing.

"I'm going to tell you a story," Suzanne said. "It's one I believe you already know. Alyssa Humphrey was supposed to fly with her brother from Chicago to Denver on August 5 of this year. But in fact, Alyssa never had any intention of catching that plane. She gave her brother the slip at O'Hare airport and caught a flight for Los Angeles, where you met her. I'm guessing that the pair of you were so pleased to see each other that you didn't turn on the television for a few hours, maybe not even for a couple of days. When you finally reconnected with the outside world, you discovered that flight 127 had crashed, killing Dick Humphrey. But that wasn't the most startling piece of news. Even more shocking than the loss of Alyssa's brother, were all the headlines about the miracle rescue of Alyssa herself from the burning plane. *You* knew Alyssa Humphrey was right here in Malibu with you. The media claimed she was in a Denver hospital. This situation made Alyssa more scared than she'd ever been." Suzanne broke off. "Does any part of this story sound familiar, Mr. Delano?"

"None of it," he said, his smile genial. "And I'm a busy man, Alyssa. Too busy to waste time talking to a woman who's clearly suffering from severe mental problems. Our marriage is old news, and I'm not enough of a hero to waste my time raking over dead coals. Whatever you're trying to prove, I'm not the guy to prove it with."

Suzanne's frustration boiled over. Moving too quickly for him to react, she leaned across the desk and grabbed his right hand. She twisted it, palm up, and ran her finger over the pad of his thumb. "Mr. Delano, those are my teeth marks. You know you tried to kidnap me last night, and I know it, too. Yesterday you wanted to talk to me. What's happened since then?"

"Nothing," he said, staring straight into her eyes. "I don't know what you're talking about."

He was putting his training as an actor to great use, Suzanne thought bitterly. He was so convincing she had to keep reminding herself he was lying. But why was he lying? Why was he so scared?

"Good grief," she said with a sudden flash of insight. "You think I'm helping Matthew and Lena! Mr. Delano, you couldn't be more wrong. I'm one of the good guys."

"Right," he said. "Aren't we all? Goodbye, Alyssa."

Frustrated to the point of desperation, Suzanne took a chance. "Adam," she said to the air. "Get in here as fast as you can. I need you."

Tony's face darkened with fury. "You're wired," he exclaimed, running around his desk and lunging at her. "I knew damn well you would be."

"Mr. Delano, let me explain—"

"How much are they paying you? Explain that, lady, and then ask yourself if it's worth the risk." He grabbed the front of her dress. On the point of ripping it open, he dropped his hands. "What the hell does it matter, anyway. You're the one who's been doing all the talking."

Suzanne ripped the tiny mike off its wires and held it out to Tony. "I'm not wired anymore," she said. "No one can hear us now."

"Damn right they can't. We're not speaking." He pushed a button on his intercom. "Isabelle, Ms. Humphrey's ready to leave right now. Tell Pedro to escort her off the premises."

"Tony, two men are here—" Isabelle's worried voice cut off abruptly. Tony ran to his door and pulled it open just in time for Adam and Bill Macguire to burst into the room, guns in one hand, badges in the other.

A panting and terrified Isabelle trotted behind them. "I'm sorry, Tony, they made me bring them over here. They say they're from the FBI."

"We are from the FBI," Adam said, thrusting his badge right in front of Tony's nose. He tucked his gun back into its shoulder holster and politely but firmly escorted Isabelle out of the door. "You need to get back to your hostess station," he said. "We can assure you that nothing happening here will cause any unpleasantness for the people in the dining room, and Mr. Delano is not going to be hurt."

"Tony?"

"It's okay, Isabelle. I'll take care of these gentlemen." Tony Delano went back to his desk and swung around to face Adam and the Chief. "Aren't you supposed to have a warrant before you come bursting into my restaurant?"

"We aren't planning to arrest you, Mr. Delano, despite the fact that we believe you are responsible for two violent attacks on this young woman, whose name, by the way, is Miss Suzanne Swenson, just like she told you." Bill Macguire sounded intimidatingly efficient, nothing like the genial, blustery Chief Suzanne had come to know.

Tony Delano lit up a cigarette. "Why are you here? And if this woman is Suzanne Swenson, why is a government agency condoning her impersonation of my ex-wife?"

Adam spoke for the first time. "Because we're hoping to prevent a crime, Mr. Delano, a major crime with international ramifications. But to do that, we need your help. We need to speak with the real Alyssa Humphrey."

Tony drew deeply on his cigarette. "I don't know if I can reach her," he said after a long pause.

"Try your beach cottage," Suzanne said. "The one north of here at Las Brisas."

Tony swung around, his chunky face pale. "She's not there."

"I read your letters, Tony." Suzanne's voice was gentle. "You and Alyssa have been meeting on and off ever since your dad's funeral. That cottage was where you took her in July, when you became lovers again for the first time since your marriage ended eight years ago. It's your personal retreat. It's isolated, secure, stocked with all the supplies you could need. I think we can find Alyssa there, Tony."

A humming noise caught her attention for a moment. She looked toward the corner of the room in time to see one of the glass panels glide open, revealing a door set invisibly into the wall. A woman stepped out from the narrow space behind the panel

"I guess it's time to join the crowd," she said. "As you can see, I'm not in Las Brisas anymore. I'm here."

"I'll be damned..." said the Chief. He crossed over to the door and looked at it with professional interest. "One-way viewing glass," he said. "Microphone. Everyone in this place is wired for sound. We're all recording each other."

"This used to be a nightclub," the woman said. "This was where the boss organized his gambling sessions."

Tony slammed his fist into his hand. "Damn it, you shouldn't have come out, Lyss!"

"Somebody had to break the deadlock, sweetie. I can't hide forever." The woman stared at Adam, her eyes darkening with self-mockery. "Well, well, well, the bumbling, namby-pamby trustee, who turns out to be a big boy with a gun and a badge. I should have known somebody as annoying as you had to work for the government."

Adam grinned. "Hello, Alyssa. I'm glad to see you haven't lost any of your old charm." His gaze softening, he turned to Suzanne and put his arm around her waist. "Okay?" he asked quietly.

She nodded, although she wasn't really okay. It was positively eerie to look across the room and see a living, breathing reflection of your own self. Alyssa's gaze narrowed for a moment on Adam's arm around Suzanne's waist, then she walked out into the center of the room, and posing with one hand on her hip, assessed her double from head to toe. Despite her air of bravado, her hand crept up and she touched her hair with a gesture that was almost defensive. She laughed, but her laughter was brittle with shock.

"Hell, I never knew I was so tall. And your boobs could definitely use some padding, honey."

Suzanne swallowed. Her mouth felt as if all the moisture had been sucked out of it by a giant vacuum. "I'm five eight, and I'm wearing heels at the moment."

"Hell, I'm barely five seven. Didn't anyone notice the difference?"

"I guess not. Hemlines are shorter this year, so your clothes fit me quite well."

Tony's fist crashed onto the desk. "Why are we having this damn stupid conversation?"

"Because Alyssa and I both feel dazed," Suzanne said. "Can you imagine how it feels to meet your identical twin in the flesh, when you don't have a twin?"

"You've had plenty of time to get used to the idea," Alyssa said bitterly. "You spent weeks in the hospital getting your face reconstructed to look like mine."

"But not from choice!" Suzanne cried. "My cheekbones were smashed from the force of the impact when the plane crashed. I was semiconscious and drugged with morphine for days, and when I woke up I'd lost my memory! I didn't know who I was, so I had no reason to protest when the plastic surgeon rebuilt my face to look as much like your photos as he possibly could."

Alyssa and Tony exchanged startled glances. "You lost your memory?" Alyssa asked. "You mean you didn't know who you were?"

"I knew exactly who I was," Suzanne said tautly. "Everyone told me I was Alyssa Humphrey. I believed them."

Alyssa abandoned her attempt to appear casual. "My God! How long for?"

"Nearly six weeks. The fact that I kept trying to convince myself I was you no doubt prolonged the amnesia."

"You really were on that plane?" Tony asked, with evident skepticism. "We figured they just took advantage of the crash to infiltrate you into the hospital and do the plastic surgery.''

''Now that's a real interesting remark,'' said the Chief. ''And who might *they* be, if you don't mind the inquiry?''

Alyssa laughed harshly. ''Who knows? The same people who were trying to kill me, I guess. After your car brakes fail two weeks in a row and you're stung by a dozen bees that just happen to be in the sun room at the same time as you, and your hair dryer short-circuits so that you'd have been electrocuted if you hadn't happened to be wearing sneakers—which most people aren't when they dry their hair—after that, you tend to think it would be smart to disappear first and find the guilty party some time later. And then flight 127 blew up.'' She tried hard to sound casual, but her voice shook. ''I guess I made my escape just in time, wouldn't you agree?''

''The bureau's gone over the evidence about that plane crash a dozen times,'' Suzanne said. ''Alyssa, it really was an accident. A whim of fate, or whatever you want to call it. Don't you think these other incidents might be accidents, too?''

Alyssa tossed back her hair. ''No. Someone was trying to kill me, I feel it in my bones.''

''But if people were trying to kill you, why did they stop as soon as I took over your life? Nobody ever tried to kill me.''

''Exactly,'' Tony Delano said, his voice dry. ''Makes you wonder, doesn't it?''

''Not really,'' Adam said. ''I can think of at least one excellent reason why the attacks stopped. Dick Humphrey died on flight 127. Maybe the would-be murderer is dead.''

Alyssa's cheeks flushed angrily. ''My brother was a power-hungry rat who couldn't tell the difference between ambition and corruption. But in his own warped way, he loved me. We loved each other. Dick would *never* try to kill me, any more than I would murder him. Of course, you probably don't think that's much of a guarantee, do you, Adam?''

"On the contrary," he said. "I don't believe you're capable of murder. I even have difficulty believing that you stole three million dollars from your own trust fund."

"Don't say anything!" Tony ordered Alyssa. He turned to Bill Macguire. "If you're going to question Alyssa, she has a right to the advice of a lawyer."

"We have no intention of arresting Ms. Humphrey," the Chief said. "We need her help much too badly for that. Besides, I'll be honest with you. Jerry Hershel's signature appears on every piece of paper connected with that transfer of funds. One expert says the signatures are forged. Another says they're authentic. Jerry's dead and so is Dick. The bottom line is that nobody's ever going to get prosecuted in regard to those funds. We have no case."

Alyssa looked relieved, and even Tony muttered something about good news.

"Why don't we all sit down?" Adam suggested. "Alyssa, let me put our cards on the table and perhaps you'll be persuaded to do the same. We know about your trips to Switzerland. We know about the bank account you and Dick opened in Zurich, and we know that Lena, your stepmother, was somehow involved in all this. We also know that Lena's been in contact with an unpleasant Dutchman by the name of Kurt Walther. What we don't know is why you needed three million dollars that couldn't be traced to your regular accounts?"

Alyssa looked at Tony and he shook his head. "I'm going to tell them," she said defiantly. "Unless I spend the rest of my life in hiding, we have to trust someone." She glanced at Suzanne and her smile became tinged with mockery. "If I can't trust someone with a face like that, who can I trust?"

"Nobody," Tony said sourly.

"Sweetie, I'm the one who looks like a total fool in this story, not you. Let me tell them." Alyssa leaned back in the chair, obviously not nearly as much at ease as she would have liked.

"Last May, Dick came to me with a proposition," she said abruptly. "He said Matthew Bradford planned a run for the presidency and needed a wife with top-notch credentials. Matthew thought I'd make a terrific first lady and he was willing to offer me the job. The price tag was a three-million-dollar contribution to his campaign coffers. Matthew and I already knew each other slightly. He was a good-looking guy. No ugly rumors about kinky sexual habits. I admired his politics. It seemed a cheap way to buy myself into an interesting marriage, so I agreed.''

Suzanne thought she'd kept her expression entirely neutral. Apparently she hadn't, because Alyssa smiled at her mockingly. ''Not everyone marries for love, sweetie. Are you going to marry Adam?''

''I don't know.... I'd like to...that is, nothing's arranged. We aren't necessarily getting married.''

Adam took her hand. ''Honey, we most certainly are. My mother's a stickler for the proprieties, and I can't go home for Thanksgiving unless you make an honest man of me.''

''Could we get back to business here?'' the Chief growled.

Alyssa poured herself a Scotch. ''The engagement went just fine at first. Matthew and I rarely saw each other. When we did, we had an interesting time planning my part in the campaign. Then Dick told me we needed to go to Zurich to finalize some transactions in regard to the three million dollars I was contributing to Matthew's campaign.'' Alyssa took a sip of Scotch. ''I complained about the transfer, pointing out that Matthew hadn't married me yet, so why the hell was I giving him my money? Dick's answer was that Matthew needed the money right away, and since we'd already agreed to marry between Thanksgiving and Christmas—Matthew's campaign manager had decided that those dates would be the most advantageous in terms of publicity—what was I worrying about? Matthew had no intention of backing out of the deal. He couldn't. He needed a wife.

''Well, I was starting to worry about quite a lot of things. I knew Matthew better now, and what I knew, I didn't like. The sex was lousy—'' She looked at Tony, cheeks hot. ''Sorry, sweetie, but you knew I'd been sleeping with him.''

"I knew," Tony agreed. "Just so long as you remember that from now on, you're a one-man woman. And I'm the man."

"Sweetie, I'm so chaste and domesticated, it's sickening."

Tony actually laughed. "Alyssa, my love, you're about as domesticated as a cougar, but don't worry about it. I love you for what you are, not for what people expect you to be."

"Do you think," said the Chief with ominous courtesy, "that we could refrain from turning this session into a four-way betrothal party? In case you've forgotten, we have a multimillion dollar crime unfolding somewhere, and so far we haven't the faintest idea where, what, when or why."

For a split second, when Alyssa looked at Tony, her heart was in her eyes. Then the brittle mask returned. "To cut a long story short, when Jerry Hershel came to me and said that three million dollars were missing from my trust fund, I suddenly started using my wits. Why did Matthew need money right at that moment? And your question finally occurred to me, Adam. Why all this fooling around with secret bank accounts in Switzerland? Why not just write Matthew a check? I finally started asking questions, and nobody would give me any good answers. When the 'accidents' began, I stopped asking questions and started looking and listening a bit more closely."

"What did you find out?" Adam asked.

"That Matthew was having an affair with someone. That Dick was nervous and beginning to wish he'd never gotten involved with the senator. That my stepmother wasn't at a New Mexico health farm when she was supposed to be. Instead she was in South Africa, meeting with a man called Daniel Schaak."

"Daniel Schaak!" Adam was so astonished that he jumped out of his chair. "My God, we knew she'd met with Kurt Walther in Europe, but we had no idea about Daniel Schaak."

"Holy bananas!" yelled the Chief. "Why didn't anybody find out she'd met Daniel Schaak!"

"Who is Daniel Schaak?" Suzanne asked.

"He's a farmer in the Transvaal," Alyssa explained. "He was married to an old school friend of Lena's but they're divorced now."

"Interesting," the Chief said.

Suzanne frowned impatiently. "There has to be more to it than that."

"He's a fanatic white supremacist," Adam said, pacing around the room, too het up to sit. "He leads a neo-Nazi splinter group of South Africans who refuse to accept the end of apartheid in their country."

"Yeah," Tony added. "I've been doing some research on him, and it turns out Schaak is one of these lunatics who believe whites are the chosen master race. He advocates armed battle by whites who see their communities threatened by integration."

"His followers are all organized into military regiments, with officers and foot soldiers, the whole crazy works," Adam explained. "Schaak was born in Utrecht and immigrated to South Africa about twenty years ago when he was a teenager—"

"That's it!" Suzanne exclaimed, pounding her fists together in excitement. "That's the link between Kurt Walther and Daniel Schaak. It's their racial views, and the fact that they both came from the same town. I bet if we had the time to conduct in-depth research, we'd find they both knew each other way back when. Maybe even attended the same school or something."

"Good thinking, Suzanne." Coming from the Chief, that was the equivalent of another person's five-minute paean of praise. "Obviously Kurt has been paid three million dollars to work some sort of deal with Daniel Schaak. But what?"

"I can make a darn good guess," Adam said grimly. "Schaak wants weapons. Kurt can provide them. He can provide anything for money. And Lena gave him the money. Three million dollars to buy guns for Daniel Schaak's army."

"Uzis and surplus Vulcans and maybe even a few cheap surface-to-air missiles," said the Chief. "Holy potatoes, can you imagine the havoc a man like Daniel Schaak will wreak with that sort of firepower in his hands?"

"Vividly."

"I'm making a phone call right now," the Chief said. "We'd better make damn sure that the authorities in South Africa are alerted to the possibility of a massive illegal arms shipment coming in from Europe. Damn and blast, how do you think they're planning to ship those suckers in?"

"We should ask Lena," Suzanne suggested wryly. "I'm sure she knows."

The Chief was already punching out complex number codes into Tony's phone. They all listened as he reported their conclusions to an unnamed—but obviously important—personage at the other end of the phone.

He hung up the phone after almost an hour of talking. "Well, that's one shipment of weapons that's unlikely to reach its destination," he reported with satisfaction.

"But we still haven't explained the real mystery," Adam said, his brow furrowing.

"What's that?"

"Why would Lena have spent the past six months planning to provide Daniel Schaak with weapons? How does she benefit? Come to that, why would Dick be willing to spend three million dollars of his sister's money to finance an uprising in a country I don't suppose he'd ever set foot in?"

"That's what Tony and I have been asking ourselves," Alyssa said. "Why were Dick and Lena both involved in such an expensive, complex scheme when it couldn't possibly bring them any advantage?"

"Maybe it brought indirect benefits," Suzanne suggested. "They both had a hefty stake in Matthew's political career. So if they tried to send guns to Daniel Schaak's army, it's because they expected those weapons to benefit Matthew here in the States."

"That's the problem," Tony said. "There's no way an insurgency by white supremacists in South Africa is going to benefit Matthew Bradford, or any other US politician for that matter."

"Matthew's known as a staunch supporter of civil rights," Suzanne pointed out.

"That's not enough," Adam muttered. "You don't spend three million dollars supplying guns to Daniel Schaak's army just so that Matthew can stand up in the Senate, or on the campaign trail, and say his record on civil rights is superb."

A bundle of disparate facts began to group themselves together in Suzanne's brain. "Thomas Van Plat is Matthew's only serious rival for the nomination, isn't he?"

"That's what all the pundits say," the Chief agreed. "The insiders consider the two of them pretty much neck-on-neck right now."

"Didn't Governor Van Plat cast a very controversial veto over some of his state's civil rights legislation?" she asked.

"Yes," Adam said. "Van Plat is vulnerable on the civil rights issue, but so what? Events in South Africa aren't his fault, even if he has narrow views on minority rights. Damn it, we're circling so close to the truth, but I still can't put the pieces together."

"Dirty tricks," Suzanne said suddenly. "Negative publicity. They're part and parcel of any campaign nowadays. Maybe Matthew hopes to find some way to link Van Plat's views to Daniel Schaak's outright racism."

"How could he?" the Chief asked.

"A false paper trail," Adam suggested. "A suggestion that Van Plat's money has been buying Daniel Schaak's guns."

The Chief frowned. "Could be. But it would be a hard sell. Would the public understand the linkage? Financial records don't make very good sound bites for the evening news. If Matthew's campaign manager is going to link Van

Plat to Daniel Schaak, he's going to need something concrete for the average voter to grab on to."

This time it was Tony and Alyssa who jumped to their feet. "But he's got it!" they shouted in unison. Tony gestured to Alyssa. "You tell them."

"Governor Van Plat is Daniel Schaak's uncle. The governor's sister is married to Daniel's father."

"By George," said the Chief. "I think we've got it. That's a link anyone could understand."

Suzanne interrupted the babble of voices and laughter. "One small problem," she said. "How are we going to prove Matthew had anything to do with this?"

Chapter Sixteen

The magnificent view of Lake Michigan distracted Matthew from his briefing papers, even though he knew they were important. He needed to have every damning fact about Van Plat right at his fingertips if he was going to impress the media when the Schaak weapons scandal broke. He looked up, irritated, as Rex came into the study after only the most perfunctory of knocks.

"Yes, Rex, what is it?" He used his chilliest voice. Damn it, he was going to be president of the United States; he deserved more respect.

Rex didn't even apologize for the intrusion. "Look at this," he said. With trembling hands, he held out a photograph.

Matthew looked. "It's Alyssa," he said. "Different hairdo. Rex, what the hell's the matter with you?"

"It isn't Alyssa," said Rex. "This is the engagement picture of a woman called Suzanne Swenson."

Matthew picked up the photo and carried it over to the giant window. He examined it carefully in the bright, early-morning light.

"Who is Suzanne Swenson?" he asked finally.

"She's the woman who was engaged to Harrison Quentin III," Rex said, his voice cracking with nervous tension. "According to all the reports, she died when flight 127 crashed in Denver."

"Make sure that she really is dead and buried, will you, Rex?"

"Certainly, Senator."

Matthew waited until Rex had left the room. With extreme care he set the picture on his desk, next to the pile of briefing papers. There was no reason for him to worry. They'd planned everything so carefully, nothing could go wrong now, not when success was so close. He, Matthew Bradford, was going to be the next president of the United States. He was going to provide true moral leadership and set America on course for the twenty-first century. A nobody like Suzanne Swenson—dead or alive—had no hope of stopping him.

His plans were foolproof. He was marching to meet his destiny. All the same, he wished that cold, clawing sensation in his gut would go away.

THE FIVE OF THEM had talked and planned until their words slurred and their brains turned to slush. On the evidence they had so far, no reputable attorney in the country would bring a case against Lena Humphrey, and the cases against Rex Clancey and Matthew Bradford were pure speculation. Worse yet, no one could think of any way to trap Matthew Bradford into admitting his part in the Daniel Schaak conspiracy.

"Let's face it," Adam said, gray-faced with fatigue. "The hard evidence we've uncovered so far suggests that Lena and Dick cooked this scheme up without Matthew having the faintest idea what they were up to."

"That's right," Alyssa agreed gloomily. "And Matthew's too wily a bird to be caught easily. He never once mentioned the three million dollars to me directly, let alone any plot to supply guns to Daniel Schaak. If I were questioned in court, I'd have to say that Dick was the only person who ever suggested Matthew was marrying me in exchange for money."

"Okay, that's enough depression for one night. We're not getting anywhere," the Chief decided. "It's midnight. Time to get some sleep. Alyssa and Tony, I'm taking you both into protective custody until I can decide how we should proceed. We'll go back to the motel, and an agent will have to spend the night in your room. If you prefer, Alyssa, you may take a separate room and a female agent will be sent for."

"That's all right," she said. "Whatever's easiest. Damn, I can't believe I said that. You know I'm tired if I don't even have the energy to argue when you darn near put me in handcuffs."

Suzanne was beyond tired; she was so exhausted that she fell asleep before Adam even joined her in bed. She slept deeply and woke up the next morning feeling like a new woman.

"Adam!" she exclaimed, leaning over to shake him awake. "Adam, I've had a great idea!"

He opened one eye, nuzzled her breasts and muttered, "Mmm, so have I."

Regretfully Suzanne decided that there was no time for lovemaking. Five minutes later she revised her overhasty judgment. Fifteen minutes later, she lay in a state of blissful repletion, watching Adam's tanned fingers weave love messages on her stomach. Then she remembered.

"I've thought of a way to make Matthew talk," she said, moving out of reach of Adam's distracting hands. "All we need to do is convince him I'm as amoral and conniving as he is."

Adam's attention was caught. "How would you do that?"

She told him.

When she'd finished, his face broke into one of its rare smiles. "By golly, I think it might work," he said. "Let's tell the Chief."

The Chief listened intently. "Holy bananas!" he exclaimed. "It's worth a try."

REX COVERED the mouthpiece of the phone. "It's Alyssa," he said, his voice less than steady. "Or at least, she says she's Alyssa. She wants to arrange a meeting with you."

Matthew frowned. Rex had been going to pieces ever since the detective agency reported the news that Suzanne Swenson's remains had never been positively identified in the wreckage of flight 127. Matthew didn't know what Rex was so scared of. If Suzanne Swenson had been masquerading as Alyssa for the past two months, then she was in no position to be making trouble for other people.

"Listen in on your extension," Matthew ordered, picking up his phone. He leaned back in his leather chair. "Alyssa, dearest, I was positively devastated when you ran out on me like that after the dinner on Saturday night."

"I assumed Lena would be keeping you occupied," she said sweetly.

Too sweetly. Did she know about Lena? "I'm never too busy for you, my dear."

"Good, because I need to talk to you as soon as possible. It's urgent, Matthew."

"Of course. How about this weekend—"

"Tomorrow night would suit me better, about eight o'clock."

"Honey, I'm supposed to be in Washington tomorrow night."

"Change your plans, Matthew. I'd prefer to meet you in Chicago. We've had so many happy meetings in your apartment, haven't we?"

"Certainly, my dear—"

"Tell Lena to be there. She's going to be very interested in what I have to say."

The damn woman had scarcely let him finish a single sentence. Matthew wasn't accustomed to being interrupted. "I have no intention of ordering Lena to attend—"

"Tell her I've got my memory back, Matthew. All of it. Every last tiny detail. In the circumstances, I think you and Lena would be smart to clear your calendars for me. I have some fascinating information to pass on to you about the banking system in Zurich.''

"I'm not interested in international finance.''

"How about my old friend Kurt Walther, are you interested in him, Matthew? Do you know he doesn't deal in seafood at all. Isn't that a surprise?''

The cold feeling in Matthew's gut spread, "What does Kurt deal in, Alyssa?''

"Guns,'' she said. "Illegal arms shipments for rebel armies.'' She hung up the phone.

White-faced, Rex jumped to his feet. "Oh, my God! What are we going to do about her, Senator?''

Matthew stared out at the waves stirring the surface of Lake Michigan. "We're going to meet with her tomorrow night, just like she asked. And when we know what she knows, we're going to take care of the situation.''

Rex tapped his teeth nervously with his gold pen. "How?''

"Leave the planning to me,'' Matthew said. "You call Lena. Tell her to be here by tomorrow at noon.''

SUZANNE MANAGED to walk off the plane in Chicago almost without Adam's support. Her legs wobbled and she felt light-headed from stress, but she figured that if she kept flying around the country like this, in another dozen years or so she might no longer become catatonic when the flight attendants gave the word to buckle up for landing.

She and Adam went straight to the Drake Hotel, while Bill Macguire departed to the local FBI offices to find out what progress the South African authorities had made in intercepting Kurt Walther and his shipment of weapons.

The first item on Suzanne's agenda was a long phone conversation with Alyssa, who had been reunited the previous evening with Jackie and was now staying with Tony in the bureau's Schaumburg safe house. Suzanne was thrilled when Jackie agreed to come to the phone, and they spoke for almost fifteen minutes with some return to the old easy intimacy by the end of the call.

Cheered by her talk with Jackie, Suzanne was tackling the unpacking of her suitcase when Bill Macguire phoned.

"Get over here right away," he said. "We have a problem."

They arrived at the small FBI office some twenty minutes later. "What's up?" Adam asked without preamble.

"We think Matthew Bradford knows about Suzanne."

"Knows that she exists, or that she's been impersonating Alyssa?"

"That's what we don't know. Our tip-off came from your ex-fiancé, Suzanne."

"Harry?"

"Yes. He contacted our local people here early this morning and said he needed to speak with the agent who was working on the Suzanne Swenson case. I returned his call as soon as I picked up the message. It seems an elderly couple approached Quentin's secretary over the weekend and said they were preparing a memorial tribute to the victims of flight 127. In response to this couple's request, the secretary gave them a photo of Suzanne. Then she got to thinking about it and wondered if she'd done the right thing. She told Quentin, who thought the whole situation highly suspicious. He called the number on this couple's supposed business card and discovered the number was a fake."

"Smart of Quentin to call us," Adam commented.

"It sure was. But now we have to take into account the fact that Matthew almost certainly knows of the existence of Suzanne Swenson. And that blows our plan for tonight right out of the water. We counted on him and Lena believing that Suzanne was Alyssa with her memory restored."

"We can still make it work," Suzanne said after a few moments of tense thought. "All we need is to persuade Alyssa to be on hand as backup. And we'll have to dress in identical clothes so that there's a maximum confusion as to which one of us is which."

"What exactly are you planning?" the Chief asked.

She told him.

"Matthew may be too wily for us," Adam said.

"It's the only chance we've got," the Chief pointed out. "Let's go for it. Call Alyssa and spell out her part in this. We haven't got much time."

WHETHER SHE WAS Alyssa Humphrey or Suzanne Swenson, she'd grown more confident since the last time he'd seen her. Matthew sensed it the moment she walked into his study. She wore a dramatic outfit of boots, black leather pants, a white silk blouse open halfway to her waist and a scarlet blazer. Her gold earrings were so huge they touched her shoulders, and her nails were lacquered to match the blazer. Even her smile was different: knowing, mocking, sexually aware.

This was a woman in full possession of her memories, all right. But was she really Alyssa Humphrey, or merely an upstart Suzanne Swenson on the make? To that question, unfortunately, he could give no answer. And who was this following her into the study? Adam Stryker. What the *hell* was Stryker doing here tonight?

Matthew put down his brandy and opened his arms wide. "Alyssa, honey, you're looking fabulous. How nice that we could all get together tonight."

She looked amused. "Matthew, don't you ever relax and talk like a normal human being instead of a politician?" She turned her back on him before he could reply and strolled over to the fireplace. "Hello, Lena, darling. So glad you could make it. Didn't your mother ever tell you that a woman over forty should never wear pink?"

Lena looked as if she was swallowing vinegar. "Hello, Alyssa."

Rex chimed in. "I don't know why you're insisting on this meeting, Alyssa. The senator had to cancel a dinner engagement with the speaker of the house in order to be here."

"I'm glad *the senator* has such an excellent sense of priorities," Alyssa said.

"Let's cut the frills and get to the chase," Lena said.

Alyssa smiled. "Certainly. First of all, I want you all to know that I'm here to bargain in good faith. Matthew announced at the fund-raiser on Saturday that we're going to be married the weekend after Thanksgiving. I'm willing to honor that commitment. I want to be first lady, and I'm prepared to do my part to see that Matthew gets elected. I don't object to getting my hands dirty in a good cause, and I agree that the end often justifies the means. Adam, sweetie, would you be a good boy and show these people our tape recorder?"

"Tape recorder!" Rex squeaked. "We don't want a private discussion like this on tape! Have you gone out of your mind, Alyssa?"

"On the contrary, Rex, I'm finally in full possession of my wits. Explain about the tape recorder, Adam, sweetie."

Stryker stood in front of the fireplace, hair neatly brushed, dark suit, sober tie, his face expressionless. The guy displayed about as much personality as a lump of lead, Matthew thought, and yet something about Stryker's buttoned-down blandness made him uneasy. He watched, eyes narrowed, as Stryker demonstrated the recorder's extreme sensitivity.

"When this meeting is over, Senator, you will be given the tape so that you can be quite sure no copies can ever be made. The tape is, in fact, our guarantee of good faith. Alyssa will never be able to reveal what is discussed in this meeting. To do so, as you will see, would render her liable to immediate prosecution. She intends to blackmail you."

Lena choked on a sip of brandy, and even Matthew felt a slight sense of shock. "And what's your role in all this, Mr. Stryker? Are you trying to pretend you're just the friendly neighborhood lawyer?"

Alyssa planted a passionate kiss full on Stryker's somewhat unresponsive lips. "Of course not, Matthew dear. Adam's my lover. We're totally devoted to each other, aren't we, sweetie?"

For a split second, Matthew could have sworn he saw a leap of desire hot enough to melt the ice in Stryker's cool, gray eyes. But there was no passion in his voice when he replied, only irony. "My dear Alyssa, I love you more than anyone on earth."

Alyssa seemed perfectly satisfied with this sarcastic response. "Isn't he cute?" she asked of no one in particular. She sat down on a small sofa and patted the space next to her. "Come and sit with me, Adam. Leave the recorder on the coffee table. Are we all ready to get down to business?"

"More than ready," Lena said, trying to sound bored and not quite succeeding. "I don't know why you need me here, Alyssa. We have nothing to say to each other."

"You're quite right," Alyssa agreed genially. "You're not worth bothering about. Matthew, please take note. My first condition for marrying you is that you stop your affair with Lena Humphrey. It's silly of me, I know, but I never could learn to share my toys. And a fiancé is such a *personal* toy, don't you think?"

Lena's cheeks burned with anger. "How dare you be so...so vulgar, when you've just admitted that Adam Stryker is your lover! Matthew, tell her that she's being ridiculous. I love you. We'll never give each other up!"

Lena's worst fault, Matthew reflected, was that she was too emotional. Sex with her was great, but he'd never said anything about love, or if he had, Lena should have known his words were simply a meaningless part of sexual foreplay. Didn't she realize that the important thing was getting him elected president, not their trivial little love affair? He frowned. "Before we leap to conclusions, let's hear the rest of what Alyssa has to say, shall we, Lena? Alyssa, my dear, please continue."

"My second condition for marrying you is that you find Adam a job on your campaign team, and when you're elected, he'd like a position on your White House staff." She gave Adam a sultry look. "I want to be sure he's close at hand when I have to move to Washington."

Matthew laughed, amused by the sheer effrontery of the woman. "Let me get this straight, Alyssa. Before you'll agree to marry me, you want me to give your lover a job—"

"A *good* job," she interrupted. "One where he can make lots of valuable contacts. We have to think about his financial future once you're out of office."

"Right," Matthew said. "I'm to provide your lover with a lucrative job in the White House so that he will be on hand to suit your sexual convenience."

"What I feel for Adam isn't just sexual," Alyssa said, and from the gleam in her eyes, he knew she was deliberately baiting him. "There's a real emotional component to our attraction, isn't there, Adam, sweetie."

"Definitely," he said.

Rex was so angry he could barely speak. "Matthew, get this woman out of here! And Stryker, too. She's crazy, she's insulting—"

"And I have information about Kurt Walther and Daniel Schaak that I'm quite sure you don't want anyone outside this room to hear," Alyssa said, and her voice was suddenly all hard business. "I'm offering you a deal, Matthew. You give Adam the job I want for him, and my information about Daniel Schaak's new supply of guns won't ever be revealed outside this room."

Alyssa's words fell into a pool of silence. The echoes rippled out, filling the air with a tension so thick breathing became difficult. "I don't know what you're talking about," Matthew said at last.

"And neither do I," said Lena.

Alyssa clicked her fingers. "Show them the picture, Adam, sweetie." She gave another of the smiles that Matthew was starting to dread. "We made lots of copies of the picture, so you can each have one."

Matthew took the picture that Adam handed him of Lena, nose-to-nose with Kurt Walther. He resisted the impulse to crush the photo into a ball and toss it into the garbage. Damn it all to hell, how could Lena have been so careless? How could she have put his presidential quest so seriously at risk?

"Who is this man, Lena?" he asked, his voice colder than death.

"I . . . I don't remember."

"Yes, you do," Alyssa said cheerfully. "It's your old friend Kurt Walther. And I've got signed statements from two witnesses who are prepared to swear in court that you met Kurt in Zurich at least five times over a period of several months."

Lena shredded the photo into a dozen pieces and dropped them onto the floor. Alyssa patted her kindly on the hand. "We have the negative in a very safe place, Lena. You should have realized that it's risky doing business with a man who's wanted by the police in three countries. So many people were watching him, you know?"

Lena looked sick. "Matthew?" she whispered pleadingly, crossing the room to grasp his hand. "Matthew, you can't let her get away with this."

White-hot fury consumed him. Fury at Lena's criminal incompetence, fury at her attempt to involve him in her mistakes. He shook her clutching fingers off his arm, recoiling from her in genuine distaste. "My God, Lena, I had no idea you were involved with a man who was wanted by the police!"

"What do you mean? Of course you did. I did it for you!"

"I never told you to contact Kurt Walther," he said. There was a ring of absolute truth in his voice because he was, in fact, telling the truth. His was the brilliant brain that had masterminded the plan to link Governor Van Plat to Daniel Schaak, but he'd left the specifics up to other people. In future he'd know better, Matthew thought bitterly.

Lena was beginning to see the trap opening in front of her. "Of course you told me to contact Kurt," she said feverishly. Matthew ignored her, and she ran back to Rex, grabbing his arms and shaking him bodily. "Tell them, Rex. Tell them how Matthew planned it all and we just helped him. It wasn't our idea. It was his!"

Rex shook his head nervously. "Shut up, Lena. The less said the better."

"It's too late for keeping quiet," Alyssa said. "I already know exactly what you did, Lena. I know when Kurt Walther flew to Bulgaria, and I know just how he plans to ship the arms into South Africa through Mozambique."

"How the hell did you find that out?" Matthew demanded.

"Kurt Walther likes money," Alyssa said smugly. "He doesn't care where it comes from, and he especially likes bribes."

Matthew's rage was so consuming, he had to swallow a sip of water before he could speak. "Get Lena out of here," he ordered Rex. "I'll deal with her later."

But Lena wasn't willing to go without a struggle. She elbowed Rex in the stomach, then—not caring what a disgusting spectacle she made of herself—she actually had the audacity to grab Matthew by the lapels of his blazer and shake him. "You aren't going to get rid of me that easily," she said through clenched teeth. "Damn it, Matthew, you don't even know for sure that this woman is Alyssa Humphrey. Why are you paying any attention to her threats?"

Lena never knew when to keep her mouth shut. The urge to strike her was almost overwhelming, but Matthew despised men who physically mistreated women, so he restrained himself. He pushed her away, hard enough to make her stumble, not hard enough for her to fall, and swung around to confront Alyssa. Or Suzanne Swenson, whoever the wretched woman was.

"Lena's made some careless mistakes, but she's right about a couple of things," Matthew said, striving to keep his voice modulated. His words would be more devastating if he spoke them calmly. "In the first place, I have a suspicion you're Suzanne Swenson, not Alyssa Humphrey—"

"Sweetie, I'm hurt! How could you doubt me?"

"Easily. And I'd like to point out that if you *are* Suzanne Swenson, you're not in a position to be trying blackmail at all. You'd just better hope that I don't decide to turn you in to the police for attempted extortion."

"Blackmailers always run that risk," she murmured. "Somehow, Matthew, I don't think you're likely to turn me in."

"You're wrong," he said. "Even if you are Alyssa, I can't let you get away with this pathetic scheme. You have no evidence whatsoever that I've supplied Daniel Schaak with guns. In fact, if you try to go public with this farrago of nonsense, all that will happen is that Governor Van Plat will be in trouble a couple of weeks earlier than I've planned. No red-blooded American will believe that I could ever have any links with human scum like Daniel Schaak."

Alyssa looked thoughtful rather than frightened. "We can prove Lena visited Daniel Schaak," she said. "And Lena's your mistress. That's a link."

Matthew chuckled, he couldn't help it. "Yes," he agreed, "and she's also Governor Van Plat's mistress. I thought that was rather an elegant touch when I planned it with Lena. She will admit to being Van Plat's mistress, of course, after a show of considerable reluctance."

He was pleased to see that he had finally succeeded in shocking Alyssa. Even the imperturbable Stryker sat up a tiny bit straighter. Matthew pressed home his advantage. "My dear young woman, I need a wife, and I'm already engaged to you, so for convenience's sake, I might as well marry you. But don't think for a moment I'm going to tolerate any of this nonsense about jobs for Adam Stryker on my White House staff. Good grief, I'll be making you first lady of the greatest country in the world. The least you can do in return is behave with some decorum."

"Don't you think Adam knows rather too much about your affairs to dismiss him so casually, Matthew?"

"If he tries to blackmail me, my dear, I'll break him. And believe me, that's a promise I am quite capable of keeping."

"I'm sure you are." To Matthew's disappointment, Alyssa still didn't appear crushed. Adam got to his feet, and she rose with him. "We have all we need," Adam said. "Let's call a halt to this sickening session."

Alyssa glanced at the tape. "Yes, he made some pretty damning admissions."

Matthew laughed scornfully. "You don't think I'm going to let this tape survive, do you? Neither of you can be that naive." He stepped forward and ripped the minicassette from the recorder, tossing it straight into the heart of the fire. The smell of burning plastic immediately filled the room. Matthew walked back to his desk and wiped his hands on a tissue.

From the doorway came the sound of slow hand claps. Matthew whirled around, and suddenly the cold, clawing sensation was back in his gut. A woman—a twin, a clone of the woman already standing next to Adam Stryker—leaned against the doorjamb, nonchalantly waving a minirecorder.

"Hello, Matthew, long time no see. Surely you didn't think we only made one recording when you and Lena and Rex were all being so splendidly talkative? My, my, Matthew, you were careless to let Adam con you into switching on that recorder. It fed straight back into our supersensitive machines out here."

"Who are you?" Rex demanded hoarsely.

She laughed. "Why Alyssa Humphrey, of course, who else?"

"Then who is she? The one with Adam Stryker?"

"I'm Suzanne Swenson, of course. Didn't you say that you suspected that all along, Rex?"

Suzanne by the fire, Alyssa by the door. Matthew's gaze darted from woman to woman, until red blazers and huge gold earrings congealed into a single dazzling blur. In a unique instant of total comprehension, his five senses drank in the knowledge of his own destruction.

In front of him, on the other side of the desk, he saw Adam hold up a silver badge. Matthew blinked and read. FBI. Of course. Now—too late—he understood why he'd always felt menaced by Stryker's imperturbable facade. From the corner of his eye he saw a burly man come into the study and slip handcuffs onto Rex Clancey. To the other side of him he heard Lena moan over and over again, "Which one is Alyssa? I don't remember which one is Alyssa." As if it mattered at this point in time.

Incredibly, just as if he, Senator Matthew Bradford, were an ordinary person, Adam Stryker was mouthing the formula for making an arrest. They were charging him with conspiracy to subvert the United States Government. How insane! How crazy! All he had ever wanted was to be president.

The stench of the burning tape assaulted his nostrils more strongly now, and the release of chemicals made his eyes weep at the uselessness of his years of sacrifice. He was one of the best, hardest-working senators in the entire United States, and he would have been the twentieth century's greatest president. Now all those chances to bring about good were lost, simply because his private, personal conversation had been recorded by those two women who called themselves Alyssa Humphrey.

But the last laugh would be on them. The width of the desk was between him and Stryker. That would give him a precious few seconds of time. Matthew had visited plenty of jails on fact-finding missions, and he knew death would be better than life imprisonment. He would kill himself, but best of all, before he turned the gun on himself, he would do his damnedest to take the two Alyssas with him.

With the swiftness and skill of ultimate desperation, Matthew reached beneath the desk surface and slid the Colt .38 out of its special holster. With deadly accuracy he took aim at the Alyssa-Suzanne woman on the other side of the desk.

Less than a split second before he squeezed the trigger, he heard Lena scream and realized she was going to launch herself in a flying leap toward him. His finger jerked back. Shots exploded. Not one, but two, and Lena collapsed in an ugly heap across the corner of his desk. But the Alyssa-Suzanne woman wasn't hurt, except that her face crumpled into an expression of total horror.

Matthew would have squeezed the trigger again, but the numbness in his hand bloomed into a sudden fireball of pain. He was bleeding, he realized with a sense of outrage. He had been shot in the hand.

Before he could switch the gun to his left hand and try again, Stryker was there, taking the gun and locking handcuffs around his wrists. Matthew looked down at the cuffs and began to cry. All he'd wanted was to be president.

TONY HAD PROVEN HIMSELF invaluable, keeping Suzanne and Alyssa away from the gruesome official aftermath of violent death, making them endless cups of hot tea and even persuading them to drink a few sips occasionally. Shocked by the horror of seeing Lena die, neither Alyssa nor Suzanne could relish the triumph of having gathered the evidence to put Matthew behind bars.

Through the long, dark hours before dawn, they discussed how they would break the news to Jackie of her mother's death. In the end Tony suggested Jackie had no need to be told of Lena's acts of conspiracy, and they all cheered up somewhat when he pointed out, with perfect truth, that she had died in order to stop Matthew from killing Suzanne. The knowledge that her mother had died a heroine wouldn't help much in the first rush of Jackie's grief, but it might help quite a lot in the years to come.

Adam joined them soon after three in the morning, bleary-eyed and his chin dark with the shadow of his beard. The case had left him heavyhearted, not least because he sensed that somewhere buried deep beneath the corruption of Matthew's life lay the ruins of a potentially great leader. His spirits lifted when he saw Suzanne, curled up on the sofa next to Alyssa, their identical blond heads sharing the solitary pillow.

"Time to go, sweetheart," he whispered.

She stirred sleepily. "Where are we going?"

He found that, despite the horror of all that had happened, he could actually smile. "Home," he said, pulling her into his arms and kissing her until he felt life and hope and the promise of new tomorrows flow back into his veins. "We're going home."

HARLEQUIN®
AMERICAN ◆ ROMANCE®

American Romance's yearlong celebration continues.... Join your favorite authors as they celebrate love set against the special times each month throughout 1992.

Next month... Spooky things were expected in Salem, Massachusetts, on Halloween. But when a tall, dark and gorgeous man emerged from the mist, Holly Bennett thought that was going too far. Was he a real man... or a warlock? Find out in:

OCTOBER

S	M	T	W	T	F	S
					2	3
4					9	10
11	12		15		16	17
18	19				23	24
25	26	27	28	29	30	31

#457
UNDER HIS SPELL
by Linda Randall Wisdom

Read all the *Calendar of Romance* titles, coming to you one per month, all year, only in American Romance.

WELCOME TO

The quintessential small town, where everyone
knows everybody else!

Finally, books that capture the pleasure
of tuning in to your favorite TV show!

Join your friends at Tyler in the eighth book, BACHELOR'S PUZZLE by Ginger
Chambers, available in October.

*What do Tyler's librarian and a cosmopolitan architect have in common? What
does the coroner's office have to reveal?*

GREAT READING...GREAT SAVINGS...
AND A FABULOUS FREE GIFT!

Each book set in Tyler is a self-contained love story; together, the twelve novels
stitch the fabric of the community. You can't miss the Tyler books on the shelves
because the covers honor the old American tradition of quilting; each cover
depicts a patch of the large Tyler quilt!

And you can receive a FABULOUS GIFT, ABSOLUTELY FREE, by collecting
proofs-of-purchase found in each Tyler book, *and* use our Tyler coupons to save
on your next TYLER book purchase.

If you missed *Whirlwind* (March), *Bright Hopes* (April), *Wisconsin Wedding* (May), *Monkey
Wrench* (June), *Blazing Star* (July), *Sunshine* (August) or *Arrowpoint* (September) and would
like to order them, send your name, address, zip or postal code, along with a check or money
order for $3.99 (please do not send cash), plus 75¢ postage and handling ($1.00 in Canada)
for each book ordered, payable to Harlequin Reader Service, to:

In the U.S.	In Canada
3010 Walden Avenue	P.O. Box 609
P.O. Box 1325	Fort Erie, Ontario
Buffalo, NY 14269-1325	L2A 5X3

Please specify book title(s) with your order.
Canadian residents add applicable federal and provincial taxes.

TYLER-8

HARLEQUIN®

INTRIGUE®

A SPAULDING AND DARIEN MYSTERY

Amateur sleuths Jenny Spaulding and Peter Darien have set the date for their wedding. But before they walk down the aisle, love must pass a final test. This time, they won't have to solve a murder, they'll have to prevent one—Jenny's. Don't miss the chilling conclusion to the SPAULDING AND DARIEN MYSTERY series in October. Watch for:

#197 WHEN SHE WAS BAD by Robin Francis

Look for the identifying series flash—A SPAULDING AND DARIEN MYSTERY—and join Jenny and Peter for danger and romance....

HARLEQUIN
INTRIGUE®

ABOUT THE AUTHOR
Born in Wales, educated in London, veteran of more moves than she cares to count, Jasmine Cresswell now lives with her husband in Solon, Ohio. Mother of four "amazingly talented children, and doting grandmother to one budding genius," she loves having her children come to stay, despite their "unceasing attempts" to get her organized.

Books by Jasmine Cresswell
HARLEQUIN INTRIGUE
 51—UNDERCOVER
 77—CHASE THE PAST
105—FREE FALL
124—CHARADES
182—HOUSE GUEST

HARLEQUIN PRESENTS
913—HUNTER'S PREY

HARLEQUIN ROMANCE
3176—LOVE FOR HIRE

HARLEQUIN HISTORICALS
6—THE MORETON SCANDAL

MASQUERADE HISTORICALS
286—THE DEVIL'S ENVOY

Don't miss any of our special offers. Write to us at the following address for information on our newest releases.

Harlequin Reader Service
P.O. Box 1397, Buffalo, NY 14240
Canadian address: P.O. Box 603,
Fort Erie, Ont. L2A 5X3

JCB10